Frozen Summer

'Absolutely stunning – a really brilliant, unputdownable book ... unconditionally brilliant ... [Crysse Morrison has] wrapped a psychological thriller, a voyage of self discovery and a romance into an addictive package'
KATIE FFORDE

'It is a dark, paranoid, edgy thriller which had me completely absorbed from the first page, but it is also so much more satisfying than a simple thriller ... a thoroughly modern novel, a suburban fairy tale in which the Sleeping Beauty awakes to find herself alone, fighting for sanity against the dragons of her own past ... As facts, discoveries and revelations drop into place one by one, the tension escalates into a climax which is both startling and inevitable'
JOANNE HARRIS, author of CHOCOLAT

Frozen Summer

Crysse Morrison

FLAME
Hodder & Stoughton

First published in Great Britain in 1999
by Hodder and Stoughton
First published in paperback in 2000
by Hodder and Stoughton
A division of Hodder Headline

A Flame Paperback

10 9 8 7 6 5 4 3 2 1

A CIP catalogue record for this title is available
from the British Library.

ISBN 0 340 74865 6

Printed and bound in Great Britain by
Mackays of Chatham PLC, Chatham, Kent

Hodder and Stoughton
A division of Hodder Headline
338 Euston Road
London NW1 3BH

My thanks to Sarah, Jill, Annabelle, Emily, Debby, and Amy, for their enduring confidence, to Serafina and Kirsty for making it happen, to Stephen for the Glastonbury '87 programme, and to Alex for the Applemac and much, much more.

ACKNOWLEDGEMENTS

With thanks to the Oysterband for the use of the following songs:

'We Could Leave Right Now' written by Ian Telfer and Alan Prosser, lyrics reprinted with kind permission of Momentum Music Ltd.

'The Oxford Girl' lyrics reproduced by kind permission of Pukka Music/Complete Music Ltd.

'The Moving Finger . . .' is from *The Rubaiyat of Omar Khayyam* translated by Edward Fitzgerald in 1859.

'The Silkie of Sule Skerrie' is a traditional folk song.

The First Week

———————⊳०००⊲———————

'Kate?'

Lifting that receiver was so scary I'm relieved that all I need to do now is say, 'Sorry, wrong number.'

'Kate? Kate?'

It's extraordinary, he must have heard me. I hang up.

A cat – probably my cat – has walked with wet paws across the notepad by the phone. I pull off the muddied page, scrumple it and drop it into the pedal bin in the kitchen. Then I start to think of how that blank page had waited to be written on, perhaps for an important message, and now it's torn off and thrown away. I sit on the bed with my head in my hands and cry. I'm not thinking, That's like my life. I'm not thinking at all. Just crying for that poor little bit of paper, and wishing I hadn't torn it up.

A child comes into the room. A little girl aged about seven. I stop crying.

'Why is your hair all different?' she asks.

Is that rude? I know nothing about children of this age.

'Different from what?' I say.

She changes the subject. 'When can we have a rabbit, Mummy?'

'I wish she wouldn't do that *Mummy* thing: it really spooks me. The psychiatrist said she had to carry on, it might help me remember, but it just feels weird.

The man who owns this house comes in. He's looking at me in that half-worried, half-suspicious way he does.

'Still in the never-never land?' he says, and then, smiling, 'I mean, it was only a little touch, it couldn't have hurt and you weren't out for more than two minutes. How long does it take to get over that, for Chrissake?' The way he says 'Chrissake' is long drawn-out and sounds so menacing. He laughs in a half-hearted kind of way, as if he hasn't seen my shudder, as if it's all a joke. He really is a most dislikeable man.

He comes over to me and takes hold of my shoulders in his big brown soap-smelling hands. I close my eyes. I feel a kiss like a blow on the head and he's murmuring, 'Sweetie', then again, pleadingly, 'Sweetie?' Close up he smells of peppermint chewing-gum and acrid male sweat.

'How long, Kirsten?' he says.

'Kirsty,' I say. 'I'm Kirsty.'

He says again, 'How long?'

I don't know. I don't know him and I don't know her and I don't know how long before I understand why they have trapped me in this house, in this place, in this curious world called 1996. It's not the world I know.

They brought me out of the hospital today. I've put on the clothes they said I had to wear, a pale blue denim top with lace sewn in, tight-fitting jeans and white high-heeled sandals. White high heels!

I stand in front of the long mirror on the wardroom door. The woman in the mirror looks at me warily. She's ages older than me, though her body's not that much different from mine. I've rubbed a ring of kohl pencil round the eyes, pushed some blusher against the cheeks. I've tied back this straggly permed strawberry-blonded hair.

'Where did I get these clothes?' I ask the man when he comes in.

'Mostly off the catalogue. Helen's catalogue.'

Helen. That name again.

'I don't know any Helen.'

'Your best friend.'

It's ridiculous. My best friend is Debs. Why hasn't she come to see me?

The medication at the hospital gave me bad dreams. I dreamed a man was bending over me, gripping my arms and shaking me. 'Kate, Kate, Kate,' he said, over and over again, whispery and intense like someone shouting down a well. Or maybe I was awake, I can't remember.

I had another dream and woke up screaming, thinking I was falling in mud and trying to push it off me. A little girl was crying, and I was walking and not walking, falling, getting heaved up to my feet. I don't know any of these people. There's this woven thing on my wrist, like a name-tag for a baby or a maniac. I pull at it until it breaks. Little beads scatter. I throw the cord of tangled threads down on to the floor. The nurse picks it up and takes it away but I can still see tiny glints of pink and purple glass rolling on the dark floor. Why does everybody stare? Where am I? Where's my tent? Where's Debs? I want to go home.

But that was all yesterday, at the hospital, before they brought me here. It must be the injection. It's making me feel so strange. And my hair is all wrong – it's not my hair, but it's growing out of my head. Panic oozes from me in beads of hot sweat, like tiny spiders crawling across my neck. I can't stand, my legs flop, I'm falling again. I want to go home.

'You are home, Mummy,' says the little girl. She makes my flesh creep.

I can hear someone at the front door, and then that grumbling man's voice. 'She's not coping very well at all — those tablets just seem to make her worse.'

What is he doing to me? Why are they doing this to me?

'I'm Kirsty Middleton,' I explain, again, to the doctor. This one wears a grey skirt and a pink blouse and says she is my GP. She will be part of my rehabilitation team, she tells me.

'Tell me about Kirsty, then,' she says. So I tell her about myself. I am just twenty, this month, and I'm on a photography degree course at Exeter University. I've just finished the first year. I live with my parents in Newton Abbot and get the train in and out to college, but I'm learning to drive. I've been doing a project on autobiography — big moody landscapes of the moors, I printed them really dark. I love those Dartmoor tors. Telling her calms me down a bit, even though everything and everyone seems to have gone missing. At least she listens.

'D'you have a boyfriend?' she says, so I tell her my boyfriend is Miles — nothing serious, just good friends. We go around in a foursome mostly, with my friend Debs and her bloke Paul. I really fancy Paul, but I don't tell the doctor that.

She's sitting there, nodding, and as my voice tails away she says, 'And who's the Prime Minister?'

'They've done that with me already,' I say cunningly. For some reason I'm reluctant to tell her.

She nods again. 'Do you want to change your answer?'

'No,' I say. 'I could hardly forget. The election was only a couple of weeks ago. Mrs Thatcher got in again.'

'And what was the date of the election?'

'June the eleventh.'

'Nineteen . . . ?'

'. . . eighty-seven,' I finish for her, as the digits linger incomplete.

'So what's the date today?'

This is where I feel a little uneasy. It's round about the end of June, but I'm not confident of the actual day. There's something I was going to do and I'm not exactly clear in my head about it. I know that term has just ended so it must be around June the nineteenth. But then another thought strikes me. 'How long was I in the hospital?'

'Only three days. You were brought in on Friday evening. It's Monday now.'

'So it's all over?'

'What is?' asks the doctor, quick as a rap. I'm puzzled. I don't really know. I thought of something when I spoke, but it's gone again now.

'Post-traumatic amnesia to this extent is very rare,' the specialist at the hospital said. 'It will almost certainly recede, over the coming weeks.'

'I want to go home,' I said, and he said that I could. 'There is really no need for in-patient treatment – in fact, it could be counter-productive. The brain scan shows you are free of major lesions. Provided you attend for therapy regularly, and let us know immediately if you have any of those symptoms we discussed, you would be far better off recuperating at home.'

But they didn't take me home. They brought me here, to this bungalow in a village where I don't know anyone. The man and the child look at me reproachfully, suspiciously. They want me to remember them. They say they are my family now.

The specialist says I must expect a certain amount of confusion. 'A certain amount of confusion is all right,' is what Dr Rahmin actually tells the grim-faced pair standing with my clothes in a carrier-bag, the child and the man, when they come to take me away from the hospital. They obviously want me to whisk behind the curtain and metamorphose into a mother and a wife. The man holds the bag awkwardly, as though it's a bunch of flowers that may wilt. The child is gripping a china ornament. She keeps trying to interrupt, whispering, 'I gave you this, Mummy,' and the man puts his hand on her head and says, 'Ssh.' He frowns, staring down, to show he is listening to the doctor. The little girl stares at me, ignoring him, mouthing, 'It's your favourite.'

Dr Rahmin continues with his list, ticking off the items on his bronze fingers. 'Erratic responses, perhaps. Muddled emotions – laughing or crying for no obvious reasons. And tiring very easily. Tiredness is a natural consequence of head injury, in most cases. In Mrs Villiers's case, the stress of this dislocated time-sphere awareness, which she is displaying, is likely to prove very wearisome. Patience. Patience and home care is the best thing I can suggest.'

They nod, both of them. Dr Rahmin presses his beautifully manicured fingertips together and we watch them mesmerically. He appears to sense that we are waiting for something more. So far his kindly words have skirted round the important part. The missing decade.

'Retrograde amnesia . . .' the doctor says cautiously, and I see the man's pale eyes flicker, he is so avid for definitive information, '. . . is not at all unusual, even with a very minor head injury like this one. The memories are filed, but the mechanism for retrieving them has temporarily closed down. I have seen many, many cases where the injured person has no recollection of events several hours, days, or even weeks prior to the accident.'

We are still waiting.

'Nine years,' concedes Dr Rahmin, 'is a puzzle. There is nothing physiologically wrong with the brain, as far as all our tests have demonstrated.'

'So there's no reason,' says the man slowly.

'No apparent reason,' the doctor corrects. 'There is nothing to be gained by further scans, I assure you. Time is a great healer.'

'Here's some dry things,' says the man.

And they leave me alone with the china ornament and the carrier-bag. I dress myself in the unfamiliar clothes and emerge.

'How do you feel now, sweetie?' says the man, rather loudly, as though he doesn't want anyone overhearing us to realise my alienation.

'Tired,' I say. And I do. He leads me out of the hospital to a dark blue car and drives me away.

My name is Kirsten Villiers. I am twenty-nine years old. I have a husband, a daughter, and a part-time job. I live in a bungalow in a small village. I repeat this exactly as I have been asked to memorise it. It means nothing to me. I have had an identity for twenty years and now the person I knew as myself has been taken away. There is only Kirsten Villiers, married, with a child.

'You were only out for a few minutes,' the man repeats. He keeps saying, 'A few minutes. At the most,' as though I have no right to complicate matters like this. 'It was only a few feet of water you slipped in. You've not even got a bruise.'

'So why did you take me to a hospital?'

'Because you didn't seem to know where you were. When we picked you up you seemed sort of puzzled.'

'And where was I?'

'At the river. We were at the place we call the lido, where we swim when it's warm on a summer's evening. The place we go to picnic, with Janey and Sam, and Helen and Jeremy.'

No wonder I was sort of puzzled.

*

The occupational therapist has said to memorise details of this room, the one they have taken me to which they say is my room now. I don't want to. I close my eyes and think about my own room, pretend this duvet is mine, pretend the light from the passage outside is filtering in from the window, behind the lilac tree at my real home.

They've let me crawl into the bed while the evening is still light and left me here to sleep. I've been given a creamy lace-trimmed nightie, not my Live Aid T-shirt. I didn't want any supper. For a while I doze, half hearing the television sounds from the next room – the *Coronation Street* theme, which my mum always watches. The *News At Ten* music. The sounds are a little bit different, perhaps distorted. After a while there is silence.

I wake into the sweet familiar shadows of my own room, intensely intimate, a soft warmth all around me. The walls are painted honeysuckle tones and there's a big blow-up colour poster of a sunflower field in France. I took the picture when I was on a school trip; it was what made me decide to do photography at college. There's a lot of clutter around – my tapes heaped up on the desk, jeans and tops on the floor. My sister and I share the big mahogany wardrobe on the landing but mostly my stuff lives in a heap.

I start to wake into this comfortable confusion but in that same second I realise there is no door in the wall where I am looking. Panic grabs me. These shadows are wrong, the angles are wrong. The tiny room imprisons me, it's not my room. And I am not alone. Beside me in the bed is a man. He's big – chunky limbs, broad back, solid chest – and he smells of sleep and unfamiliar maleness. He is not my boyfriend. I don't know him. It takes only two seconds to shift from my own, familiar, room to this place. My heart pounds, my breathing is shallow. I want desperately to cry but I am too afraid.

Waking is the worst part of the nightmare.

I've been pleading for Mum and Dad. I was really surprised

they didn't come to see me in hospital. He says they are coming as soon as they can – 'when they can get a flight.' This makes no sense.

'A flight, from Devon? You said this is Somerset here. That can't be more than a couple of hours' drive.'

'From Spain. They live on the Costa Brava, now, Kirsten.'

Impossible. I was with them only a few days ago.

I'm trying to remember the last thing anyone said to me before I woke up in the hospital ward. There are voices in my head, woolly and whispery, and I can't recall whose they are. Maybe it was my sister being her usual infuriating self while I was packing. The last thing – this is so stupid – the last conversation I properly remember was about a dead fly. A bluebottle, actually. I remember as clear as yesterday coming into the kitchen and finding Suzy whining to Mum that I'd put a dead bluebottle on the white icing of her sponge cake. And I said, 'Don't be pathetic, Sooz. Do I look like I'm fussed about your fondant icing? The thing just dive-bombed it and stuck, obviously. Why would I do that, anyway?'

'To pay me back for getting nail varnish on your Bon Jovi tape,' she said, with a look of pettish triumph that was particularly irritating since I didn't know she had. So I said, 'Oh, grow up. And yes, I did stick a dead fly on your stupid cake, and I spat in the mix too,' But she knew I hadn't, so I snapped on, 'And that skirt makes your knees look fat.' Her face went soggy then, like a puckered paddling-pool, and she ran off to her bedroom making those snorting noises she does when she sobs.

I wish I hadn't. I wish she'd walk in right now, in her creased-up zip-front denim mini, and I'd tell her she looked like Madonna. But now I suppose she wouldn't want to.

I try to remember what they have taught me in the hospital. My name is Kirsten Villiers. I am twenty-nine years old. I have a husband named Clyde and a daughter called Janey.

I can see my real life so clearly. Our kitchen, with the old enamel sink that needs changing (Mum says, on a daily basis) and the sun coming through the window so that the tradescantia trails long shadows over the scrubbed-pale wooden table. The table is so big it fills our poky kitchen, with a long cutlery drawer filled – not with knives and forks (they only ever inhabit the draining rack) – with pencils and pins and pop-up toaster instructions, bits of string that have lost their purpose and elastic bands that have lost their ping. This is the room where everyone does whatever they're doing, in our house, so there's usually a jumble of papers and jumpers at one end of the table, pushed back so's we can sit down to eat. Mum moans, but it's not just my mess, it's all of ours.

Was. Of course, I have to say it was. Someone else lives there now, and the old table will have been junked.

I know it, but equally I know it's impossible. I can see it with absolute clarity. Mum had bought herself a bunch of freesias and put them in the middle of the muddle on the table, in the slim-stemmed glass vase with the blue-tinged, bubbled, ball-shaped base. I love that vase. I can see the dark shadow of elegant stems falling across the table top, I can see the way the sapphire shadow of the glassy bulb swells, elongating the air bubbles into myriad magic eyes. I took a photo of it.

It's like yesterday I was there. It is yesterday. It has to be – I can even smell the peanut butter. I was making a sandwich while the idiotic squabble about the cake was going on. Smears of peanut butter on my jacket cuff. I swabbed them off with a bit of kitchen paper. My rucksack was on the floor ('Right where we can trip on it,' said my mother, so I left it there, and then tripped on it reaching for the kitchen roll). It was Friday teatime, and I was waiting for a lift . . . somewhere.

Clyde comes over with a pile of photo albums. 'The OT said . . .'
'I know,' I say. 'You brought them into the hospital.'

He stands there looking like a slapped kid and then says stubbornly, 'Well, she said we should keep trying. You hardly looked.'

It's true. I had opened one page, the page with a lank-haired, shiny-faced woman dotingly holding a tiny baby, then pushed them all away.

He puts one in my lap and tries to pat my head. I jerk away. I'm not a puppy, I want to say, but he looks so dejected and the little girl looks so hopeful. They make me feel accused.

She snuggles up to me on the settee. I make a real effort, give her a forced smile. 'Are you going to tell me who everyone is?'

She nods self-importantly. Together we open the book. It's full of wedding photographs. The sky is pale as pearl, it seems to be a cold day. Here's me, looking pretty much the way I know myself, with long straight hair. I'm in an ivory dress with a very full skirt and flowers in my hair. I am the bride and Clyde is the groom. He looks terribly happy. His hair is thicker in the pictures, I notice, though he still seems to be older than me. My parents are smiling out at the camera, and there's my sister Suzy, but I don't recognise the church. Janey is pointing out people and naming them but I can't concentrate: I've thought of something else.

'Where are my photographs?'

'What photos d'you mean?'

'My own — my black-and-whites.' Apart from the installations, which were too big, I've kept all the work I've done on the course. As well as the autobiography stuff there is a whole set of environment work. After Chernobyl last year I started a series on all the different issues that were in the news, like the acid-rain thing. I have some really lovely close-ups of leaves and webs with raindrops on.

'Your black-and-white photographs?'

I'm struggling to get up, I'm panicking. He's trying to calm me. 'They're in the spare room,' he says. 'Shall I get the box?'

The thought of a box in a spare room scares me even more. I imagine something dusty, overlooked, full of crushed, discarded images. I feel the loss of my beautiful pristine prints as painfully as though they have been slowly torn to shreds before my outstretched hands.

I say, 'No. I'll look later. Let's go on looking at these ones now.'

I try. I really try. After a while it's obvious I'm not taking in anything more, and he says to Janey, 'That's enough for Mummy, she's tired. She's only been home for a day, remember.'

Janey drags the album on to the floor and bends over it silently, her face so close to the pictures she can't possibly see them properly. Clyde doesn't tell her not to, he just stands there with his hands on his hips looking at her helplessly and then looking at me. I lean back and close my eyes.

He says, 'D'you want a cup of tea?' and I hear him in the kitchen, boiling a kettle and getting Janey a drink of juice. She's followed him out and she keeps changing her mind. I'm glad he's dealing with her: she seems rather fussy.

I go to the patio doors and look out over the garden. All neat and tidy, like the bungalow. The sun is low but it's a bright, clear evening. 'She's only been home for a day, remember,' Clyde said. The thought of endless days here is terrifying.

He comes in with a tray. He's a big man, burly and tall, in his mid-thirties, I suppose. His hair is reddish brown. He wears glasses and his face in repose has a slightly dour expression. He is absolutely not my type in any physical way and I can't imagine any possible emotional rapport with him.

I gesture to the discarded photo album. 'Why . . .'

'Why what?' He sits beside me on the settee and Janey climbs back too.

'Why do we live here?'

His right foot starts tapping: this is a struggle for him.

'You wanted it. You wanted to be in a village.'

'But . . . I mean, why here?'

'My job's in a garage in town. It's not far – I drive there in ten minutes. You wanted Janey to grow up in a village.'

'Oh.'

'You thought you'd like village life.'

'And did I – do I?'

He laughs, gets up, sits down again. 'S'pose so.'

'But what do I do? I mean, you said I work in the pizza place some evenings while you're babysitting. What else do I do?'

His face is flushed. The knee is jerking rhythmically. He swings round. 'Look, do you want to stay? Yes or no?'

'I don't know,' I say.

He puts his face close to mine. 'Yes or no?'

I turn away. Janey starts to cry.

Now he's down on his knees beside the settee, trying to hold me. 'I'm sorry. I'm sorry, Kirsten. This is all so difficult. I know it's difficult for you too, but, hell . . .'

Janey snuffles into quietness. I stare down. His thumbnail wants cutting: it's broken jaggedly. Somehow I find this quite moving. I don't know what to do but I don't want him to bully me again so I put my hand on top of his, and there we sit like one of those children's games. Who will slide away first? Luckily the phone rings.

Janey nips off to get it. Clyde says, 'Thank you,' to me. He sounds so humble it makes me feel curiously ashamed.

The call is for me: it's Suzy, to say Mum and Dad are coming over to visit me.

Suzy. My fifteen-year-old sister – podgy, sulky, wannabe punky – had turned up to visit me in hospital in a trouser suit her hair bobbed and hennaed. She told me she works for a commercial insurance firm in London and has a flat in Hammersmith. She insisted she is twenty-four. I thought about the story of Rip van Winkle and found I was shaking. That's when I began to realise my family has gone, has left me utterly alone in this terrifying place. They won't come back.

Suzy seems impressed to find I still don't remember, as if I'm doing something rather wild and trendy. She keeps saying, 'Definitely? This is so bizarre.' On the phone, where I can't see her, Suzy is easier to recognise. That typical tactlessness. She rattles on, and I get the feeling she's become used to extensive sister-type calls. But I never confided in Suzy – a kid with Madonna posters and green hair-wings at the weekend. I can't start now. I simply don't know what to say.

I do try. 'Bizarre? It's doing my head in,' I say.

She gives an uncertain laugh, as though I'm quipping, and says, 'Brilliant excuse if you've got detector vans in your area and no TV licence, though.'

Suzy is better at finding silver linings than she used to be. But her jokes still don't make me laugh.

Clyde comes back from getting Janey some supper or something. He sees me looking at a colour photograph propped on top of the television. It's Janey in a bright blue v-neck jumper, big bow-tied bunches at the sides of her head and a rather cheeky smile. Clyde says, 'Her first-year picture. Remember?'

'It means nothing, absolutely nothing.'

He looks around, then says, in an angry whisper, 'Can't you try, for her sake?'

Try? Try? I feel like screaming. How obtuse this man is. He keeps going on about his child as though he can't comprehend my feelings or my fear.

I wake in the night with one of those absolute certainties that shake you from head to toe. Suddenly I understand everything. Kirsten is my sister, she isn't me – she's an older sister, lost long ago. That's why I don't remember anything, and why I don't belong here. It's a case of mistaken identity. Like tiny babies sometimes are, we have somehow been mixed up in the hospital.

Incredible relief floods through me and my tense muscles relax. In that same instant I realise with dreadful sadness that this scenario is hopeless and absurd. It explains nothing. I am twenty-nine years old, I have lost my life and I don't know who I am. Kirsty is gone, spinning down a black hole of time. Her world will never come back. The pain cuts me, my head and gut ache and my pillow is sodden with tears.

Beside me in the bed Clyde groans in his sleep. The horror of being here is choking me. I stare at the grey shapes in the unfamiliar room and wait helplessly for rescue.

I've been looking through the black-and-whites in my old college folder in the spare room. Clyde got the box out for me. He methodically moved aside two suitcases, some blankets in plastic wrapping, and a box of Christmas decorations. It was horrible. Seeing my important things relegated, stacked behind all this transient and unnecessary stuff, I felt the last dregs of my personality crushed out of me. Watching him fumbling with the box when it finally emerged I had a sudden sad, wild feeling that all my pictures would have turned into dead flowers. I imagined them tumbling and falling from the half-open butterfly lid, frail and pressed and paper thin, dwindled by the heavy weight of time.

The box is full of my old essays, my contact sheets, plastic pages holding my negatives, and a few test strips. Also my precious folder, with my best images printed up on resin paper. I turn the pages. There seem to be quite a few missing.

'Your mum took some, to frame up for their new house,' Clyde tells me. 'The views.' He's standing in the doorway, watching me, as I search through the prints and contact sheets over and over again, as though I might find a key to understanding what's happened to me – or maybe a door I can squeeze through to get away from this place.

The pictures are strong and fresh and clear to me. They are

places and people I know. Moorland landscapes. Debs with her tongue out, a punk in slashed leggings and safety-pins swigging cider in the precinct. She spat at me for taking that one. A portrait of Paul and Miles, one rainy morning. So little light they had to stay still for half a minute while I used the table for a tripod. Miles's smile is slightly blurred but Paul's luscious eyes are bright as a hawk's.

Here's some of the landscapes and textures I did for my auto-biography brief. When I'd done the moors and tors I couldn't think of anything else original to say about myself so I went round the university grounds – which are really nice – and did all my family as trees and bushes. The waving tree is Dad, because it's incredibly high with a single lofty branch that looks like that one arm waving free, in one of his hippie songs. Mum is the rhodo-dendron by the scented garden. Suzy is pampas grass. She objected and said. 'Can't I be that flowery climber on the clock tower?' And I said, 'No. It's my brief, do your own.' But she's not doing art as an option. It felt good to know I could do some-thing better than my pushy little sister. I got the idea from the mad tree at the end of the road by the station with the two low branches thick enough to sit on, where we first met Miles and Paul last year.

Not last year. Nearly ten years ago.

I close the folder and zip it slowly. I'm still on my knees, stroking the black leather; I can't seem to find the energy to get up.

'Don't I take photos any more?'

'Well, holidays, and special events you do, sometimes. Or I do.'

'Pictures, I mean, not family snaps. Where's my Pentax?'

Clyde looks away. 'You've got a new camera,' he says, 'a proper one. I gave you one.'

I can't work out his tone. It sounds grudging – blaming. Did he stop me taking photos?

My certainty that I am Kirsty Middleton, photography student, is beginning to falter. Everyone around me is so sure that she has gone and there is only Kirsten now and there's all this stuff around that doesn't belong to me yet is supposed to be part of my life.

It's so hard to find the shape of a person in this empty space. I'm looking for the outline of the person I have to be, but this place is as spick and span as a show house, as quiet as a retirement home. I've been looking for music, but there's no albums, not even a record player, just CDs, and a few tapes. One with no cover and some scribbled writing on the label. 'Everything must go,' it says. Not my handwriting.

I spend a lot of time sitting curled in the flowery wicker-backed chairs among the mist-green slub-silk cushions. Often the cat comes and sits on my lap. All the seats face the telly but I don't put it on. I concentrate, sometimes, on trying to remember the room.

There's a ribbon of floral frieze; above it the walls are hazy blue and below they are blue with kind of green lowlights, splashed and splattered on in blotchy splodges. Rather fussy-looking.

'You did that,' says Clyde. 'You went on a Saturday course, at the college, and learned how.'

I try to imagine it. I picture the room with newspaper over the carpet, the seating moved aside or swathed, the telly and the glassy walnut-look cupboard with its beady-eyed diamond glass doors covered in old sheets. I think about me, kneeling at the forget-me-not skirting, swabbing with dribbling sponges of lagoon blues.

Sponges. Well, it has to be sponges, doesn't it? Or is that a fragment of memory?

I stare at my hand and picture the weeping colours trickling across my fingers – no, glove. A yellow rubber glove.

I'm sure of it. I'm holding my breath, holding tight to a tiny slice of something I may actually remember . . . But it's only one of the photos I'm remembering. Not a real breathing moment, just a Polaroid snap wedged sideways in the album. I saw it last night. Me with my hair piled up like a posing Maya, kneeling on the floor, turning to smile. Someone stood in that doorway and called me, and I turned round at the instant the flash caught me, and smiled, and I don't even know who that person was.

Small things like that distress me for hours. Like, I'm looking round for a clean towel, and I've been told where the towels are kept so I go there, open the cupboard and pull one out from the folded pile. And I know it. It's my swimming towel. Suddenly, in the middle of this routine of careful memorising, there is something I really know, and I clutch at it wildly like it's lost treasure. A lost child, I nearly said, but I don't feel much like clutching at children at the moment. I feel like a lost child myself. But this towel, it should be so fluffy with deep bright colours and it's flat and pale. I know, as I touch it and smell it, that it really is nine years older. A tiny thing like that, insisting to me that this is not a bad dream but a waking day, can make me cry and cry.

Finding my Walkman was nearly as bad. The belt clip is broken and there's different headphones on it, tiny instead of the spongy ones I expected, but it's definitely my Walkman. So is this all that's survived of Kirsty Middleton's? A Walkman and a towel. There has to be more somewhere.

I've been going through all the clothes hanging up in the bedroom. Perhaps with every door I open I'm secretly hoping I'll find the path out of this dense dream world back to my reality. It's certainly not through the wardrobe. Looking at these clothes feels like prying into another woman's life. A couple of things have been worn and not yet washed; they even smell of another woman. A flowery, sweet sort of fragrance. Not mine, not me.

There's nothing here I want to wear.

It's not that this stuff is really horrible, it's just that I can't imagine wearing it – more, I can't imagine the woman who wore these clothes. It's all so fussy. Even the jeans aren't the sort of jeans I buy: they have little butterflies embroidered on the hip, and there's a pale denim jacket to match with more butterflies, slightly shaped at the waist. There are some white jeans too, which look like a really tight fit, and they've got teeny bits of satin sewn along the pocket edges. There are lots of tops, which all have these little bits of detail, and several have masses of lace sewn into them, around the neck or sleeves. There are some dresses too, mostly with quite long skirts, mostly patterned.

I'm trying to picture the personality of the woman who wore these things, and I'm not impressed. I'm searching for some evidence of her interests – a skating skirt, or walking boots, even a *Come Dancing* frock with sequins she sewed on herself. But, apart from an aerobics outfit and a couple of swimming costumes, it's mostly that sort of smart-casual, feminine stuff. One little-black-dress, nothing funky, more the sort of thing that's called 'effortless elegance' and clamours for sheer black tights. Smart, OK, but not me.

Maybe I'm not really here at all but strapped into some horrific experiment with hallucinatory drugs. I'm not really moving around this place, not really seeing and touching these alien things. My captors are probing my mind; they are devoid of pity, devoid of any emotion except curiosity. *Interesting but illogical,* notes the ersatz child in its report. She certainly watches me enough to be my analyst. And they move things about. Maybe they want to observe my reactions. There was that card-mounted photo of Janey in school uniform on the telly yesterday, and it's gone today.

Clyde comes back from work. He's staring at me.

'What?' I take off the headphones.

'I didn't say anything.'

But his face did, it was a big grimace of angry puzzlement.

'I was playing that tape I found by the bed to see if I remembered it.'

'Do you?'

I shrug. He goes away.

I'm trying to do normal household sort of stuff but I can't open the washing-machine. Everything seems to have stopped spinning and there's no water left but I can't find a handle to this circular door at the front. There's a button with a light, which I've pressed; the light goes out. I press the other buttons. A tray for detergent starts to slide out, that's all. I'm beginning to panic. Clyde comes over. I gesture, wordlessly. He stoops and presses somewhere I hadn't seen and the door clicks open. 'This technology is quite old, actually,' he says.

His tone is pretending-jokey, pretending not to challenge. *Actually*. What is he really saying, about me? That he thinks this is all fake, everything I'm doing, and he's caught me out on a bit of historical detail? The cruelty of this feeling of being accused makes me gasp aloud with anger. Suddenly the kitchen floor is full of tangled still-wet clothes, his shirts, sheets, everything I've dumped at his feet.

He stares at me. I don't know how to defend this moment of retaliation now. I want to say something that will convince him, that will make him stop sniping and help me, but I don't want his help, or him, or his washing. So there isn't really anything to say. I walk out, leaving him stooping over the mess, silently lifting and sorting the things.

I go out into the garden and sit on one of the patio chairs. I can understand Janey not accepting that I don't know her. For a little girl that must be scary. And I do at least recognise her now, and I know her favourite teddy, which is not actually a teddy but a rather ugly duster-yellow lion, called Sinbad, I think. So I expect she's convinced herself that my forgetting is all behind us, un-important now. But I can't understand Clyde. Sometimes he says things like that about the washing-machine, as though he is sure that I can't have forgotten everything, not everything. I'm being wilful, or lazy, maybe just not trying hard enough. And I wonder,

What kind of a stupid man did I marry if he thinks I could sustain a trick like that, what kind of a brutal one to think I would want to? Then I wonder what kind of a bitch I was, if he really believes me capable of this. And that really scares me.

I close my eyes and let the sun soak my face, let the warm and scented air console me. Distantly I hear wood pigeons. I think about Devon and my friends. Especially Miles, and Debs and Paul.

And Nico hangs around with us too. What a joker, what a jerker.

Nico is this crazy guy who's always juggling. Or he's playing spoons – everywhere, on tables, walls, on his legs or someone else's. Or he's counting one–two–three. He's got green eyes and a wispy-wiry little beard, which runs down his long chin like a squirrel sliding down a ski slope. He wipes his hands down it, left, then right, then left, one, two, three times then slaps his knees and starts a little drum-roll. Anywhere. On the side of the pool table.

Paul dabbed towards him with his cue like a jousting knight. 'Fuck off, Nico, you spazzo,' he said amiably.

Nico backed away till he reached a tray of empties then he grabbed three cans and started to juggle. A fine spray and a scent of lager. We laughed as Paul wiped his hair and swore. 'Serves you right,' Debs said, 'for being so offensive.' And Paul said, 'You're right – it's insulting to spastics to call them Nicos.' Debs kicked him and gave Nico a little lip-pouty wink. He blinked back and wiped his hands along his chin some more.

Nico doesn't mind the teasing. He's a sweet guy. He's gone off grape-picking in France now. We all went with him to the junction to watch him hitch his first lift. He was dancing on the grass verge like a puppet on a string and we were killing ourselves laughing. 'His grapes won't need trampling,' Miles said. 'They'll be fermented when they leave his fingers.' After we'd watched him climb into a tanker cab we went into the motorway café for drinks. It was hot and we took them outside. I leaned back in the long grass listening to the traffic noise, constant like wind in my ears. I felt so free, and happy. As if something really exciting was about to happen.

There's a shadow on my eyelids. Someone standing looking at me, someone blocking the sun in the shimmering sweetness of the garden. I open my eyes and it's only Clyde, staring down. 'D'you want anything?'

I shake my head slowly and my eyes spill. I blink away the scorching tears. He begins to walk away in the blundering, shambling way he has. Then he pauses and comes back a step. He moves behind me and puts his huge paws on my shoulders. They tense instantly at his touch but he strokes them gently. It's nice. I can feel my muscles relax a tiny bit. I can feel somewhere under the taut skin that my nerve ends recognise this caress. My mind is dismayed but my disloyal shoulders are purring ever so slightly like a cat lazing in the sun. Something deep within me does know this man's touch. Betrayed by my own body now, I feel the hot tears fall.

The Second Week

The actual layout of this house isn't taking long to learn. It's all the other stuff that just won't come — the associated feelings. What I liked and what I only tolerated, what I was planning to alter. I mean, did I choose this hand-lotion, or was I given it? Were those jade green towels a present, or did I buy them? And if so, did I shop for hours to find that shade, or were they an impulse buy in a market somewhere? Why do I keep that jug with the crack? Was I just about to throw it away, or did I cry over it nostalgically and put it sadly back on the shelf?

I can't ask these things. Well, I can, but who would know? Everyone has their own private thoughts about everything around them. How could that man know whether soft-set fruit jam is my passion or my compromise to family pressure. 'We all like that,' he says, then glumly, 'Well, me and Jancy do.'

Clyde tries, but it's obvious he doesn't know. It's obvious my questions are driving it home to him how little he knew his wife. I don't see why he is acting so hurt — no one really knows someone else, do they? Not all those intimate, internal things. Why does he take this so personally? Is this a man-thing, or a Clyde-thing?

And then there's the whole peculiar uncertainty about significance. When I find things, I don't know if they are important or simply trivial. I mean, there's a diary in the big navy shoulder-bag that is supposed to be mine, but it's one of those slim ones with no room to write anything and nothing much written in it anyway. There are numbers, some underlined, some crossed out, and I don't know if any of them matter. There are some times jotted against some of the dates, too. Last Friday has '10 p.m. Friends!'. When I ask Clyde about this he peers across my pointing finger and says it's a programme on TV and I was probably going to video it. Is that the limit of my life? And if not, what is? Why don't I wear a watch? Why are my rings lying in a scalloped saucer beside the kitchen sink? The engagement ring is one of those glittery things pictured in catalogues with starburst effects and A-Diamond-is-For-Ever in wispy writing. The wedding ring has tiny splinters of diamond in it too. Clyde tells me I take them both off for doing the washing-up but that sounds dubious to me. Aren't diamonds supposed to be the hardest substance there is – harder than domestic crockery, anyway – and aren't wedding rings supposed to stay on even through major operations? Clyde appears to have no opinion on these questions. But perhaps Clyde doesn't always tell the truth.

If Clyde was my husband, I must have chosen him and I need to know why. Maybe if I can get a clearer picture of our first days together it will help. I get the photo albums out again.

The wedding pictures are the earliest ones I can find. There are lots of baby ones, and pictures of a toddler standing naked in a paddling-pool – Janey, I suppose. The most recent ones seem to have been taken last summer. There are some pictures of children wading in a river. The sun is shining through a clump of reeds, making the long leaves look almost fluorescent green, and the water is a dark clear brown. There's a close-up picture of Janey the way she looks now with her hair in a scrunchie and her face painted all over with flowers. On another page there are several different views of a complex of Spanish-style houses against a baking blue sky. Jasmine trails around the arched porches and there are loungers set around the parched grass. A woman waves from the doorway, so brown she almost disappears into a bright smile in the shadows. She looks a bit like my mother.

I've found a box of cards too, a mixture of Christmas and birthday cards, with some holiday postcards, spanning the last few years. Most of the names I don't recognise. Some of them I can't even read, and there's one here that says 'to Kate'. I don't know why that was kept. There's a card with a drawing of Glastonbury Tor on the mirror in the hall with handwriting inside that I don't recognise. 'What a perfect day!' and then a scrawl, with a big P and a clear L and a kind of loop in the middle. It's dusty on the fold where it's been hanging over the mirror for so long.

'Who's it from?'

'Can't you read it?' He's looking inscrutable as he shambles over. He takes it from my hands and I think of a bear pulling up a plant.

'Pol,' he says flatly, as he gives it back.

'There's no date,' I say, waiting for more. He is my self-appointed memory-jogger, after all.

He frowns a bit, as if he's weighing up the evidence. He reaches a verdict. 'Last year. You went off to the Chalice Well. Just the two of you. You climbed the tor.'

Pol . . . That means nothing. 'Was she . . . is she a special friend of mine?'

'Not really. Just another mum.' He seems uneasy. He says, 'You must have seen her, she goes past the house every day taking Alice to school.'

His certainty infuriates me. 'How would I know that?'

'She collects Janey. They go together.'

I haven't been taking much notice of Janey's comings and goings, to be honest, other than that these arrangements don't seem to have much to do with me. I say, 'Did we go out together a lot, me and Pol?'

'Only that once, I think. I don't know.'

I put the card back.

There's nothing from Miles, nothing from my college friends.

I miss Miles. But mostly I miss Debs, and the crowd I went around with. I sit on the floor with the box, pretending to study these baffling exhibits, turning them over and over like complex jigsaw segments, but really I'm thinking about the friends in my proper life.

Debs and I go way back, and we still hang around together although she went on the teacher-training course. Her guy Paul is a first-year journalist. Miles is on my course. In fact we got together in the first term for our joint project and we just seem to have stayed together. We haven't really any plans for the future. Miles is more ambitious than me: he wants to go back to London and get commissions from the heavy papers and become a major name in photo-journalism. I just want to make pictures. And Debs, of course, wants to teach. Paul goes on at her about that. 'Education is all washed up,' he says, so she says, 'That why you're a student?' Miles is just as bad about my ambitions too: he teases me I'm using uni as an arty-farty finishing school, and I'll end up a housewife within a year of getting my degree.

Debs says, 'Oh, ignore them both. Who's getting the best grades? They're only jealous.' It's true I surprised everyone, myself included, by how well I was doing. My tutor said if I carried on like that I was set for an upper-second degree at least.

My tutor is Andy Gray. He's good-looking in a black-leather-jacket sort of way, with hair that's short on top and long enough for a ponytail at the back. He's pushing thirty but he tries to act like the students – last time he saw us in the bar he called out, 'Probably see you at one of the festival gigs,' so everyone would hear and know he was going to Glastonbury too. In other words, he thinks he's cool but he's actually a bit pathetic. I got on all right with him in my first two terms but he really hated my last project. I had a set of landscapes around Hinkley Point and I'd pasted on Chernobyl headlines from the newspapers.

He spread out all my prints on the desk and looked at them without saying anything for a while, whistling through his teeth. Then he said, 'What's this all about?'

'Well, the fact that we've got a potential nuclear disaster here, and—'

He interrupted, 'You can get off your soapbox, Kirsty, I'm well aware of the context. I asked you to talk to me about your prints. Why, for example, is all this foreground detail out of focus?' He was tapping at the cow-parsley and grasses, which fringed the picture in a softly fragile tangle. 'What's wrong with your tripod? You do have one, I presume?'

I said, 'I didn't use a tripod. I was walking—'

'—and it was too heavy!' he finished for me. He pushed his hands in his jeans pocket and stared at me from under half-lowered lids without his usual bland smile.

I tried to look humble but even though Andy was being so heavy I couldn't really feel like I was being told off. The atmosphere was charged with something indefinable and I liked the way he was concentrating on my images, focusing on my ideas and taking me seriously. 'Protest as decoration,' he said, slowly and sadly, like a pilgrim who's lost his faith, and he rubbed his fingers hard across his forehead. Then he got terse again. 'Technically, I'm marking you down on this assignment,' he said. 'You need to think about what you're doing far more closely. You could be a perfectly competent stills photographer if you practise what you've been taught instead of spending your time with professional malcontents. Think for yourself. Don't waste your time on posturing and green-washing campaigns.'

I felt quite puzzled when I left his office.

'Andy comes over as totally radical when he's lecturing but he doesn't believe I'm entitled to my own opinions,' I complained, when I told the others about my assessment. The tripod thing was beginning to rankle now.

'You should make a formal complaint,' Debs said. We were in the student bar and she had to shout over the general noise and Whitney Houston on the juke-box.

'I'll leave it. Forty-nine per cent is a pass, just about. I'm disappointed, though – he can criticise my photography if he wants, but it's up to me who my friends are.'

'Professional fucking malcontents!' Paul sounded quite pleased. 'That's me, isn't it? He doesn't trust journalism one little bit.'

'It's me too,' said Miles. 'He was moaning at my Wapping stuff, calling it naïve neo-activism. He is a dog. I reckon he just wants to get into your pants, Kirsty.'

'Tripod too heavy!' Debs exclaimed. 'You could get him for that, Kirsty. Tell your head of year you were aiming to be inconspicuous but Andy accused you of not being able to carry the equipment. That's sexual discrimination and harassment. He can't do that.'

'It was a bit mean,' I agreed, 'but he was right, in a way. I didn't want to carry the tripod round with me.'

'But that's not the same as couldn't manage! You really ought to go for him, Kirsty. For the sake of all the other women students. Send a letter – say you've been thinking about it since, and it upset you.'

But I didn't write. I talked to Mum about it and she seemed quite shocked at the idea of complaining about a member of staff. Dad just laughed. 'You should have stood up for yourself at the time,' he said. 'There's no point now. Forget it.'

Forget it. Dad says that a lot. If Mum tries to argue with him, he brushes her off with 'Forget it.' Sometimes when Suzy is annoyed she says that too, in a shrill, huffy way, and Mum lashes out at her for being rude. She never says that to Dad, though.

I just miss them all so much.

I put the box of meaningless mementoes back in the spare room.

The spare room is more of a junk room, really, and I've had
to rule out the idea of asking Clyde if one of us could sleep here,
even for a short while. It's not set up as a guest room – there is a
bed but it's a folded put-you-up and there is absolutely no room
to open it out. There is a small desk with a computer on it with
just about space to sit down, but the rest of the room is storage
for boxes and tea-chests and what looks like bits of car – head-
lamps and black bits with wires on. I don't know why, the garage
is huge. Clyde says he hasn't damp-proofed it yet. He seems
uneasy when I prowl and question. He would obviously rather
that I concentrate on the colour snaps in the living-room. But I
keep wandering back into the spare room and looking up at the
shelf, and he must have taken pity on me because this time the box
is on the floor beside the doorway, its flaps already opened.

I pull out my familiar black folder and unzip it slowly.

The pictures in their plastics are still smooth and fresh. They
look like I filed them away a couple of weeks ago.

I study my landscapes. I've printed in the skies to look dark
and moody, almost as though a storm is coming. There's the one
with Hinkley Point in the distance with wild flowers in the foreground. I look at it for a long time. The flowers are soft and the
picture looks crude and amateurish.

I tear it slowly.

'Crap,' I say aloud. 'It's all crap.' but I can't see the others,
because I'm crying so much. I'm still sobbing as I butterfly up the
box and push it away.

Clyde sits on the two-seater settee, lolling awkwardly against the
flowery cushions. The suite is one of those wicker-back affairs
and the flowers are kind of honeysuckley, on a grey glazed cotton
background. He doesn't look comfortable. But he doesn't look
like a man who could find it easy to be comfortable in a pretty,
prissy living-room like this.

I look at him and think about Miles. Miles sprawling on the red-ribbed bed cover of his single bed in the room he shared with Paul. Perhaps I could phone him. Clyde says I haven't seen any of my college friends for years. 'Not since I've known you,' were his exact words, as he stared lugubriously at me as if I was asking for the moon. But when I'm alone I remember Miles's face better than his.

Sometimes they merge, though Miles, of course, is younger. His chin is always so smooth. Pampered is the word I think of. He shaves twice a day whether he needs to or not (he doesn't). Sometimes I've found tiny babyfine splinters of down swirled around in the scum of their wash-basin. Debs says I shouldn't clean it for them. She says let them pig it, if that's what they want. But I like messing with water. I always have.

God, where are they?

I'm still waking in the night, every night.

I wake abruptly, sticky in this silky stuff I wear. I won't lie naked next to Clyde so I'm drenching hot and my pulse is pumping and I'm in panic because I've forgotten something terribly important. My chest tightens round my heart and fear is a solid pain. I lie tense and listen to the dark tapping of my heart-beat and wait for the vortex of terror to stop whirling my head around. But it won't stop because it's true. I have forgotten something important. Me. Every scrap of me, the thoughts, the sighs, the sobs, the very skin of me, all gone. Sometimes I think I will simply melt away in white-hot terror in the night, in the comfort-lessness of dread.

There isn't even a shop in this village. I don't know how the people who live here manage, having to think on a weekly-trip basis. Getting in provisions. It's like being at the North Pole or something. I found I was bleeding this morning and had a really panicky half-hour hunting for Kirsten's tampons – why doesn't she simply leave them in the bathroom like Suzy and I always did? I tracked them down in one of the compartments of the chocolate box she keeps her jewellery in, together with a nearly-used wheel of pills. Obviously I should have been taking them all along. Why didn't he tell me?

I've been looking for things like ornaments that I can recognise. I found some little porcelain animals that look like mine in Janey's room, which gave me a weird feeling, but the bits and pieces round the house aren't mine. I found the missing school photo, incidentally, under Janey's bed, cut into little pieces. I don't think she should be allowed scissors if she's going to mess about like that. I can't find my clock, or my little jade otter. Clyde mostly says, 'Wedding present,' if I ask him where things have come from. He claims he doesn't remember who gave us what, though when I said, 'Who would give anyone a bloody awful lamp like that?' he gave me a stiff look and said, 'My mother.' My mum and dad apparently funded that front-loading washing-machine. You use plastic ping-pong balls filled with liquid instead of washing-powder.

The garden here is nice – both gardens, in fact. The front one is full of peach and white roses and lavender bushes, and the back has a kind of paved area and a little lawn and beyond our back fence are fields right into the distance. The bungalow is set back a bit from the road, and on a corner, so we have no distinctly next-door neighbours. Opposite there's a long high wall hung with raspberry pink valerium, and further along on our side of the road there's a little terrace of houses. I have seen an old woman in the first house, the one closest to ours, which has a little path to her back garden on the other side of our fence. She has one of those circular washing-lines and she was out there slowly pegging up a basketful of washing. She didn't see me and I didn't speak. I don't feel up to neighbours yet. I've told Clyde I want to try to memorise a few things before I meet anyone else. At least bring myself up to date with a few topics of conversation.

Janey is quite good on my favourite TV programmes, up to her bedtime anyway. This is less helpful than I hoped, and the new sitcoms don't seem very funny.

'Why don't they show good stuff like *Black Adder*?' I complain to Clyde.

'You'll be able to see them again,' Clyde says. 'We're getting cable next year. Forty-eight channels and most of them do repeats.'

He doesn't understand. I don't want to watch these programmes repeated on forty-eight channels, even if that's true and not a wild exaggeration. I want them to be new and fresh. I want them to be now.

The soaps all seem different too. Den and Angie have left the Vic, and there's hardly anyone I know in *Coronation Street*. At least Janey isn't fazed by me wanting to know all these things. She seems to quite enjoy giving me little scraps of information when she thinks of them. But it's all connected with her things – who gave her what toys and clothes. She's done me a family tree of our pets. The cat is called Dandy and it had five kittens, all named by Janey – 'They were so sweet!' – before we gave them away. Dandy is now 'newted', according to this document. Even the goldfish in the pond are named, and Janey has included, I notice, 'Rupert Rabbit (lop-ear)' at the bottom with excited orange rays crayoned around. I take this to be a reference to the conversation that always ends, 'Daddy says he'll make a hutch.' This seems rather manipulative so I haven't commented.

I get Clyde to go through the things in the fridge and tell me about them. But having to ask seems to make everything worse. Picking up a pack of margarine spread and demanding, 'Do we always get this sort, or was it on offer?' leaves so many more questions. What's the advice about cholesterol, these days – and where did I buy this anyway? It underlines the emptiness where all my routine experiences should be stored. The whole structure of decisions that led to these choices is gone. And I keep thinking,

OK, the margarine doesn't matter, but what else has been erased? Are there important things I should be doing right now, wiped out along with the trivia? I don't know. I just don't know.

On Thursday evening Clyde will drive us to the supermarket in the town. He's been getting me to practise my signature.

He fetches the little notepad from beside the phone and watches while I write my name. Not Kirsty Middleton, my new name.

I write *K. Villiers.*

'Pretty much the same,' he says. He gives me a shrewd look.

'I suppose it would be,' I say, irritated. 'I haven't had a stroke.'

'Yes, I suppose it would be,' he echoes, and then he adds, 'Or you wouldn't be able to buy anything, would you?'

'What's that supposed to mean?'

I know what it means. It means he doesn't trust me.

I'm suddenly furious. I scrumple up the page and throw it across the room; I try to tear the notepad and he takes it from me silently.

He looks so angry it occurs to me that if he hit me I might have a way out. I could call the police and get him excluded from the house. Maybe he deserves that – maybe he's bullied me for years. He's never properly explained how I got hurt at the river, not so's it makes any sense to me. Why is he so insistent that *actually* I slipped – that it was *actually* the riverbank I hit my head on? I know I don't flinch from him but maybe that's only because I've forgotten. Kirsten might have a journal somewhere chronicling a whole series of assaults, and he's found it and hidden it away.

But Clyde does not hit me, and I don't have the energy to be more deliberately provocative.

That's the trouble. I don't seem to have enough energy to be anyone. Kirsty Middleton, twenty-year-old student, is what's real to me; the towns and moors of Devon are what I know, but here

33

is where I am. Being here seems to take all my concentration so these other things are becoming fuzzy. They are still real, still more familiar than this alien place, but there seems to be a sheet of thick glass between me and the world I know.

So I do a list and we go shopping.

The supermarket is nothing like the ones I know. It has automatic double doors like an airport and when you walk in the first thing you see is flowers, big tubs of mixed bouquets and bunches of roses. Then racks of magazines, then CDs and videos – it's like a whole shopping mall in one hall. And the scent! A kind of succulent just-baked smell, like the patisseries in Paris I remember from my school trip. There are shelves and shelves of French sticks and croissants – *pain au chocolat, pain aux raisins* – I'm about to ask if this is a special French promotion when I see loads of Italian breads too, and American bagels and muffins, and Danish pastries . . . The whole world's baking is here in a transparent wrapper.

This place is unbelievable. Big broad aisles absolutely bulging with food. 'It's enormous,' I say to Clyde, but he says this is fairly small, actually, there's a bigger one in Bath that has clothes. I'm glad he didn't take me there, this is quite freaky enough. I've never seen so many cheeses – a whole wall of them, and then a lot more at a delicatessen counter, along with loads of salads and five sorts of olives. The fruit aisle is like a huge colour chart. Pinks and reds of summer berries, then a swathe of golden apricots and peaches; dark, mellow greens of melons, with a cascade of citrus colours at the end – oranges and grapefruit, lemons and limes. There are so many exotic fruits too – star fruit, prickly pears and tiny fruit like Chinese lanterns.

The veg is just as amazing. Plastic bowls of ready-made salad, already cut, washed and layered, and a sachet of dressing too. Lettuce, which I thought meant those floppy green things you hold under the tap and then swing for hours in a wire shaker, now means pretty frilly things with purple tips, or bags of tiny leaves with unlikely names like lambs' tails. Here's a whole aisle of tomatoes — tomatoes like marbles, tomatoes like mangoes, plum-red tomatoes and golden yellow tomatoes, mounds of loose tomatoes, sprays of tomatoes like grapes on a vine.

I'm beginning to feel there's something almost obscene about this abundance. Walking between these piles of shiny fruit and washed vegetables you'd hardly know what country you were in. The fruit of the planet is spread out for us, and I can't help wondering if some of the people who grow and pick and pack it ever eat this well. 'How many air miles d'you think it took this lot to get here?' I say to Clyde. He contemplates for a moment and then says, 'Shoppers like choice.' He indicates a family pack of tomatoes with 30 per cent extra free and Janey plops it into our trolley.

Janey knows all our favourite brands. Clyde reaches them down and she puts them in our trolley and pushes on. I'm quite surprised to see vegeburgers going in, but Clyde says that's because of the BSE scare. From what he's told me, this makes people's brains turn into sponges and they die; if that sci-fi tale is really true, I'm amazed anyone's eating meat at all these days. Janey tells me Alice is a vegetarian and she thinks she may turn into one too. She seems to feel it's out of her hands, like a jelly can't choose what shape it will turn out of the mould.

'So how can we be sure any of the beef cuts are OK?' I say, but Clyde says he'd rather talk about it later, it's a contentious issue in a rural area. He covers the vegeburgers with a one-extra-free pack of choc ices and we push on.

A lot of these packages look more like toys than food. The yoghurts are all done up like cartoon characters, little mermaids and Mister Men, smiley trains and zany turtles — I keep expecting them to jump up on little feet and start tap-dancing along the chill cabinet. It's not just the children's stuff either: everything seems to have bright labels and extra sachets stuck on, as though we all need coaxing to eat up.

Waiting at the checkout I find I'm staring disbelievingly at our trolley-load. All the labels look strange. For one thing, they have so much information on them. I lift out a little tin of tomato purée. ' "Twelve calories per serving. Made with genetically modified tomatoes." What's that?'

Clyde replies, without looking, 'Scientifically developed.'

'That doesn't sound very healthy.'

'Well, get used to it. They'll be doing it to everything soon.'

This is alarming. 'That sounds a bit stupid, after all that fuss about the beef. That was caused by interfering that went drastically wrong, wasn't it?'

He looks at the tin. '"Less waste and reduced energy in processing",' he reads. 'And it's cheaper.'

'You mean our health's not worth it? Or you agree?'

'No. I don't. I don't agree with messing about with nature one bit. But they aren't going to ask me, are they? They're going to do it whether we like it or not, and if we make a fuss they won't even tell us that's what they're doing. Come on, we can't start an argument about genetic engineering in the middle of a checkout queue.'

Why not? That seems a pretty good place to me. But it's our turn now, so I shuffle forward.

Prices are amazing. Even with all the economy packs and special offers it's still over seventy quid to fill a trolley. I can't believe our plastic cards will keep covering all this.

Kirsten has so many plastic cards. I had a cheque guarantee card and a donor card, and even that was paper, but she has a little leather wallet full of them. There's cards for the gym, for the car breaking down, for the phone; there's credit cards, bonus cards, and several store cards. I need two just for the supermarket. One gives me points and the other pays. The paying card will pay for anything. Clyde and Kirsten don't really need a cheque book: the plastic card does it all.

Janey knows about all this stuff. She knows which cards to

offer at the till where a boy pushes everything through and it gets checked as if by magic. There is this little box on the till like a mini departures board at an airport, and it knows everything I've bought, even down to the colour of the grapefruit. Every now and again it does a little sum and Janey sings out, 'Multibuy', or 'Buy one get one free!' or 'Extra reward points.' She talks about our shopping in slogans as though this is real conversation.

The supermarket car park has a paper bank and a bottle bank. Clyde drives over to them and starts dumping some stuff from the boot, then stops and gives me a newspaper from a big stack of old ones he's collected together. 'You should have a look through,' he says. 'Might ring a few bells.' Its still folded at the page about the European cup final he watched last Sunday.

'Maybe,' I say. Or maybe not. I stuff it in my bag. Clyde sighs, gets back in the car.

On the way home he starts pointing out traffic to me. 'That's a car you'll remember,' he says.

'Why? Whose is it?'

'I mean the model. It's a 1986 Sierra. You'll have seen that around.'

Clyde is clearly trying to be helpful. He seems more relaxed in the car. He has abandoned his look of rueful suspicion and is trying to get into the spirit of the last decade. He is car-spotting for me, to help me feel more at ease. The limit of Clyde's disorientation in my situation, apparently, would be seeing vehicles on the road that he couldn't put a name to. He points out an E-registered Honda Prelude, and then a Cavalier. 'Very distinctive styling.'

I can't think of any comments but I don't want to discourage him. He's obviously given this aspect of my trauma some thought.

'I suppose modern cars look quite space age to you,' he says. Actually they look like big sucked sweets but I nod non-committally.

'That's the CD factor,' Clyde goes on. 'Coefficient of drag.

They're tested in a wind tunnel. Better fuel efficiency these days – more aerodynamic. And green.'

'They seem mostly shades of grey to me,' I venture, and he chuckles like a little boy.

'Green, like ecologically efficient. You're keen on that. I've fitted a catalytic converter in ours and we use unleaded fuel. That was your idea too. Good one.' He sounds quite proud. I'm not sure if this is about the catalytic converter or the fact that we'd agreed about something.

'Escorts have changed quite a bit,' Clyde tells me, warming to his theme. 'The basic design has developed a lot over the last ten years.' I nod more vigorously. I know this because Clyde's car is nothing like Paul's. I try to think of things to say about this Escort. It appears that I drive it, too. In fact, it will be good for me to get back behind the steering-wheel, Clyde decides. This scares me. 'You used it every week,' Clyde says. 'It'll come back to you.'

'But I'm – I was still learning to drive at college,' I say. 'What if . . .'

He says, 'I'll sit in with you, if you want. On Saturday.'

I'm still not sure.

'I'll drive it to somewhere quiet, and you can practise. That's what we did before, when you went for your test.'

'You helped me pass my driving test?'

He nods. He seems pleased about all this. It doesn't seem to depress him, like everything else I've forgotten. Maybe it's because this is something he can actually get hold of, not the grey fudge that seems to be around most things. I can understand that.

Next night the phone rings and Clyde answers. It's already rung a few times before he got home but I don't like answering it. Last time it was another of those weird 'Kate, Kate' calls. Now I watch him as he stands with one hand in his trouser pocket jingling change. 'I know,' he keeps saying, 'I know.' Then 'I didn't want to trouble you.'

He turns round, passes the phone to his other hand and fiddles with the spirals of the telephone cord. 'We're fine,' he says, 'we're fine.' Then, 'Yeah, she's here.'

I stiffen in my chair but he holds out the receiver to Janey, who's been kneeling on the floor looking at the TV papers. She jumps up and takes it and says, 'Hello, Granny Vee.'

'My mother,' mouths Clyde, sitting down again, while Janey chatters on. It's clearly part of a familiar ritual that Janey deals with the dialogue.

'She's heard about what happened to you,' Clyde tells me. 'I didn't want to tell her till you were better but she's found out.'

I can't work out from his tone whether his caution was to protect his mother or me. 'Is she upset?' I say.

'Not really. She'll probably come to see for herself, though.' I start feeling all panicky and weepy at the thought of a strange mother-in-law arriving to stare at me. I say, 'When? When will she come?' but he only shrugs.

Janey is saying, 'Well, I'd better go now, Granny. Yes, you too. Bye-eee.' She hangs up without offering the receiver to Clyde for further farewells. She never even looked at me.

On Saturday morning Clyde reminds me about the driving practice. He takes me to a big car park on the edge of a wooded estate. I still feel a bit apprehensive but when we swap places I find it's easy-peasy to drive the car around, park up, reverse, and generally control it. He's giving the orders in a serious instructor voice, and I'm obeying without speaking, smooth as silk.

'Well done,' he says at the end, and he pats my knee. Janey – she's come with us – flings her arms around my neck from the back seat and kisses me, and I do feel quite touched by their pleasure.

He gets out, indicates to me to move back over so's he can drive us home. I obey again. I feel oddly tired.

He drives quickly, not the way we came but to a pub. It has a long beer-garden, with grass and trees. He parks the car and escorts me towards the wooden tables. 'Celebration,' he says. 'Or – would you rather go inside?'

I'm beginning to feel wobbly. I shake my head. 'It's lovely out here,' I manage to whisper.

Janey dances off to a table with bench seats under a huge horse-chestnut tree and I follow. She's quite a confident, happy little girl. I'm glad about that. Wouldn't it be awful if she was a whiny child, and it was all my fault?

Soon Clyde's bringing out a tray with drinks. A pint, a white wine, an orange juice, and three big grainy baps, their fillings spilling out, all garnished with bright salads.

'That looks delicious,' I say, and he smiles, a proper smile. He looks so much more likeable when he smiles.

He puts the tray down. 'Well?' he says.

Now I know why I feel shaky. It's a kind of test. I take the wine.

'Yes!' squeals Janey.

My queasy feeling sinks lower. They have planned this. 'If she gets the driving right,' he's said to our daughter, 'we'll take her to Our Place. We'll get Our Meal, and Click! We can switch her back on.' It's not the conspiracy that's making me shake: it's because I can't do it. I feel so sad – for them, not for me. For the first time I see this as something terrible happening to these two people, and not just to me.

I stare at the three baps with their visible fillings. Prawn, Cheddar, Stilton.

'They all look lovely,' I hazard. I look at Janey. Her eyes are flickering round all three. Clyde is looking intently at me.

I'm thinking furiously. Not Cheddar, that must be his. But would a child eat Stilton? The Stilton must be his. I haven't really noticed what he eats.

I reach out.

I take the prawns.

There's a moment when even the birds stop singing. Then

Janey says, in a small voice, 'Which is mine, then, Daddy?'

I'm crying and crying. I want to go home.

'We'll go home,' he says. He's sounding scared. As though he's become part of it now, not outside it. Now he's able to make it worse. I want to tell him I don't mean his home, I mean my home, in Devon, my mum and dad's house where I used to live. Where I still live, in my head.

We got through the lunch, in the end. I couldn't bear to see them walk away from the tray with its pathetic pile of dashed hopes.

'I'm sorry,' I say, when we get back, 'I really—'

'I know,' he cuts in. 'You don't remember.'

'It was worth trying, though. It's worth trying all these things.' This takes me quite an effort. I want to say, 'Don't ever trick me like that again. The emptiness is bad enough without unhappiness like that.'

He says, 'I feel so useless. It's like you've rubbed me out of your life.'

I know I should say, *I can learn to love you again — we can turn over a new page.* But I don't want to say that. I feel too bruised to want to touch anyone. Maybe Janey's warm little hand, but not this big heavy man full of anger and unhappiness. How much did I put there? How much did he put in me? There is no such thing as a new page, is there? Not when the book's already printed.

There's a kiwi fruit in the bowl beside the kitchen window. The bowl is transparent plastic, bright blue, and the sun spills through it on to the worktop making a pool of brilliant shadow. I've been looking at that kiwi every day and watching the mossy skin slowly turn bruise-dark. It has a pulpy, puckered look, as if a fingerprint touch would linger on the dull surface. I've been wondering why no one's eaten it. Maybe it was bought to decorate some dessert that never got made – there's a packet of cheesecake in the cupboard and Janey is into those sweet, synthetic things. Maybe we were planning to make that together, only no one's got the heart to remind me now. Or maybe I'm the only person in the house who likes kiwi.

And I just don't know. It's so absurd, and so painful. But I keep on thinking about it because this problem is small and safe. The tiny dilemma of why this one kiwi remains in the bowl is less agonising than lifting my eyes to ask why this kitchen, this house, this village, this life, this everything. Why now, why ever? No, a soggy kiwi is easier to hold than all that.

By the evening I'm tired again. I look through the stuff at the side of the bed where I sleep for something to read – I was half-way through Miles's copy of *The Wasp Factory* – but there's only magazines here, a glossy one and a couple of mumsies. There's also some tapes called things like *Relaxation* and *Balancing Your Chakra Energy Colours*. I put one in my Walkman and press the play button. *Feel the light at your temple shooting forward into the black void, crossing the barriers of time, transcending the limits of the known universe. This power can be used to make contact with etheric world intelligences, should you so desire.*

I take off the headphones and find I'm crying, sobbing noisily and despairingly. Clyde appears in the doorway. 'Aren't there any books in this house?' I say. My voice sounds querulous, imperious. Clyde disappears, then comes back with a paperback, a novel called *The Ghost Road*. I take it from him and see the name 'Polly' pencilled in the front. The marker is at page ten. 'You borrowed that,' says Clyde, 'but I don't think it grabbed you.'

He's looking at me with that awful yearning look that's even worse than the puzzled, fucked-up look he usually has. I open the book quickly, as though I haven't heard him say quietly, 'How long, Kirsten?'

He says this often. *How long, Kirsten?* It fills me with panic and revulsion. At first I thought he meant, How long before you remember me? which freaked me, or, How long before you admit that you remember me? which made me furious. Now I realise it means something else too. He means he wants me. The big bed with its sprigged quilt is between us as I meet his eyes and turn away.

My OT is called Jemima. She wears plaits and hair extensions and she tells me neuropsychology isn't really her bag but she's getting supervision. I say I don't think her specialism matters much because in the end it's me who has to do the remembering. She looks a bit shocked, as though I've downgraded her profession-alism. But if there is some kind of fuse blown in my system and a switch that needs turning back on, as my GP has explained it to me, then I can't believe these tests have much effect either way. I don't mind doing them, but I can't pin any faith on them. It seems more helpful when we just talk. She suggests I make a list of things I'd like to know about Clyde — what music he likes, his favourite meals and animals, that sort of thing. And then we can work through it like a sort of game.

I've made my list. I tell Clyde about it as soon as he comes home.

He just stares and then he says, 'That's my shirt.' I'm wearing this dark red cotton shirt I found. I've rolled up the sleeves and tied it above the waist. And I've found my old trainers. I went hunting in a black bag of stuff in the spare room — mostly baby dresses — and there they were.

I say, 'D'you mind me wearing it?'

He says, 'You look different.'

That's not really an answer, is it? But he doesn't seem to mind. He looks puzzled but not annoyed. He says, 'You look really nice.' Then he looks worried, as though I may frown or turn away.

And what I want to know is: is that because I'm different to him now, or is Clyde always nervous of saying things like 'You look nice,' to his wife?

It's strange and scary knowing he's waiting to be allowed to have sex with me. He hasn't tried yet, which I am seriously relieved about. Waking up beside a stranger is traumatic enough. I haven't even looked at him naked. He sleeps in pyjama bottoms, thankfully. The hairs on his chest and under his arms are gingery and curly. Did I tangle my fingers through them? Did I passionately suck the drops of sweat from them? It's difficult to think about these things.

His overall top is pulled down because it's hot, so the sleeves are dangling; there's a big smear of dirty oil on his rather naff acrylic T-shirt – one of those polo-style ones with a navy stripe along the collar. I think looking grubby improves it. He says quickly, 'I'm going to wash,' and goes into the bathroom.

I can hear my heart thudding. I know when he comes back I ought to kiss him. I don't think he will compel me, but that moment was the closest we have come to tenderness without tension, and I know that I can't let it slip away without making some effort. If he is my husband, if this is going to be my life, then I have to give it a try.

So he comes back into the kitchen slowly, watching me, walking right up to me. His face is freshly shaved and smells of something musky. He's pulled off his dirty clothes and put on jeans but not another T-shirt. He's taking his glasses off and putting them on the worktop. That big bare muscular chest is close but not quite touching me. I have time to decide, myself, to sway slightly towards him, and I hear his tiny gasp, which is almost a groan, as our bodies touch all the way down. I move my thigh across self-protectingly and he doesn't push against me there, but his chest is really close to mine, hard and heavy and warm.

His mouth is seeking mine. He keeps his eyes open so I close mine. His kiss is tender but soft. Really, I like hard-lipped kisses, but I don't know how to say it. After a while I pull my face away but slowly, and not moving away so he is still cradling me. He seems pleased with our first embrace.

I turn so he won't see that I can't stop myself from wiping my mouth, rubbing my fingers fiercely across the licky kind of sensation he left on my lips that suddenly felt unbearably like slime. He's putting his glasses back on and I really don't know if he saw.

We settle down and I start on the questions.

'Favourite colour?'

'What for?'

'Anything – a colour you like.'

'I dunno. Red.'

Maybe this isn't going to be very revealing, after all.

'You're not trying,' I complain, but he says he is, and what's my favourite colour, if it comes to that, because it's not a thing we've ever discussed?'

I let the list drop, but he picks it up and says to go on.

'What's the point? You're right, a relationship isn't a collection of facts about each other.'

'It's a start,' he insists. 'Come on, ask me some more.'

'Favourite place for a holiday,' I say grumpily.

'Here.'

'Favourite person to play with, when you were a child.'

'My brother.'

That seems useful. I ask about his brother, but Clyde says, 'He was run over when he was nine. I was seven.'

This startles me, and gives me a funny feeling I don't like. I'm trying to push away a picture of Clyde not big and self-sufficient but a little boy grieving, frightened and lonely. It makes me want to hug him and that scares me.

'I'm sorry,' I say flatly.

'Is that all the questions?'

So we go on. I'm writing down his answers. Favourite recording artists (mostly soul singers, surprisingly), favourite TV shows (*Top Gear*) . . .

'Favourite sport?'

'To watch or to do?'

'To do – or something you'd like to try.'

'Microlight. Or hang-gliding.'

I get this image of Clyde dangling in the air far above me, a kind of Icarus, not flailing and falling but suddenly soaring. The sun flashes on his glasses and the sky is very blue. Up and up he soars, until he is tiny in the distance.

'What about you?'

'Oh . . . water,' I say. 'Something with a splash. Windsurfing, maybe.'

'You liked the chutes when we went for Janey's birthday. You liked them better than she did. The high one you said was like death by orgasm. And I said I'd wait for the real thing.'

In my mind's eye Clyde drops to earth with a thud. He shakes off the canvas wings. We are alone on the windy hillside.

I look down at my list of questions. 'What sort of things do we row about?'

'Row? How do you mean?'

I don't really know. It's Jemima's idea for a question, that one. 'Rows . . . like, arguing. Shouting.'

'You don't do that,' he says.

There have to be rows in every relationship, Jemima says. I don't think that's true, actually. My parents never row, not so's you'd notice. Dad used to say, 'If you don't think you're going to like the answer, don't ask the question.' Mum sometimes got angry about things in a tight-lipped sort of way and banged a few doors, but he never retaliated. He would just go quietly away till it was all over – whatever it was. Mostly I never even knew.

'Well, I'm glad,' I say. 'I think it's better for the kids if parents don't argue.'

'Yes,' he says. 'I know you do.'

His flat tone puzzles me. 'Don't you?'

He doesn't answer right away, and then he says, 'When I was

eleven I was the biggest boy in the school. When I was thirteen I was taller than my teacher. I learned early that if there was a row I would be the one blamed. I was labelled a bully before I even knew what the word meant. No, I don't like rows.'

This is the longest speech I've ever heard from Clyde that's not about cars. This game is getting heavy. I flip to the end of my list looking for something lighthearted.

'What's better than sex?'

I expect him to say 'cars', but he doesn't. He looks at me, hungrily. Then he says quietly, 'Better than sex with you? Nothing.'

There is a silence you could split with a sighing breath. Then he says, 'I love you.'

This big, serious man says *I love you*, and I don't know what to do and I don't know how many times or hundreds of times he's said it before or even if he's never said it before. For me it comes absolutely new, and it shocks me.

He recovers quickly. 'But other things are good too. Watching Janey run on sports day, that was great. Bacon and eggs. Going flat out on a good road.'

I'm grateful. Soon I'll have to make some decision about this matrimonial-expectations thing but, please, not today, not tonight.

Janey comes in from the garden and I put my notes away. I haven't learned much, really, except that Clyde loved Kirsten. And now he says he loves me.

Thinking about that hungry look of his reminds me of Miles. 'I'm hungry . . .' he says that. Used to say, I mean. He whined it, quiet and meaningful, looking at me under his lashes. Hungry for love. '*I'm hungry, hungry, hungry* . . .' He meant lustful, and he knew I liked that.

I realise, thinking about Miles now, that it's not too surprising that we lost touch. It was never exactly a flaming passion. We started being an item almost accidentally, the day Debs and I took

Miles and Paul to Dartmoor. As they were both city boys we insisted they had to visit the tors, the famous granite rocks on the moorland.

Paul had a car of sorts, a heap of rust that spent more time off the road than on it. It is – or was in its youth – a silver Escort and it only cost him a hundred pounds. Originally it was a hundred and fifty but the price dropped along with the bottom of the doors while Paul was hassling his family for the finance. The problem wasn't the car, or even the petrol, it was the insurance. He'd been trying to persuade his aunt Miriam to help with this (Paul had absentee parents – his father was something posh in the embassy in Italy). When Mim's sub finally came through, so did our trip to the tors.

We got Paul to park off the road near the biggest of them, Hay Tor, and then trekked through the bracken towards the grey mass of rocks ahead. The stones are splayed about, huge and half hidden in scrubby grass, then you find a clump together piled maybe twenty or thirty feet high. It's cold up there, even on a warm day. The wind was blagging us as we started climbing the rough steps hacked into the granite. Half-way up Hay Tor there's a big gap you have to swing yourself across. I showed them how. But Paul was hungover that day, and he said, 'Forget that, I'm fucked,' and jumped down on to the outcrop below. He untied his jumper from his waist, dropped it on one of the flat boulders and flopped on to it. Debs sat down quickly beside him. I was already on the final stone, climbing the crudely carved steps, which curl round the tor, clinging on as the wind cut me. It was too late to go back.

Miles was following close behind me. 'Wimp,' he called back, and laughed. I laughed too but Paul didn't reply. We reached the top.

By the time we got back down to the ledge, where the rock sprawled out below the chasm, Debs and Paul were entwined on the scrubby grass, oblivious of the gorse and rabbit droppings.

Miles held my wrist, steadying me, harder than I needed. He pulled me round to him. I half screamed as I wobbled in the blundering wind, and he pulled me towards him. Balanced together, precarious, high above the jagged rock outcrops, he kissed me on the lips. His tongue felt cold as it forced into my mouth; I was afraid my chattering teeth would bite it. He held me there until we heard Paul and Debs call us from below and knew they had separated and seen us. We climbed down to join them. Paul's jacket was round Debs's shoulders; Miles held my chill hands to warm them. And it was done. He was hers, and Miles was mine. That's how it started, and we never talked about it. Miles was nice enough, but safe. Come to think of it, he looks a tiny bit like Clyde. Nothing special.

After supper I ask Clyde something that's been on my mind since we did the quiz.

'Did we ever try for more kids?'

'You only wanted one.'

'And you?'

He shrugs. 'I've always treated her as my own,' he says, and then, seeing my expression, 'Janey's not my child. Kirsten, it's obvious – you must have worked that out.'

But I haven't. I haven't been in the mood for doing mathematical calculations recently. Clearly I should. Janey is not Clyde's child. She is my last connection with Kirsty and the summer of 1987.

The Third Week

Janey's school is perfectly pleasant. It's a long, low building with a small playground at the front and a biggish grassy area at the back, with trees, which looks nice for playing out on summer days. There's not much space for parking but Janey always walks, she tells me, with her friend Alice and Alice's mum who is an assistant there. I've been leaving it up to Alice's mum, Polly, to keep this going without any intervention from me but Jemima is keen on me getting more involved with the Janey aspect of things.

This is an arranged visit. I have arranged with Mrs Crabbe, Janey's teacher, to sit in her class this morning. Apparently I sometimes came in on a Monday to 'hear' the children – one of a rota of reading-support volunteers. The idea is to see if this activity will trigger any recent recollections. I'm not optimistic. I've looked at Janey's books when she brings them home and none of them means a thing to me.

This whole Janey thing is doing my head in.

When Clyde said she wasn't his, I believed him straight away. It's like a little piece of jigsaw quietly clicked into place. But instead of making the picture clearer, it made everything more confusing. It's as if, in this jigsaw in my mind, that new piece has shown me that something I had nearly got sorted out is really something else – like a patch of blue I thought was sky is really water, and I have the whole picture upside-down. That's how I feel now.

Janey was eight at the end of March, so she could be Miles's child. Why didn't I tell Clyde? Why doesn't Miles send us money or something? Why were we so careless anyway? I keep telling myself I really must start thinking about all that, but it's too confusing and awful. I can't get my head round it. I'm putting it off, now, until Mum and Dad come. Obviously they will know about it even if Clyde doesn't.

In the meantime I may as well take a look at Janey's school. Janey is here in my life whether I like it or not, and I'm part of hers. Everyone's gone in already – I insisted on avoiding the other mums at the school gates – and I take a deep breath as I follow Janey through the door.

Inside there's a wide corridor full of neatly labelled kiddie pictures. 'Today is lundi' a sign informs me, and a sunny picture tells me 'Il fait beau'.

'What's that?' I ask Janey, trying to show interest. From what I remember of junior school people were always asking you things they actually knew, just to check that you knew too. Janey barely gives it a glance. 'Top year,' she says blithely. 'They do different topics.'

Janey skips along to a big room full of little desks and tables. I follow her in. It's milling with children all about her size, all wearing blue V-neck sweaters, which is a bit unnerving on a warm day. Janey is pointing round and announcing names in a singsong voice. Some of the children look up at me and smile, some are busy with those inscrutable childish debates that seem to absorb all their attention and leave no room for consciousness of others. Lucky them, I think. I smile feebly.

Janey points out a little girl with freckles and announces that this is Alice. Alice flashes me a benign smile and carries on with her drawing of a chameleon. Alice is coming with us next time we go to see my parents at their villa, where those photos were taken.

We go there for our holidays, Janey has told me, but not till the summer is over because the sun prickles her and she gets ill if it's too hot. Their video shop apparently takes pesetas hand over fist from sundried ex-pats on the Costa Brava. Which is why, when my parents come to see me next week, they are not driving up from Devon but flying over from Spain.

Mrs Crabbe strides in and my legs go all school-phobic and turn to jelly. I found it really difficult to explain to Mrs Crabbe on the phone, and in the end I got Jemima to write a letter for me. I hand this over now, feeling as if I'm trying to get excused from PE, and she reads it, frowning.

'No problem,' she says. 'We've been reading about Sleeping Beauty, and she had a century to catch up on.' She gives me a feisty smile and I decide a naff joke is better than concealed embarrassment.

Mrs Crabbe wears leggings and a big baggy T-shirt, and has short messy hair. She looks like a woman who owns dogs, if you know what I mean. She doesn't fuss the children in that sarcastic way I thought all teachers did, she lets them bounce around until they settle naturally. She's sent a kid to get another proper-sized chair from the hall for me, and I sit beside her desk watching as she ticks off the names in a register by looking round the room instead of calling out. When she sees one of them looking at her and waiting to be ticked – they obviously know her head-turning route – she pulls a silly face, and they giggle. They do go quiet, though, when she closes the register. She holds it out without saying anything and a small girl takes it and disappears from the room.

'Big assembly today,' says Mrs Crabbe. 'We've got something very special happening, but I forget what it is.'

I decide I like Mrs Crabbe. I don't remember her, though. I don't remember this room, or these faces; or the sunny, daisy-spotted field outside the window, not even the schooly sort of smell. In fact, I could say with absolute confidence that I have never been here in my life before this morning. But once again I'd be wrong.

The children are getting out reading books from desks and bags. Some have gone to a sort of screen with books tucked in behind elastic and done some swapping and ticking-off on charts. It all seems fairly laid back. I sit in the chair feeling detached.

'Do you want to hear Daniel?' says Mrs Crabbe. 'He needs extra attention – and a lot of encouragement.'

I look at Daniel. I think, I'll bet he does. This is a child who needs a good bath, a haircut, and a hug every night until the crease between his stubby eyebrows is smoothed away. I sit down beside him in one of the little chairs.

'Hello Janeysmum,' growls Daniel.

He's staring at his book and for a moment I think that the reading has begun. Realising that this is a greeting gives me a shock. I should be prepared for it, of course. Presumably every child in the room has seen me before and recognises me, even with my 'different hair'. But I've done a kind of ostrich thing. Because I don't recognise anyone, I've let myself assume they don't know me.

'Hello, Daniel.'

What Daniel has is not a proper book but a folder with some cut-out words tucked into sort of little shelves. They say 'Daniel' and 'Dad' and some others, like 'dog' and 'ball'. Three of them are pushed together to say 'I play ball'.

'D'you want to read me that?' I say.

'Football,' he says instantly, then swings round to me. 'D'you see the matches last week, Janeysmum? D'you see England? We won lots, din't we? Din't beat Germany. But we beat Holland. Beat Spain.' He looks at me with shining eyes and a glittering nose.

I get out a tissue and do something about the latter. I remember that in my bag I've still got the newspaper Clyde gave me, the one about the cup final, so Daniel spends his reading time poring over match reports and telling me about the players in the pictures with a bewildering blend of affection and slander. He also designs a second strip for the England team, which would be better than the bollocks they had for the semi-final, he says.

At the end of this session the children go off for a bit of a break before assembly. Daniel slings his folder into a desk and plods after the squealing horde and I say to Mrs Crabbe, 'I hope that was OK. He didn't seem very keen on reading.'

'No problem. It was fine. Didn't . . . spark any memories, then?'

I shrug. It must be obvious it had not.

'You always had a soft spot for Daniel,' Mrs Crabbe says. She laughs. 'If you don't mind my saying so, your approach has changed fairly dramatically.'

'Why? What was wrong before?'

'Oh, nothing. You were more orthodox.'

'So was I wrong today?'

'Certainly not. Daniel's scheduled to have extra class support from September. You should apply.' She picks up her bag. 'Coffee calls. D'you want to come to the staffroom? Helpers can. It might . . .'

I know that nothing there will ring any bells, or whatever chosen phrase half forms then falters. But I feel comfortable with Mrs Crabbe. She seems straightforward. She says, 'I won't tell anyone about your amnesia unless you want me to. Volunteer assistants are fairly anonymous people here anyway, and you may find it easier just to learn who's who again from scratch, without explaining anything. I'll sit with you and keep you on course, if you want.'

I realise, suddenly, that for the last two weeks all my queries have been answered by subliminal versions of the same reply – 'You shouldn't be starting from here.' The idea that I can simply start from today, meeting people and getting to know them, is very reassuring.

I give her a grateful look. 'I'd prefer that. I feel enough of a freak as it is.'

As we're walking out I see a crayon picture of a cat displayed by the door. There's a poem underneath, too, in careful, round-handed script, with a coloured border. It's the name underneath that catches my eye. Janey Villiers. I can't help feeling rather pleased.

'That's nice,' I say.

'Yes,' says Mrs Crabbe, looking round. 'Her best work this term, probably. You were quite upset when one of the other mums said you'd helped her. Well, you were in tears one day and you said that was what it was about.'

'Was I?' I can feel a slow blush soaking my face. What a stupid thing to get upset about. 'Who was the other mother?' I say, trying to shrug, trying to smile, trying to find out if there was more to it than Kirsten's pathetic paranoia.

'Helen Montague. She gets her off-days, so I shouldn't worry.'

'I'm not worried,' I say. But I do feel anxious. That name again. My friend Helen, whom I haven't yet seen. Perhaps she's having a string of her notorious off-days.

'You know, you're different today,' says Mrs Crabbe, as she sits beside me in the staffroom balancing a coffee mug on one knee while opening her post.

'What was I like?' This is such an absurd question. I'm smiling to show I know how ludicrous it sounds, willing her to tell me straight, willing her not to say anything I'll hate.

She chucks her post in the bin and concentrates on her coffee.

'Well, you're more laid-back now, for sure. More — it's funny, because you must be under quite a strain, but you come over as more relaxed.' While I'm digesting this and sipping coffee, she adds, 'Have you considered hypnosis?'

I shake my head.

'It's a thought. Isn't it?'

'No way. I feel out of control enough as it is. The idea of

losing consciousness again scares the shit out of me. And how would I know if the memories I came up with were right, and really belong to my life here? I've got no ordinary certainties any more. I could end up convinced I was Cleopatra.'

She pulls one of her faces. 'I see what you mean. And that's another way you're different, by the way. I never heard you say "shit" before.'

Janey's school is a lot nicer than my primary, with its high walls and tarmac playground. Mine was an old building, the same school my mum went to and it wasn't even new then. Of course, being in the centre of town didn't help. Here they've got a feeling of space in the playgrounds: you can see all the way to the woods and fields in the distance, which is very different from the bricked-in views we had. I used to go traipsing home beside the tall wall where the houses were so high you have to go up steps from the road to reach the pavement. Then round the corner to the big square with a church in the middle. When I was little I didn't understand about the square: it seemed so huge I thought there was another road on the other side of town with the same name as ours.

Our house had a long front garden with a cobbled path beside a wall with a flat top which you could walk on. When it was high, Dad used to lift me on to it at the gate so I could walk up to the front door, as tall as his shoulder. Over the years the wall somehow got lower until it was low enough to sit on. The house became less enormous too. All the houses in our road got smarter as I grew older – actually smarter, I mean, as opposed to the metamorphosis of growing up that dwindled the square and the garden wall. They became fashionable, and smart firms bought them up and painted them in tones of cream and green to suit the Georgian fronts. Dad did ours up, too, though he groaned about 'going bourgeois', as though it was worse than going bald.

Debs always talks about *parents* as if they are really boring but I often feel mine had a more interesting life than I have. Debs's parents are teachers, so maybe she's right in her case – though if so why is she doing a teacher-training course? But mine are quite interesting. Dad was a bit of a flower child, back in the sixties. Then he got a job at a home for delinquents down in Devon, which is where he met Mum, who was trying to be a painter and sculptor and pulling pints in a scrumpy bar at the same time. They didn't get married till I was nearly five – there are pictures of me at the wedding in a blue taffeta dress with cornflowers in my hair – and only then because Gran was ill and Mum wanted to make her happy. They had the ceremony at the church opposite her house, in Devon Square. I remember Gran looking fierce and elegant in navy, with gold hoops in her ears like an aristocratic gypsy, leaning on her stick. She died soon after and we moved into the house. Before that we lived in a flat in Teignmouth but I don't remember much about that.

Dad bought a shop down the road and called it The Corner Shop, although it was in the middle of a terrace. I think my earliest memory is of bagging up potatoes, the earthy smell and the pebbly feel of them, the way the soft grime came away on your fingers. We used to have meals of weird combinations of food, what Mum called our sell-by meals. When the new regulations came Dad stopped doing most of the fresh food and started a video library. It really took off: by the time I was at university we opened from ten till ten and the whole place was videos.

By then it was pretty easy work. When I was doing my shift I just had to sit at the counter reading, or watching the TV, and booking the videos in and out. No weighing or bagging and not much calculation. One pound a night's hire, or one-fifty for the new releases. And, of course, I got to see them all. *The Breakfast Club, Pretty in Pink, Ferris Bueller's Day Off* – I was first to see all the smart films on video.

Debs wanted us to get a flat together, in Exeter. She thinks

I'm lame for not being keen. 'What's the point?' I say. 'We can't really afford it, and I'd still have to go home every weekend to help out in the shop. I owe my parents that much, at least, the amount they're forking out.'

'What's the point?' she says, miming, jeering. 'Kirsty, freedom is the point! Men are the point. Wouldn't you like to have somewhere a bit more comfortable for you and Miles than the cemetery or the back of Paul's car?'

But I'm not sure that I would. I rather like the sudden thrill of finding an unused room at a party, or sneaking into the woods at night, or even making the dustbins rattle in a back entry. It occurs to me that with a bedroom always to hand Miles would develop expectations. I think I prefer things the way they are.

Now, on the other hand, if I had Debs's Paul I would probably feel rather differently. In fact I would be in the mood all the time, without needing a bit of illicit frisson to enthuse me. Paul is drop-dead gorgeous. Debs seriously doesn't appreciate him – she actually says she's always rather fancied Miles.

'Miles!' I'm fascinated.

'Don't make him sound like a slug in your salad, Kirsty. He is your boyfriend so you must fancy him too.'

I suppose I must. But Paul . . .

I wonder what Paul looks like now. He used to have a great body from playing a lot of sports at his school. I remember eyeing him up as he went racing up and down the beach in his boxer shorts the day we all cut lectures.

It was nearly the end of the summer term but not quite. We'd met up on the stone wall by the Cathedral Close. We often meet there because I walk up from the station and the boys' room is on the far side of the college buildings – it's also about half-way between where we have our lectures and where Debs has hers. It was mid-morning and much too nice a day to do any work. We should go to the seaside, Paul decided. Torquay. And Debs said no, Torquay is either pensioners and Pekinese or else it's vulgar T-shirts and games arcades. Teignmouth is better. So we went to Teignmouth.

Teignmouth is about twelve miles from Newton Abbot, about half an hour's drive from Exeter for a sensible driver, or twenty-three minutes exactly if you go with a lunatic like Paul. We hadn't got towels or cossies or anything like that with us so we went to the pub on the quay for crab sandwiches and beers. We were sitting outside watching the sailing boats and Miles saw the little black-and-white-painted ferry chugging across the estuary to Shaldon. He said, 'Where does that go?' We told him, and they both wanted to go on it.

'It's not worth going there,' Debs said. 'It's a really boring place, just Georgian fronts and a village green and a few posh new houses up the back.'

But Miles had found a leaflet about Shaldon having a smugglers' tunnel to a beach below the high cliff and he insisted we had to go. So we queued on the beach for the ferry and twenty minutes later we were offloaded on the opposite side of the bay. The smugglers' tunnel smelt of piss and the beach was tiny and stony.

'I told you it was boring,' Debs said, but Miles said, 'How can you say that when there's jet-skis about?' And he went charging into the water still wearing his jeans and trainers and started rushing up and down pretending to be a jet-ski. Paul pulled off his jeans and followed him in. They were charging around in the waves making zroom-zroom sounds. Debs and I were killing ourselves laughing. Then they had a go at being speedboats and water-skiers, each taking it in turns to be running behind with both arms held out like they were clutching tight to a tow-rope, then with one hand, then the other, then – 'Aaagh!' shouted Paul, as Miles did a sharp turn, and he keeled over in front of where Debs and I were standing, falling dramatically into the shallow water and splashing us so totally we thought we might as well take our jeans and T-shirts off too. A family with a frisbee nearby moved their windbreak further down the beach in a marked manner and we all cracked up laughing again.

When we got tired of this, and of speedboating and surfing in the shallows too, we sat on the sea-smoothed boulders and watched tiny crabs, almost transparent, wavering under the seaweedy rims of the rock pools and argued idly about whether it was worth going to look for chips. Eventually, when the blue sky started to pale and we were beginning to get shivery, we walked back through the prim little village with its trim rose-bush gardens and over the long roadbridge to Teignmouth.

I remember it so clearly. Paul put the Oysterband in the tape deck he had wedged in the glove compartment and we sang along.

I wonder where Paul and Debs are now. I wonder where Miles is.

The thought of Miles is preying on my mind confusingly. His image is becoming less clear now, and I get a different sort of lonely feeling that is more despairingly painful than the rest of the big muddle of bewilderment that floats around me. The fuzzy, foggy feeling is because each absence is still more real than the concrete things around me. I can still list each piece in the pattern of my life, but I have to put a denial in front of every item. No college, no student's union bar, no morning scramble across the park to the station to get the train, no Miles meeting me by the tree with the dromedary branches, no routine rows with the stores about borrowing the five-four camera, no Andy eyeing me over the coffee cups, no Debs's crucial laugh, no Paul's sweet silhouette at the window where he sits to smoke his tiny roll-ups. Impossible to accept that all this has vapourised utterly, not instantly but with the passing of years.

I stay at Janey's school all day, doing different things. For the last lesson I leave her class and help some of the little ones get changed back after PE. They're quite sweet. Only five, some of them.

The arrangement today is that I'll walk home with Janey and Alice, and Alice's mum Polly, the one who Clyde says is 'just another mum'. She seems quite old – nearly forty, I reckon. I've had to explain to her about the forgetting, though, in case we sometimes had some different agreement. It's a panic-making thought that Alice and Janey might be left uncollected after a forgotten dance class or something, but Polly says she usually does the accompanying. When I get through to her that I really don't remember this, or even her, she doesn't seem offended. 'We'll take it as it comes,' she says, offhandedly.

As we're going out of the noisy playground Janey says, 'Sometimes I go home with Sam.' She's been pointing out various kids all day. I can't take it all in. Sam is one she's named a few times, a sparky little boy with loads of confidence and expensive trainers. He's climbing into a pale grey Peugeot parked beside the rail – right where you're not supposed to park, actually, because then the lollipop lady can't be seen properly. The woman in the driving-seat has sunglasses pushed up into her auburn hair and she's looking in the driver's mirror. She seems to be watching me.

'Why?' I ask Janey, 'It's not far enough to need a lift home.'

'Sometimes we play at his house,' she says, 'and I stay for tea.'

The child is in the back of the car now. He pulls the door shut, waving in a generalised way, and the woman slides the glasses over her eyes and drives off.

I feel really tired when I get home. There's a cat, probably our cat, crying somewhere. I can hear Janey talking to it, then the rattle of dry pellets in the bowl.

I really ought to do something about this rabbit Janey keeps pestering about. It seems to have become something significant, as though getting this creature will be like saying an enormous yes to everything, giving in to all the things I don't under-stand. As though once there is a rabbit there will really be no way out.

The radio is playing a song I've heard before. Something about things being ironic.

I've been doing more rummaging in the spare-room boxes, but warily. I keep thinking of the story of Pandora. There are lots of scribbles and crayoned pictures – Kirsten must have kept every drawing Janey ever did. I've also discovered my old certificates and Record of School Achievement, a bundle of reports with a red spiral binding. I flip through. Ticked boxes. *Can do, can do.* Then some handwritten comments. My art teacher gave me A grades and wrote 'Kirsty has a great deal of untapped creativity. I am pleased she is seeking a career within the arts.' And here's my head of year, summing up. 'Kirsty should try to be more decisive. Under her noncommittal exterior she has much to offer, but really needs to find out what she can offer and what she wants from life. She must be prepared to take the initiative.'

I put the folder away and go back to the kitchen. That song is still playing. Ironic seems about right.

Clyde is doing veggie sausages and beans, with those potato waffle things Janey likes. When I go in he gets a third plate out. 'D'you want any?' he says, but I'm not hungry. I pour a mug of tea from the pot and go out into the garden.

This morning in Janey's school seems totally unreal now that I'm back here, like a video film that's reached the end and won't rewind. I wish I could put it away in its box in a spare room somewhere and get up into the life I know.

I can't believe it's all gone. I feel so certain it was only a few days ago we were all talking about coming back in September as second-years. It was after we'd been to see Nico off as he hitch-hiked to London on the first leg of his journey to France. We'd waved to him as he climbed up into the lorry cab then walked back to the services and sat on that steep grassy bank outside drinking Clausthaler lagers.

'It's going to be well cool to be second-years,' said Paul. Debs pushed her sunglasses up into her hair. 'Hey, I'm a second-year,

I'm coo-ool,' she mocked. Miles and I were lying back on the grass and my head was propped against Miles's chest. I had my camera round my neck. I started focusing on a nearby clump of wild flowers. There was a big refrigerator truck beyond and I thought it made a good picture.

'What's your angle?' said Paul.

I checked the zoom lens. 'Wide-ish. About thirty-five.'

He laughed. 'I meant yours, not the equipment's. Here – make it a statement about environmental pollution.' He drained his lager and slung the bottle into the shot.

Debs giggled and nearly choked on the grass stem she was chewing. 'Yeah, right! Subversive daisies.'

Miles said, 'Paul expects everyone to manipulate the truth because journalists do.'

'All media manipulates truth,' Paul said. 'Photographs can lie just as much as words.'

'I think that's probably true,' I said and, as Miles shook his head, 'What about that Don McCullin picture about the famine in Biafra? That starving woman with a child trying to suck her. It wasn't even her baby.'

'Yes, but there's an essential integrity there that's more important than the facts,' Miles argued. 'He's showing the truth about the aftermath of war.'

Debs shuddered. 'I'd hate to have a baby in a war. What a nightmare responsibility.'

'I do my best to avoid it,' said Paul, grinning, 'Like, I'm a pacifist.'

Miles flipped him lightly on the head. 'You lying dog. You'd start a war today if it gave you a story.'

The thought of Paul and Miles in battle fatigues sweating in a jungle somewhere while army helicopters whirred overhead was making me feel quite faint with excitement. I lay back and listened while Miles and Paul argued on about the rival depravity of words and images. 'We follow the wars, but the wars follow you,' Paul insisted. 'You photographers make things happen just by being there. Of course you do – every kid will make a face for the camera. What about that television reporter, that Kate Adie woman? Everywhere she goes there's instantly a battle.' And Miles conceded but countered, 'What about that guy in the Congo, or wherever? "Anyone here been raped and speak English?" Intrusive reporting like that is part of the problem.'

'Let's face it, we're all part of the problem,' said Debs. 'One person's solution is another person's problem. Just accept it.'

I love it when we talk like this. I can never think of anything smart to say, but it feels so cool to be part of the analysis, knowing we are the media-makers of the future.

Paul had been picking off daisy heads and laying them in a line down Debs's leg. 'So you reckon we media men have the future of the world in our hands,' he said.

Debs said, 'Media persons, actually.' She twitched her leg and the flowers fell into the grass. He began picking them up and re-creating his white petalled road on my arm. My skin, already sticky from the sun, melted a little more at his fingertip touch.

Then Paul sat up and leaned over me on his elbow and said, in a grave voice, 'Your mission – should you choose to accept it – is to look into the future.' He swept all the daisies up in his hand. 'Come on. Cross my palm with daisies and make a prediction. Five years from now –' he jumped up suddenly '– five years from now, what will we be doing?'

None of us answered straight away so he changed the challenge. 'OK. What d'you want to be doing?'

'I don't know,' I said. 'Just taking photos somewhere. Making images.'

Debs decided, 'Teaching, abroad probably.'

Miles said, 'Well, five years on I should be self-employed – travelling, of course, but with a good base somewhere.'

Debs said, 'Married?'

'God, no.' Miles gave me a quick look and laughed. 'Not yet, anyway. That's still the woman's dream, isn't it? Even after all these years of feminism.'

And Debs said, 'Not mine. I want to travel.'

I wonder where Debs is travelling now.

The doorbell goes. Someone to talk to Clyde, about cars, I suppose. Clyde seems to work such odd hours I don't know how any of his friends know when to catch him in. I hear a snatch of quiet conversation at the front door and come out of the living room to see Clyde on the step with his back to me, leaning on his elbow on the doorframe in his usual way. I can hear another man's voice but I only take in the whispered words after I've heard them. 'Has she really forgotten everything?' is what his visitor said. That bastard Clyde must have hinted secretly to him that I might be faking it, for him to ask that.

Clyde says, 'That's right,' with a dry satisfaction that drives me wild. He keeps quizzing me as if he doesn't believe me, and now I hear him say, 'That's right,' like that, as if I'm a performing animal that he's been teaching tricks.

I go back to the garden.

Later on that day – that other day, I mean, from the time that feels like *now* but has whirled into the black hole of *then* with all the rest of my life – Debs asked me if I minded what Miles said about not getting married. And I said of course not. Actually, I was probably a bit miffed that he hadn't protested a burning desire to hold me in his life at whatever cost, but I knew he was right anyway. I knew it wasn't a time to be finding life-partners. 'It's not like any of us is in love, is it?' Debs agreed. And I agreed back, though my breath was suddenly tight because I was thinking, Except maybe I am just a little bit in love, with Paul. How ironic if he was secretly a little bit in love with me too. But I only said, 'There's no point in getting possessive. Miles and me just go around together, like you and Paul.'

Dad likes Miles – used to like Miles – but I made sure they

didn't meet that often, to protect him from Dad's ageing-hippie routines. 'Students today don't know how to protest,' he told us, last time I brought Miles back to the house. That was only a quick visit to borrow some boots and a waterproof coat, but Dad went on about ''sixty-eight' like it was a great old steam locomotive from glory days gone by. Days that changed the world, he said, and he reeled off names, inching out a swaggering kite of rebels into a wide blue sky. Nelson Mandela . . . Tariq Ali . . . Peter Haine . . . Che Guevara . . .

'All men,' said Mum, handing round sponge cake.

'Well, you lot have done your best to redefine radical politics. Feminism!' Dad said, with a mouthful of soft crumbs. 'Can't open a door for a lady without getting your hand slapped.' He winked at Miles.

'Exactly why I don't bring friends home,' I said, to the world at large. 'Dad, you're so gross. You know perfectly well we're women now, not ladies.'

'You're ladies on the loo doors,' said Miles.

'And you're a bad influence,' I told Dad. Not that Miles took much notice of him, really.

While we were out in the garage looking for a groundsheet I asked him if he thought my dad right about students today being an apathetic lot. He said, 'Dunno about apathetic. Realistic, maybe. All due respect to your father, Kirsty – I know you idolise him – but flower power went out with flares. And when do we get any time to be radical?' Quite ironic, really, as we had spent all that afternoon on a grass verge making daisy chains. I mentioned this. 'You know what I mean,' he said. 'We probably work a lot harder than your dad's generation back in the sixties when they were chanting about times a-changing on a herbal high and a full grant. Plus, also, what's the point of being militant? Protests makes fuck-all difference in the end.'

'But if we think it's pointless, and we're the people that show everyone else what's going on in the world, then what hope is there for the rest of them?'

I really wanted to know, but Miles didn't. He simply kissed me.

Clyde is tidying round, putting out the old Sunday papers. We have two, a big one and a tabloid one. I see a name I know in a headline and say to Clyde, 'Gorbachev? What's happened to him?'

'It's Yeltsin now,' says Clyde.

'But his reforms – did they work?' I grab the newspaper back and try to scan the article but it's analysing things I know nothing about.

Clyde says, 'They brought down the whole Soviet Union. There's no Communist government in Russia now.'

How extraordinary. How unbelievable. Something as big as that and we're just walking around the same. So the Cold War that hung over all my growing-up years has ended: no more bombs, no more weapons bases. On the other hand, nothing to hold back capitalism. I say, 'Is that good?'

I'm completely in the dark about Clyde's politics. I don't even know which way he votes. He could belong to the better-dead-than-red brigade, for all I know – a possibility that makes me quite anxious. 'I mean, do you think that's good or bad?'

He just shrugs. 'You don't think people over here get told all the ins and outs of what's going on over there, do you?'

He's probably got a point, but his indifference infuriates me. I simply don't know what Clyde thinks about anything important.

Mum and Dad always disagreed over politics and in the end they never even discussed it. Mum said the rule of manners that banned religion and politics as topics of conversation was probably a good one. Dad used to laugh at her view that we needed a 'strong woman leader'. He said it was typical of a woman that in the end it all came down to a gender thing. There was a time when they got quite bitter about their differences. Dad would get angry about what he called the capitalist greed ethic, and she'd snipe back, 'Well, they've done very nicely for my mother's nest egg, or would you rather we were back on the poverty line?' Eventually they seemed simply to agree to differ, or maybe they don't differ as much. Dad says he has grown out of politics.

But I don't believe Dad has stopped caring. How can he, if it was so important once? It's different if you've never been interested at all, like Miles and Paul and a lot of my friends. I don't really know where I stand exactly. Maybe the Greens have the best idea.

It occurs to me now that I don't even know if there is still a Green Party. I fetch the bag of newspapers from the hallway waiting to be thrown out. I haven't looked at any of them properly, and suddenly I want to know what's been happening. Everywhere.

I can't understand why I didn't think of this before. Of course I won't find my lost world in a house or a schoolroom. Here is the news, here is what is happening around me in this altered world, in these different days.

I turn the pages over and over, searching intently. I'm trying to get an idea of how the world has changed and why it's still the same.

Wednesday's paper has a story about a man attacking a classful of children with a machete. The paper is saying 'like Dunblane', and Clyde says that was a gunman who massacred about thirty kids, just shot them all. And this murdered little girl Jade, why is this 'like the Bulger case'? Clyde talks about child-murderers, and it takes me a spine-creepy moment to realise that the phrase means that the children are the killers not just the victims.

'Why would two little boys kill a toddler?'

'How the fuck would I know?'

This is a bloody weird world I've woken into. Half the news is about million-pound prizes, the other half is atrocity. Some lottery. Adults killing children, children killing each other. I wish there was someone I could talk to about all this stuff. Someone like Debs, but here, someone who could explain how we got from then to now. While I was growing up some awful things were happening, like famines and acid rain, but once they were 'news' we thought the problem would get solved. That's what I believed: that knowing something was wrong is the first step to making it right. What's happened to hope, I want to know? What's happened to feeding the world, peace protests and Rainbow Warrior?

The floor is smothered with scattered papers. Clyde stands looking helpless while I crouch over the newsprint, still turning pages. The trouble is, this is all written for people who already know what's happening, who only want an update. I have a whole decade to understand.

'I'm no expert,' says Clyde, with that testy look he puts on. As though I'm only doing this to annoy him. 'The news is on the telly most nights. Don't you listen?'

No, I don't. I let the sound glide over my ears and the images slide over my eyes. Everything sounds jagged and looks sharp-edged. Everyone looks wrong. He doesn't understand.

'I don't know what you want me to tell you,' Clyde says. 'I can't see it your way. Things just happened, bit by bit.'

OK, he is saying he doesn't remember. I can't really complain about that. There is a difference, though. His memory isn't totally wiped clean like grime from a glass mirror; only little bits of it, like rubbed at by a licked finger.

I try again. 'What are the really important things?'

'Well, Nelson Mandela was freed and he's President of South Africa now.'

I jump up and hug him, I can't help myself. 'That's fantastic.'

'Yeah,' he says. 'You were pretty pleased.'

'Don't you think it's fantastic?'

'Of course I do. I've got used to it, that's all. Like the Berlin wall coming down. We were all excited about that for a while. But life goes on, and the problems soon start showing.'

Clyde's hopeless. I want to talk to someone who will understand what I'm trying to ask. There doesn't seem to be anyone around here. I could phone Suzy and ask her to come and stay. But when Suzy came to see me in hospital I just got confused about how much she'd changed from the spot-picking teenager I'd expected. All my energy seemed to go on making this stranger into Suzy and I couldn't take in what she was talking about at all. I need my college friends for this. Maybe they are cynical but they wouldn't be blasé about extraordinary news like that. Or maybe they would – maybe we all were, and that's where the energy got lost.

I go back to the pile of papers. 'Don't people want international news any more? Look, this front page is all film stars' affairs and cheap trips to France for duty-free booze!'

Now what? Why is he standing there in the doorway looking at me like that, like I've done something wrong?

'I'm glad you're ready to save the world,' he says. 'You must be feeling better.'

I don't think that deserves an answer but I can't help myself. 'You want me to know who I am, don't you? I've got to start in my head.'

'You could start with your daughter,' he says, and bangs off. Bastard.

She's in her room playing. She spends a lot of time there. It's easy to forget she's around. It's actually quite a strain, this child-in-the-house thing; having to keep check on where someone else is all the time, like being a permanent babysitter.

I make sure that when Clyde comes back inside I'm in Janey's room, listening to her reading. She chooses a story about some children who journey to the end of the rainbow looking for a crock of gold. 'Of course, it's just a story,' she says dismissively, as she closes the book. 'There isn't really gold there. There can't be.'

'Why not?' I'm wondering if she'll give me a little lecture about prismic light, from a Mrs Crabbe-type scientific project.

'Because there aren't any fairies, of course. But I'd still like to go to the end of a rainbow. It would be so beautiful to see the different-coloured raindrops dripping all around.'

Janey just amazes me. She can set the video, heat her own tea in the microwave, and use the phone, yet still somewhere in her head is this magic place where, although there are no fairies, rainbow droplets can fall like jewel-bright coloured crystals if you can only find the end of a rainbow.

I've just met my neighbour from the end-of-terrace house with the garden nearest to ours. This old woman lurches her mottled arms over the fence and calls out plaintively, 'Have you seen my washing?'

I don't know what she's on about. Her circular line is full of the usual shapeless stuff the colour of porridge; she's wafting it round and round with one hand and her quizzical face keeps disappearing behind billowing bloomers as they circle in the breeze.

'Have you seen my washing?' she says again, in this anxious, peremptory way. 'All my things are missing. The christening gown. Hand-made lace, my aunt tatted it herself, all around the hem. And the little smocked polka-dot frocks! I washed them all this morning, and pegged them out to dry. Someone's taken everything. Everything!' And she stares with dismay at the clumsy garments slowly swaying round her.

I keep smiling, shaking my head, and retreat back up our garden to the bungalow. This is one hell of a weird place I've landed myself in.

On Sunday afternoon Clyde says what about going strawber-
rying, and he escorts us to the far side of the village where there's
a house with a sign on the gate saying 'P.Y.O.'. The landscaped
garden is enormous, with rows of strawberry beds on a high slope.
The woman gives us a basket and tells us the fruit is ending, this
is the last week, and we'll have to pick carefully.

Janey is brilliant at this: she should go for a job with piece
rates. She squats beside the lines and sorts through the bright clus-
ters of berries like a little squirrel, quick and meticulous – she
even threw out some of mine that didn't pass her stringent quality
control. She eats a lot of them too, cramming them blatantly into
her mouth, dribbling scarlet-pink juice down her chin. Clyde
doesn't stop her. In fact, he's quietly munching too.

'Isn't that pinching?' I say primly.

He shrugs. 'They don't weigh you when you arrive and when
you go. People are bound to taste. Try one yourself.'

I'm stooping over a big clump of very red fruit, heavy and
drooping low over the carpet of leaves and black matted earth.
The berry in my hand is hot from the sun. As I pull it from the
stem the firm fruit yields slightly to my finger pressure. I put it
in my mouth. It is warm and sweet and succulent. I eat it slowly.

Clyde is watching, smiling. 'Not like the shop ones, are they?'

'I've never tasted anything so delicious.'

He half starts to speak, but instead eats another strawberry
and smiles. He has a nice smile. Not goofy or gapey, like some
big men. He keeps his mouth mostly closed but the muscles lift
it quirkily to one side. It makes you feel suddenly delighted inside
so you smile too. I notice Janey smiles in the same way, which is
interesting.

When we get back Clyde puts some of the fruit in bowls with
ice-cream from a big soft-scoop tub in the freezer. He brings
them out into the garden. We sit around the little patio, on the
green plastic chairs under the stripy parasol.

I look at the garden and take in for the first time what a lot of work has been done on it. By Clyde, I presume. Perhaps Kirsten dead-heads a few of the pungent peachy roses occasionally. But I can guess who made that pond and who clips the borders.

Janey puts the fountain on and shows me the fish. They glint below the surface, sultry red beneath the creamy water-lilies. She shows me the place where she wants to put the rabbit hutch. The grass is long and lush there, overhung with nasturtiums.

'And the reason you don't have a rabbit is . . . ?'

'Daddy says it's up to you.'

'And what do I say?'

She looks at me cautiously, picks her nose a bit, and then she says, 'You say, "I'll see."' Anger at Kirsten floods over me.

'Well, I've seen and you can. Not right now, but very soon.'

She rushes at me, hugs my waist, warm sticky hands tight on me, little head digging into my groin. I try not to think about the commitment of the rabbit-pledge. I sit on the grass so she can cuddle me less uncomfortably. Her hair smells sweet.

'Did you wash it yourself?' It looks so abundant.

'Daddy helps me.'

I want to say, What about me? Is that why Kirsten left? She just did less and less, and then she faded away entirely?

In the evening, when Janey is asleep, I decide to stay up with Clyde to watch the movie on TV. It's called *The Piano*, about a woman who is wilful and deceitful and controls everyone around her with tantrums. It's supposed to have a happy ending because when she's cheated on her husband she goes off with someone else, but it seems to me that the traumas she's caused will mess up her daughter for life.

Clyde asks what I thought of it. He's looking particularly noncommittal. It occurs to me that he may have the erotic scenes in mind: this woman seemed to get turned on by yielding against her own reluctance. Perhaps he has a similar scenario in mind for us. 'I didn't like her at all,' I say. 'She dominated the little girl, then shut her out when there was something she wanted more.' Clyde doesn't discuss it any more. I'm sure now he only watched it for the fondling scenes and I felt a bit uneasy. I'm fairly sure he won't try to fuck me without me indicating in some way that it's OK, but I don't want him to start talking about that sort of stuff. Mostly the empty space between us is solid and impassable but sometimes it gets so thin I am afraid. It can happen with a look, one of his slow, quiet glances, or just something funny Janey says that makes us both suddenly smile together and our laughter touches in the air.

I sense that these things sometimes tumbled us into bed: I know that's what Clyde wants. But I can't. I don't know if I ever will.

Right now the phone rings, and Clyde goes through to the hall to answer it. I hear his low mumble. I follow as far as the doorway and watch him hang up.

'That was Helen,' says Clyde. He seems to be flushed. Angry, or blushing?

'My friend Helen?' I say. I'm trying to sound cool, trying to suppress an anxiety at his evasiveness, which has crowded out that other tension.

'Yes.'

'My mysteriously invisible best friend?' I'm humming that ironic song in my head. 'Is she coming round, or what?'

Clyde doesn't answer me. He stands there looking big and stupid, and I hate him. I want to throw something at him and scream but I don't want to wake Janey.

'Let's take one step at a time,' he says, in that slow, irritating way. 'Your mum and dad are coming tomorrow.'

I remember the spare room with sudden panic. 'Where will they sleep?'

'They'll be staying at the Bell. Like they always do.'

I hate him so much in that moment, hearing his supercilious

singsong voice. I don't throw anything, though, and I don't answer him either. I take comfort from the certain knowledge that soon, when my parents are here, I shall get some answers. And if I don't like what I hear, I won't be staying. I shall go home with my mum and dad, and never ever come back to this house again.

The Fourth Week

Dad has got older. He's a little bit shorter, and his hair is thinner and greyer. He's still quite muscly, but the skin around his neck and throat is soft, the tan kind of grizzled. Mum is really brown, with a fan of crinkly lines around her eyes like ammonite markings. I suppose that's Spain for you. The part of my mind that didn't really believe they'd moved there, even after those fuzzy phone calls where everything you say goes echoey, is silenced now.

They spent last night at Suzy's 'because it's nearer the airport' – in other words, so that my sister can fill them in on the mystery, maybe break it to them gently. Maybe ask Mum not to get upset and Dad not to look so baffled. If she did it's not working.

I cling to Mum. I want to go home. I'm crying inside, *take me home.* But there's no point, is there, when I don't know their 'home'? So I just cling on to her. Her arms are all brown and soft and smelling of shower-gel and mumsiness. She's stroking my hair and saying, 'It's all right, it's all right.' Dad has brought a big packet of photos of their place in Spain and he's trying to show them in the car while Clyde is driving us all back from the airport. I think he hopes I'll take one look and sing out, '*Oh, yes, of course, a pool! Now I remember everything.*' He's fidgeting with them and smiling. It must be one of those awkward situations when you need to have something to do with your hands. I feel really sorry for him, but sorrier for me.

When we get back the photo pack comes out again while Clyde is bringing in their luggage and Janey is fighting with the Cellophane on some unsuitable-looking sweets. I was never allowed to eat rubbish like that. Clyde says, 'Tea?' in his lugubrious way, but I had heard a clink in the carriers so I say, 'What about a glass of wine?' So it all comes out, the duty-frees and bottles of Elegido. It's almost like a party.

I can't get over Mum moving abroad. She's such a Devonish sort of person – she even ended up back in her home town after art college.

'Wasn't I surprised when you told me you were going?' I demand. 'Did we discuss it at all?'

She laughs, looking at Clyde as if for support. (At Clyde! My mother.) 'You knew all about it, darling. You agreed it would be wonderful for you too, for the holidays.'

So I smile, appeasingly. But how will I ever know what I really thought? Perhaps we never talked about it properly before they went away. Mum pours more wine, says, 'We always intended to go, when you and Suzy were grown-up. That's why your dad never let you have a dog.'

I consent to go through Dad's Spanish photos. They moved three years ago, so Janey is quite little in some of them. Some do seem slightly familiar, but that's because we've got duplicates. I flip through our album to show what I mean, and Dad seizes on that photo of Janey in the paddling-pool.

'You couldn't take that today,' he says, sighing. 'They wouldn't print it.'

Clyde glances at the page and agrees. 'The lab would probably hand it over to the police,' he says. I'm puzzled for an instant, then jolted by a feeling of disgust at his meaning as I look again at the innocent little pubes and that trusting smile. Is this what Clyde fears, or what he really thinks? I'm surprised at my dad, though – and Mum nodding too.

I wish Dad had brought some of their old pictures from when we lived in Devon, but Mum says I have to concentrate on the last few years. The missing years, she means. She gives me detailed anecdotes about all the snaps till my head is spinning and I'm relieved when Clyde suggests they should check in at the inn. He walks them down the road and I'm glad of the quiet.

When Clyde gets back he finds me looking at our albums again. I've gone back to our wedding photos. I'm trying, again, to make sense of them. I can see now that the full-skirted dress masks a very rounded stomach. I try to identify the venue but I don't recognise the wall in the background. It's not the right sort of stone for the church in Devon Square, which I know well because it's so close to our house. My parents' old house, I mean. Clyde tells me brusquely it's in the town where he works when I ask where we got married. I have a feeling I've asked him that before. In the picture there's a glum-looking woman in a chocolate-coloured hound's tooth suit with a pink handbag. This has to be the mother-in-law threatening to appear, large as life, before long. I'm flanked on one side by Suzy and on the other by a bridesmaid I don't know.

Clyde peers at my pointing finger. 'That's Leila. Your flatmate.'

'Tell me . . .' I say, and he looks at me mutely so I add '. . . again. Please?'

And he tells me that I left university to take up a job at a printing firm in the town where they specialise in photographic books. I worked in the colour-separation lab and I shared a flat with another girl who worked there. Leila. And then I married him, and came to live here.

'So how long did I share this flat with Leila?'

'Less than a year. Summer 'eighty-seven till spring 'eighty-eight, when we got married.'

'Do we ever see her now?'

'Not a lot. You've had lunch with her a few times. Catching

up on the gossip.'

I suppose this is Clyde's idea of women. Men do things together, sports, talks, man-stuff; women catch up on the gossip.

I want to know more about the flat. 'So are there any photos of where I lived with Leila? In another book?'

'There might be some in an envelope somewhere, from parties at the flat. We can have a look tomorrow.'

But I have already mentally scheduled tomorrow's research. Tomorrow my parents will be here early and as soon as Clyde is out of the house I intend to spend the entire day asking questions. They must know so much that he can't tell me. There's the whole whose-baby thing, obviously, but I feel that one may need working up to. I intend to start where I left off, at the beginning of the summer of 1987.

I wait till Dad is messing around with Janey on some computer game and take Mum out into the garden with mugs of coffee. We settle on the green plastic chairs below the tasselled parasol. I'm getting more used to how Mum looks now, though her smile still dismays me. She has slick red lips but there are tiny lines feathering out from her mouth like thread veins bleeding. As if she's blotted her lipstick on something sharp. She never used to look like that.

'You do have a lovely place here,' says Mum, and then tells me, again, how well Clyde looks after it. And Janey, and me.

I agree routinely, and then say. 'Who told me about the job in the printing firm, that summer?'

She sips. She puts on her sunglasses and leans back to face the sun. 'Your tutor, that Mr Gray, came up with the idea. He phoned you in the first week of the holidays. The placement details had arrived too late to go up on the noticeboard, he said, and he thought it would be a good opportunity. He knew you were looking for summer work and he thought it would suit you. Dad drove you up for the interview, and they took you on straight away. You met Leila that day too, and arranged to stay with her for the summer, until she got another flatmate.'

I sit silently for a while, thinking about this. I can see why this would be ideal for the summer holiday, learning colour separation at first-hand, so I could do really well in the second-year theory assignment. 'So it was just a temporary job, and I intended to carry on with my degree?'

Mum is twisting her tissue into tiny scrolls. 'Well, of course. Then the next thing we heard, you had packed in your studies to stay with the printing firm, and moved in with Leila. And then, of course, you were getting married. To Clyde.'

'And we didn't talk about that, either?'

'Well, we could see you were pregnant when you came home for Christmas, obviously. You never talked about it, though, darling. You had simply made up your mind and didn't want any questions. And Clyde seemed such a nice chap. I did say, you know, there's no need to get married if you don't want to. No one does, especially these days. And Clyde would have supported you. He would have paid the maintenance, no doubt about it.'

There's not much I can say to that. My mother obviously thinks that Janey is Clyde's child. It appears that I married for maintenance because I had no other way to acquire it. My parents clearly have no idea of this. I wonder how low their opinion of me would drop if they knew. Is that why I never told them? Is that why I lost touch with Debs and my other friends? Was I simply too ashamed of myself to show my face, to tell anyone what I'd done?

And what had I done?

Janey summons my mother to see some score that she and her grandad have achieved between them and I stay outside finishing my coffee, glad to be briefly alone. I'd hoped so much that Mum would know everything. It really hadn't occurred to me that she might not. I wanted to gorge on every detail like a baby bird fed beak to beak. I wanted to find and lay down, piece by piece, the bits of this jigsaw that so utterly baffles me.

After a while they come back out into the garden again. Janey is going to demonstrate how she rides her bike. Cries of disbelief from my father about her dexterity and skill – I don't remember him ever praising me like that in my cycling days, incidentally – and then he says, 'Isn't she beautiful? Getting more like her mother every day.'

Janey does look like pictures of me when I was young. Same shape face and chin, anyway. Same tawny hair. He kisses the top of her head. 'Got her daddy's blue eyes, though,' he says. 'Hasn't she? Lucky girl. Your looks, and Clyde's blue eyes too.'

This visit isn't really working out. If it was just an ordinary family visit it would be OK, we could go on trips with Janey and explore new places. But my parents are concentrating on retreading all the steps we took together, as if intent on rediscovering ancestral songlines. This necessitates a lot of discussion that teeters precariously close to argument between the pair of them, with Janey an indifferent arbiter.

Mum seems to think that in my vulnerable state any new experience will tip me further into confusion. I catch her looking at me with careful intensity, as though without this magical attention I will suddenly jump up and say, 'Who are you, anyway?' I don't blame her, but it's upsetting to see my mother at a loss. Even when I didn't agree with her, I always used to think she was confident that she was right. Seeing her perplexed like this makes me feel even more disorientated.

They are trying, so obviously, to jog my memory. It's not working. Sometimes I think I do recall some little thing, and then I remember Clyde showed me it a week ago. It's all still new to me, just some not quite as new as the rest.

I've been trying to recapture a sense of easy intimacy with my mother but this is so far from happening that I'm beginning to wonder if my recollections of rapport are just rosy delusions. There are sticky moments between us whenever I get close to confiding my feelings or asking about hers, and I don't know if that's because of this forgetting thing or a deeper silence that has grown between us over the years. Maybe she thinks I let her down when I packed in the course. Perhaps she told me so at the time – maybe we had an enormous showdown that left her so drained she decided *never again*. Maybe wounds were bandaged but never really healed, and when she left for Spain instead of hugging and weeping there were just quiet handshakes all round and Dad saying, 'I think this is for the best.' Or maybe I'm wrong, and everything went on being ordinary and loving at home in Devon, and I phoned her every week and said, 'I wish I could come down and see you more often, but . . .'

But what?

I follow Mum into the kitchen where she's making drinks, and when she's filled the kettle and plugged it in I ask her, 'Did you mind when I left?'

She meets my direct gaze with a wide-eyed insouciant smile. 'Darling! We just wanted you to be happy, of course.'

'But what about your feelings? Weren't you even disappointed?'

She says again, 'We wanted you to be happy.' She's fingering her string of jet beads where they loop across the soft hollow in her neck that is crêpey now where it used to be supple. I know with an echoing kind of sad feeling that she will not tell me what she really thought. I begin to understand that she never did tell me, but I wait anyway.

The kettle whines and she pours some of the water briskly into the teapot, slops it out into the sink then busies herself with teabags and mugs and searching round for a tray. 'And of course we love being grandparents!' she's saying, and then she adds, quietly and unexpectedly, as the scalding water steams between us, 'You know how stubborn you could be, when you didn't want to discuss something.'

No! No, I don't. I want to remind her that that's wrong, I was never stubborn. I need a light and breezy voice so we won't quarrel, but while I'm swallowing hard and waiting for it, anger buzzes like a humming-bird caught in my head. So I say nothing, and Mum goes blithely on inventing history. 'And your dad used to get so angry, it simply wasn't worth it – there was no point in arguing once you'd made up your mind. I said that to the college counsellor—'

Now Mum stops, bright crimson. She presses a finger to her pimento-painted lips as if she's trying to squash that snippet of information back in. I think I've found the necessary light voice at last, but it comes out sounding more exasperated than breezy. 'What on earth were you talking to Brenda Billinge for? She's nothing to do with students leaving their courses.' It sounds to me as though my mother wasn't happy at all about me quitting university. If she was talking to bloody Billinge, why didn't she talk to me?

And if she did talk to me, why didn't I tell her?

Mum rearranges the mugs on the tray for a while without answering me, and then she says, 'Darling, that was a long time ago. Water under the bridge, like your father says. You must think about now, and getting better.' She gives me a radiant smile, as though this idea has really cheered her up, and advances into the garden calling out, 'Refreshments, everyone!' I follow her hurriedly. There's one more question burning me from that taboo time.

'Mum, Clyde says we met in July. Janey's birthday is at the end of March.'

My mother doesn't falter in her careful pace. 'She came a little early,' she says.

'Really? Aren't first babies generally late?'

'Oh, not always.'

Mum has a supremely indifferent air. Whatever she surmised or suspected back then is buried so deep I know I'll never uncover it.

Jemima has suggested that my parents should go right back to the beginning. 'It's like learning to walk again,' she said. 'You have to go through crawling first, to get your co-ordination.' So we've had lots of d'you-remember conversations about my childhood and my schooldays, but they always cut out at the same place. That summer of 1987, sort of round about the end of June. The early stuff is fine; it's family folklore, lots of it cute and funny, and we all know the lines by heart. What's frustrating is that by my teens we were already diverging so much. The 'friends' they remember for me were only on the sidelines of my life; they don't know how I felt about anything. And by the time I was going to university they don't really know me at all.

And they don't realise this. They obviously think we share the same recollections right up to the day I stopped remembering anything. All that time when I thought I had an intimate family life they were listening without hearing, in a world which looked the same as mine but wasn't. As if Kirsty slipped away a long time ago.

And I know I shouldn't blame them. Childhood is a kind of cocoon, and growing up means struggling out to soar away. But you're only supposed to fly off once, aren't you? Most people never need to do it all again. For me this is like falling on to a safety-net in shreds, and knowing it must have been me who cut it.

So we have these stilted conversations during the day, with Mum and Dad talking to me carefully as if I'm a convalescent whose illness mustn't be mentioned but can't be forgotten. And for proper, ordinary conversation they wait for Clyde. They sit around in the evening with him, drinking red wine and watching the telly, and they chat easily about anything under the sun.

Until now I would have said that I could talk to my mum about most things. Thinking back, it seems to me we never really talked about the important things – in her life, or mine. Like, why did she give up art? And why did she destroy the Totem?

In the Devon Square garden, all the time I was growing up, there was a sculpture that Dad called Your Mother's Masterpiece. It looked, at first glance, like a silver mannequin – aluminium, not totally solid but very heavy. Mum had made it when she was at art college, casting it from a mould she made from a shop-window model. She had used acid on the immaculate high-boned cheeks to etch down a stream of tears. There was a scroll on it saying 'Totem'. Mum never talked about that sculpture, or any of her other work, and I don't remember ever asking her. Then on the day Dad hired a skip to clear away the old garden shed, I came back from school to find Mum in her cotton dress and sandals dragging the Totem down the path. She cut into my incredulous protests. 'Help me,' she said, and together we lugged it the last few yards and heaved it over the side of the skip. It clanged like an enormous gong. I laughed involuntarily, nervously. I looked at Mum, wanting a reassuring smile, but she just straightened her scuffed skirt, turned away and walked back to the house without a word.

I never asked her why, and I never heard Dad mention it either.

We go for walks around the village. Mum wants me to remember local landmarks – personal things, special trees we liked on the green, an engraving of the old mill. 'There's that lovely old chapel, remember, that's been converted into a design studio. It's got a colour copier and all sorts of equipment. One of your friends rents it – we've seen inside.' Have we? I follow my mother around, listening to her prattling memoranda with a don't-remember, don't-remember refrain clicking at my heels like the spattering stones. Almost I get defeated and submit. I almost decide simply to remain here in my own not-knowing world, a hybrid, out of my own time and resisting theirs, walking through the days with no comprehension and no commitment. Almost, but not quite.

We go further afield, little jaunts to nearby attractions. An Italian garden – 'I remember that lovely medieval music they were playing, and the candles' – a stately home with vast grounds you could lose yourself in and a sculpture trail through the woods. 'There's the lodge, where they have a children's fête. I remember last year you sent me a sweet photo of Janey with her face painted all over with blue flowers.' Mum's taken to musing aloud about her own recollections as a variant to chivvying me about mine. Now she enlists Janey for a double-pronged attack. 'Do you remember that, darling?'

'Sam got done too. He was Spiderman,' Janey volunteers diplomatically.

The energy that these excursions take is exhausting me. I go to bed early, longing for sleep, but then I wake in the night feeling utterly alone. Sometimes in the dead heart of the night I fear that this is all a conspiracy and something else is wrong with me. I am mad, completely and utterly mad, and this façade has been created to control and contain me. Perhaps I am not young at all, I am a very old woman in the blizzard of mental illness. They pretend to me that I'm still young, and sometimes the fabrication holds, but my faded mind can't grasp a single era so it slips back again, further back, and that's why I'm caught in these two time spheres. And neither is real.

'It must be nice for you to have your mum and dad staying,' Jemima says, when I phone to tell her I won't be coming in this week for my check-up, and I say yes it is. 'Nice for hubby, too, to have a bit of help with the caring,' she says. I'm about to say that Janey doesn't need much looking after when I realise she means me. My parents are helping Clyde to care for me. I ring off mortified and weepy, and slink back to bed.

My parents' visit has clarified one thing: what a muddle this whole bloody mystery is. It must have been a pretty good job to make me chuck my course – but, then, I chucked the job too. Then there's all these new people in my life. I didn't know Leila or Clyde at the beginning of the summer, but I married him the next year and she was close enough to be my bridesmaid. Even though I don't remember the other eight years either, that first summer seems the most threatening. I've had three weeks' practice at living in this place now, so though I still feel flaky about meeting people at least I can cope with day-to-day routines. It's how I got here in the first place that I'm desperate to know. I made some crucial decisions in those missing months, and if my parents don't know why then I can't see how I'll ever find out.

Leila is the first link in the chain. Clyde claims he hardly knew her. He tells me she was 'only a friend of a friend'. And no, he isn't in touch with that friend any more, he was a bloke at work who's been left ages. And he says, with unbelievable hostility, 'It was nearly ten years ago, Kirsten.'

Mum says I shouldn't get in a state and Clyde didn't sound hostile to her. Why does everyone hate me? She can't help about Leila either. She says she never met her till the wedding.

And there's something else happening in all this struggle of emotions. Like in a dream when you realise you've forgotten something enormously important, and nameless anxiety swells and swells – it's that sort of feeling. As I'm looking at Mum this evening suddenly I know what it is.

'When's Glastonbury?' I say. 'Have I missed it?'

Mum looks at Dad and he says, 'I thought we'd be hearing

that, sooner or later,' and she says to him, 'Ssh.'

Clyde says, 'There's no Glastonbury festival this year.'

Suddenly my eyes are streaming tears. My face is so wet I can feel them dripping into my mouth, hot and salty. It's strange because I'm not sobbing or wailing, just pouring tears. 'Is it all over, then?' is all I can manage to say.

'No,' says Clyde. 'There'll be another next year.' Dad says, 'Kirsty, love, you haven't been since 1987.'

Mum says soothingly, 'You went with some of your college friends.'

'I know,' I say. I'm surprised I never thought about it till now.

We drove down in Paul's car, the four of us. Me and Miles, Debs and Paul. We had two two-man tents and we pitched them down in the Green area. Miles and I crashed down in Debs's one leaving her and Paul with his. It's coming back to me as clear as if it were last week. I'd been looking forward to it for months – I can't imagine how I forgot about it.

Mum has her hand up to her throat with excitement. 'It's coming back to her!' she whispers. She's getting all flushed and agitated, like this is the drip before the deluge. She's completely mistaken – I still feel like Kirsty and it's still 1987, as far as I'm concerned. But I do remember the Glastonbury festival. It actually feels as though I've only just come back, as though I'm exactly at the start of the summer holidays.

'D'you remember how wet you were? Everything soaked through,' Mum says. I feel that odd crumbly-inside feeling again.

'No,' I say.

'You didn't know much about it then, either,' says Dad.

Horrible, this is really horrible. Now there's another bad dream inside this nightmare. It's all their fault – I was longing so much to see my mum and dad and now they've come they don't look right and everything they say is wrong.

'Do you mean,' I say, 'that I've done this before? Are you trying to tell me I've lost my memory before?'

Mum starts patting my arm. 'Nothing like this,' she says, giving Dad one of those you're-not-helping looks. 'When you got back from the pop festival everything was soaking wet and muddy and you didn't remember why. That's all.'

'Probably been chewing funny Smarties all weekend,' says Dad. He laughs, but his mouth is tense. It looks like this was an old argument – though a bit hypocritical from a guy who used to grow marijuana in the greenhouse when Suzy and I were young.

'No,' I say. 'I know you're wrong, Dad.'

And I do. I'm not going to say I never scrounge stuff – or, rather, used to, since the me now doesn't seem to do anything much – but I didn't score at all at Glastonbury. We didn't take anything with us, and only a clown would buy there because it's costly and it's probably rubbish. And why pay for pricy tickets and then bomb out so you don't know what band you're hearing? And anyway – if you want another reason – we had four wine boxes with us, stashed in the back of Paul's car, and that seemed enough mind-altering stuff for a couple of days.

We got to the festival field on Friday, late afternoon. It took ages to get on to the site. We'd none of us been before and it freaked us out to see how big the place was. I got a programme and the seller said to memorise where we put our tents up because the fields get unrecognisable as they fill up, and that we should use the lock-ups because of thieving. So by the time we'd done all that, and made a start on the wine box, it was around nine and the Oysterband was due on. They were on one of the smaller stages but there was a really big crowd and Debs and me had a wild time bopping to their new song with a really catchy chorus. 'Never had a chance to prove them wrong,' we yelled, along with everyone else, until our throats were sore. The guys didn't dance but they stayed around and sang along too.

Pretty soon it was obvious that it was going to be hard to stick together as a foursome. It was still light but there were so many distractions – street theatre and dance music from the stalls, circus dragons and laser lights – and every time you stopped to look at something a whole crowd of people seemed to surge up and separate you. Debs and I stopped to buy those liquid light wands that glow pink and silver and blue. You fasten them into a circlet and then you can wear them as a headband. By the time we'd got that sorted we had lost the guys. And they had the booze.

'It doesn't matter,' said Debs. 'We know they're headed for the Womad marquee. We'll probably see them there.'

But we didn't, and we didn't see them at the Bhundu Boys either, though by then we didn't care. We were dancing like maniacs to the throbbing rhythms and having a brilliant time. After the last set of the night had been played we went down to the Green field to see if there was any impromptu drumming there.

There was. A guy wearing raggy cut-offs with white-rasta hair was showing some people how to copy the drumming pattern he was doing on a big *djembe*. It sounded fantastic as more and more of them joined in on different drums. 'This is a Zulu rite of passage for the young women,' he said, and Debs immediately stuck out her bottom and began swinging around in what she imagined was an African dance. The drummer called out, 'Slower, slower. You're walking back to your family now, walking with attitude.' So we both prowled around with attitude, sassy and sexy, and then when the drumming became more vehement and the rhythm more insistent we devised our own wild dance, swaying and stamping and jumping, and I knew people were stopping to watch, and I loved it.

By Saturday morning we were all feeling pretty haggard. I crawled out at about eleven and found Debs sitting outside staring at the cooker. Someone had nicked our proper gas cylinder and left a little one with a bit of pipe. Last night's fires were out but not burned out, the charred wood ominously damp. 'It looks like it's going to rain,' she said. 'I can't be fucked to twiddle around with this. Let's go to the Tiny Tea Tent and get some breakfast.'

I thought about the inert figure in the sleeping-bag in our tent. 'Should we leave a note for the lads?'

'No, sod 'em. Unless you think Miles will wake up and care tuppence. Paul won't.' She strode off frowning, adjusting her unnecessary sunglasses.

I picked up my bag and caught her up. 'Not a good night, then?'

'Paul is hopeless. I feel like going backstage somewhere, anywhere, and tapping up a roadie. Someone who knows what they're doing.'

I thought, Paul looks like he knows what he's doing. In fact, some of his lingering looks are quite excitingly knowing. Almost encyclopaedic.

I said, 'What went wrong? Too rough, too quick?' We'd discussed erotic style preferences enough times for me to know Debs's views, though she'd never complained about Paul's skills before.

'Too drunk,' said Debs. 'Not bloody interested. The first night we have ever spent completely on our own, in our own room – sort of – with no interruptions, and all he wants to do is pass out. What was Miles like?'

'Like Miles,' I said. 'Tender.' Tender, gentle, conscientious. I thought about Paul's beautiful body, collapsed in the tent, and I wanted to run back and lick him all over, pushing my hand slowly and gently into his crotch to hear him groan with wanting.

'Tender . . .' said Debs longingly. 'Oh, fuck, Kirsty, I could just do with some of that. Why don't we swap?'

The thought made me tingle. But I said, 'Thanks, Debs! You just told me Paul's impotent.'

'Not all the time,' she said quickly. 'When he's horny he's amazing.'

We talk about sex a lot, Debs and I. We discuss things like, what's the most sexy thing about sex? For me it's being wanted. I start to get that luscious fudgy feeling inside as soon as I realise that the guy I'm with is getting hard and longing. I love to watch them stare and fidget, trying to look nonchalant; I love the way their breathing gets shallow, they flush and can't concentrate on what they're saying, their eyes get wide and glittery. I like moving against them, ever so slightly, just to feel the promise of their greediness touch my tingling thigh. I'm not a prick-teaser, or a slag; I'm judicious, I like to think. But for me this secret fore-play, before anything is asked or promised, is the whole of the thrill. I love to see myself as they see me in their mind's eye — beautifully naked and potentially, yearningly, theirs. I don't care how quick or selfish they are when we finally get there because I'm quivering at the first touch and I only have to look at that flushed face and feel the first thrust and I'm there.

Which is why, I suppose, the men I fancy mostly have a kind of needy look about them. I've read that men think about sex most of the time; well, it's surprising, then, how many of them won't show what they're thinking. I suppose they've been reading these *Cosmo*-type quizzes when women say What Really Turns Me On, and it's always a sense of humour and a nice bum. Of course those are OK, but they're a long way lower down my list than incipient lust. I like men with lascivious eyes, and a certain way of lightly touching their lips with their tongue, as though quietly flexing it. I enjoy those wordless pauses in conversation that tremble with unspilled desire. I don't like double meanings and crass hints: they have no elegance. The economy of pure lust is what turns me on, and as soon as I know that I'm the object, I'm simmering up to the boil.

Debs disagrees, of course. 'You are merely a temporary icon. When a bloke says he fancies you, he only means he fancies his chances with you.'

'So? I'm not looking for a life partner. Just a good time with someone who's safe. The sort of blokes I fancy never have to disappear into the pub loo with a handful of change, they're always well-equipped.'

But she goes on about Miles, how he never plays the field and it's really not fair of me. 'Unlike Paul,' she says, 'I never know what he's been up to. But, then, I suppose you wouldn't mind that, would you?'

The festival was coming slowly alive. We toured the market and explored all the stalls. There was so much brilliant stuff – gorgeous fabrics and jewellery, wind chimes made of twisted cutlery, hookahs, postcards, just about everything you could imagine buying. I got a festival T-shirt and Debs bought herself a kind of sixties long dress in swirly psychedelic colours, and we went back to the tents.

The guys had surfaced and were eating giant burgers and drinking cans of lager. Debs was flaming. 'We go to all this trouble to bring food with us to save money and you can't be bothered to open the coolbox.'

'Well, I won't be spending my money on new frocks,' said Paul. He winked at me. I told Debs there was no point in getting annoyed, it left more for us anyway.

We sat by them on the groundsheet, drinking lager and looking through the programme to plan the rest of the day. It had begun to drizzle.

Of course I remember the rain. I don't know why my parents are making such a mystery of it. I probably didn't want to be drawn into some stupid inquest about getting the camping gear in a state. Mum probably thought Debs and I ought to have been a bit more houseproud, and I didn't feel like explaining that I had shared with Miles. And Dad, in spite of being the original sixties wild child, has got this irrational protective thing going now. Why are old people so hypocritical?

Now that I've remembered the festival I'm feeling less muzzy. I almost feel confident. There's still this huge mystery, but I feel I've got something to get hold of now – a date. I can remember my last weekend or, rather, I can remember which weekend was my last. Until 20 June 1987, at least, my life is in order.

My parents' flight home is on Friday, but it's so early in the morning that they have to leave really late on Thursday to check in. Mum says I needn't come to the airport to see them off because it will be such a late night for Janey.

'She'll sleep in the car,' I say, but Dad says it would be better for us both to get a proper night's sleep at home. So I say OK. I don't care: if they don't want me to see them off they can suit themselves.

Now that they've gone Clyde is looking at me warily but I don't feel like crying any more. I've got a new feeling, a kind of resilience, which is almost cheerful. Maybe this is what it's like for prisoners on a long sentence; when they begin to really assimilate that this is the life they're stuck with, a kind of grim buoyancy pushes them up from the depths. If I'm going to be abandoned in this time and place, isolated for ever from every familiar face, then I'll have to make some kind of new start. *Kirsty must be prepared to take the initiative.* I've been going around like a zombie. I've been letting Clyde walk me round like a doll in a pram, trotting around with Janey as though I'm eight years old too. I think it's about time I met some people my own age and started to get a life.

A woman is walking up the path. She's got auburn hair, tinted, I think, and minty green sleek-fitting jeans with a white camisole top. Even through the window I can see embroidery detail in matching green around the neckline. She looks at me intently when I open the door, then clasps my arms and presses her face towards my ear with little oh-oh noises.

'Helen,' I say.

'Oh, Kirsten! You remember. You do—'

I decide I'd better interrupt. 'I'm guessing. I recognise the style.'

She steps back. She's looking like I've slapped her.

'I'm sorry,' I say. 'Clyde says we've been friends for two or three years. Since Sam and Janey started school together. I'm sure he's told you, though it's all completely gone.'

She's biting her lip and nodding. She looks so troubled you'd have thought it was her mind that was shot to bits not mine.

'Best friends, he says,' I add. 'So why not come in, now you're here?'

'Kirsten, don't be angry. I did want to come before but with you not knowing me at all in the hospital . . .'

She's following me to the kitchen. It seems a familiar route to her.

'At the hospital?' I'm surprised. I unhook two mugs.

'You don't remember that either?'

I'm struggling a bit here. I do remember a woman crying and shouting at the hospital but I didn't know her and I thought she was much older than me so I didn't take much notice. And then she went away.

'I'm sorry,' I say again. 'Post-traumatic amnesia, I suppose. Or possibly culture-shock.'

We both laugh, though I don't think she knows what the hell I'm talking about. Still, I feel a little bit easier.

The kettle boils.

'Coffee?'

'Decaff for me. It's here, by the herb teas. And, Kirsten, I always have this mug.' She's fetched out a porcelain mug with berries on it from a cupboard. 'You don't mind my mentioning, do you? I thought it might . . .'

'Not at all,' I say. 'Every little helps. What do I use?'

'You're not picky,' she says. I'm relieved.

'Do I have decaff too, when you visit?'

'Usually. Kirsten, do you really not remember any of this?'

How can I answer? I don't even remember why she thinks I should remember. I am a stranger to this kitchen and these mugs. I don't know her and I don't know me.

I just say, 'No.'

But I do remember something odd. I don't mean a break-through, I mean from the week before last, when I came out of the school. The woman in the car, waiting. Watching me. A little boy climbing onto the back seat, her pulling the sunglasses down from her glossy hair over her eyes and driving away. That was this woman, that was Helen. My best friend. Something isn't adding up.

I give Helen her decaff coffee and offer her the cookie jar. She pats her midriff and pouts, then peers in and finally selects a small Bourbon. I feel like pulling out three and stuffing them in my mouth together, but I don't because I want to make friends again with my best friend Helen.

I'm wondering what to talk about. Debs and I talked about periods, men in general and men in particular. What do married women talk about? Helen doesn't look like she broods much on stomach cramps, or gets the day-late panics.

'Sam's made a wonderful hand puppet for drama,' she begins helpfully. 'He's going to be artistic, like his father.' She looks at me enquiringly, as though expecting corroboration, so I nod and make reflective murmuring sounds. 'And he has perfect pitch,' she adds.

'Oh, good,' I say inanely.

'Your Janey still writing those lovely poems?'

'I expect so,' I say, relieved there's no cat-verse conspiracy-theory today.

'So clever. Both of them. We're both so lucky.'

She doesn't look like she's feeling lucky. Her hand on the table shakes slightly as though the weight of her rings is almost too much to bear. She sips her decaff sombrely.

'Apart from the kids,' I say, feeling this is a sufficiently generous helping of Sam and Janey's uncanny abilities, 'what did we, mostly, talk about?' I add the 'mostly' to make this request seem less abrupt.

'All sorts of things.'

'Like?'

'Well, those healthy-eating recipe cards in the supermarket, for instance. We were trying them out and comparing notes. And we often talked about what we'd watched on TV.'

I consider these options. Debs and I used to discuss whether spunk was a source of protein but not much else in the recipe line, so I ask, 'Did we talk about things in the news?'

'Oh, sometimes. Charles and Diana, of course.'

So we start there. She tells me about the breakup of the royal marriage and how everyone's taking sides, women with Diana and men with Charles. 'We feel Diana has been treated shabbily,' she explains, taking on the role of spokesperson for our gender rather than assuming majestic plurality. 'She's been the scapegoat for a dysfunctional royal family.' I'm intrigued. Royalism used to mean cutting out pictures from magazines and standing in drizzle waving flags. This new-style monarchism, of idolising by disparagement, seems a bit unhealthy.

'And she's so courageous,' says Helen. She circles the rim of her porcelain fruits-of-the-forest mug with a sharply manicured oyster-coloured fingernail and sighs. I think, Courageous? She's a princess. I could tell you what needs courage: it's getting up each day isolated and afraid, not knowing who to be for the rest of your life. Like me.

'Tell me more,' I say, and she does. She gives me more data on Princess Diana's disorders than I know about my own.

What is interesting in all this is how attitudes to baring your soul must have changed. Dirty linen, it used to be called, and you didn't wash it in public, not if you were posh. There was a girl in our year who was supposed to have bulimia but it was only a whispered rumour. Self-induced vomiting wasn't on everyone's lips.

I want to say this to Helen but I'm not convinced she'll laugh. Debs would.

I could say anything to Debs. I could come out with whatever I found myself thinking which, right now, happens to be: If a lion-tamer suddenly thought, What's the point? would that be the moment that the lion would attack him? I don't feel like discussing this with Helen. Without my friends, my college friends, who is there I can say things like this to?

(Well, there's Jemima, of course. She's interested, at least. But she'd say something like, 'Who's the lion? Your husband? Or you?' Which isn't really the point. Is it?)

So Helen and I keep on easier topics, like other people's business and beauty routines. Whatever is bothering Helen, she clearly finds it easier to talk about Diana's troubles than her own. I get the uneasy feeling that what's bothering her is probably me – the way I look at her as if she's a total stranger.

I try to explain I look at the mirror that way too, but she can't seem to grasp why. 'You're a very good-looking woman,' she says. 'And you look really young! No one would take you for nearly thirty.'

Helen is thirty. I feel she would like me to say the no-one-would-guess-it thing back to her, but I can't because she does look thirty to me, and so do I. It's only older people who blur these things and go, 'Oh, you don't look that age!' Older people are always saying to Mum, 'A daughter at university! You don't look old enough!' and, of course, she does, she looks like most of the mums. She did, I mean.

I've studied the woman in my mirror and I can see she's fussed with face-creams and stuff but there are tiny tension lines and a different sort of definition to my face. I'm fit enough, though – probably fitter than I was. Kirsten has looked after my body well.

Helen is going to show me how I do it. Helen is taking me on one-of-our-days-out next week. 'I would have before,' she says.

'but I didn't think you were quite ready. You seem so disorientated.'

Our-days-out apparently comprise a workout at the gym, lunch, and a little shopping. Helen comes with me into the bedroom and shows me which workout stuff I wear – not what I had taken to be my aerobics kit ('Full kit is terribly tacky now, it makes one look in an eighties time-warp,' says Helen. Thank you, Helen) but a pair of dark red cycling shorts and a crop top. She gives me a potted provenance for other wardrobe items while she's at it. As Clyde said, Helen was clearly very much my fashion guru.

'I'll expect you'll want to buy some new clothes to make you feel better,' she says. 'Something . . . feminine.'

I'm wearing a black vest and a pair of khaki drawstring shorts, knee length on Clyde (they are his) but longer on me and still baggy, though I've put a chunky belt with them. This outfit clearly doesn't accord with Helen's notions of femininity – or Kirsten's, I suspect. I rummage among the jewellery in the chocolate box on the dressing-table for a softening touch, and choose a rather lovely moonstone on a silver chain. I've already asked Clyde if he gave me this and he said he didn't. He just shrugged when I asked if he remembered where it came from.

'Did I ever tell you where I got this from?' I ask Helen now, as she hooks it for me. Helen, like Clyde, obviously prefers the gold chains and sparkling gemstones to the sulky lustre of the moonstone.

'I've never seen you wear it before,' she says. 'It's very . . . sweet.'

I had a life before I married Clyde, of course. I had the start of one summer when I went to a new job, and met new people. I worked with them and partied with them. Maybe the moonstone belongs to this piece of the missing years, jagged hidden edges that catch me everywhere I turn. I try explaining to Helen. 'It's like walking on eggshells,' I say.

'Eggs, surely,' she says. 'That's what people say, if they have to tread carefully. Like walking on eggs.' But I don't think I mean that. It feels like the eggs have all broken. I'm walking on slime and sharp, painful edges of crushed debris.

Before she leaves we've planned a day out next week, with Janey spending the day at Helen's house. Helen says her husband won't mind looking after the two children. He works from home, she says. His name is Jeremy.

Saturday night. I've been dreaming. I was on the ledge of a very high building – a skyscraper, miles high. All around me the city was laid out like building blocks and the glittering river ran below. A voice behind me was saying, 'Fly, fly! You can do it!' But I knew I couldn't. I knew if I tried to fly I would plunge to my death as the toytown below became huge and real; I knew it would rush towards me and devour me.

Clyde groans ever so slightly, rolls sideways, and puts his hot thigh heavily across mine. I can feel his swollen dick against my hip. I lie absolutely still, wide awake.

It occurs to me abruptly, and with piercing certainty, that Clyde has been lying to me. Janey is Clyde's daughter. 'Got her daddy's blue eyes,' my father said.

I'm choking with anger and contempt. Janey is my husband's child, and what kind of manipulative monster does that make Clyde? I married him trustingly and it must be his cruel psychotic games that have half eroded my mind. Now he's playing the innocent and making me feel to blame for all this. I'll never believe him again. I'll never love him.

I lie rigid and after a while Clyde, still sleeping, rolls away.

In the morning I watch Janey as she carefully smothers her toast with peanut and chocolate spread. Clyde stands by her at the worktop, humming along to the radio. 'It's Oasis,' he says defensively, looking up, seeing me watching. Like I care what he sings.

Clyde's eyes are pale grey-blue. Janey's eyes are blue too. Indigo blue, lagoon dark, exquisite, bright as sapphires. They are full of expression and mercurial emotions. There is no way that Janey has Clyde's eyes.

Janey is not Clyde's child. He is not a liar.

My I-can-cope feeling has somehow dissipated. Earlier this week I felt really good about getting clear in my head when my 'proper' life stopped, as though I had finally found my own hard edges in a fuzzy world. And at first I thought that would give me the confidence to make relationships on my own terms. But then I started thinking how Helen is absolutely not the kind of person I would ever choose to hang around with, and the nonsense logic of it just leaves me nowhere. I tried to talk to Clyde about it, pretending to joke. I said, 'Helen's nice enough, but she's not the sort of woman I'd choose for a friend.' He just gave me that look that says it all. I did choose Helen for a friend, his look says, the same way I chose him for a husband. We both know what I'm thinking about that, too.

By Sunday night my upbeat feeling has totally gone and I'm distraught and panicky. It occurs to me that seeing my parents here didn't give me a proper chance to talk. I need to see them again, on my own and away from this place. Their phone number is on a memory key and I call it up while Clyde is reading to Janey before she goes to bed.

The line is muffled like I'm talking into cotton wool. I'm trying to speak clearly and calmly but the echo of my voice is high and weepy.

'Suppose I come and stay for a bit?'

'Oh, darling! We've got such a houseful! We've kept your week, at half-term, of course — and remember, Clyde and Janey do find it a bit hot in the high season.'

'Mum, I don't mean this family. I mean me.' The other caller on the line, the one who parrots everything I say, sounds whiny and petulant. And my mother tells me again about the houseful, and Suzy's friends, and old Uncle Tom Cobleigh and all, and I want to say, *What about me?* I need to go home, and where they are is the nearest I'll ever get now. But she's saying, 'I don't want to take sides, so please don't make me – you'll have to sort things out with Clyde. He's been good to you.'

What is she talking about? Take sides about what? I'm so angry I hang up. What did bloody Clyde tell them before they left to turn them against me?

The Fifth Week

'Don't rush back,' says Jim Wiseman.

'I won't,' I tell him.

The Pizza Parlour doesn't look too bad a place to work, but why on earth, when I started a degree course in photography, would I want to be working here? Jim has just made a point of telling me his polystyrene packaging is free of CFCs but I'm sure these lurid toppings must be full of additives. I never really liked pizza. Perhaps personal relish is not a prerequisite for this job.

'Which one is my favourite?' I ask a boy in a white coat. He doesn't look up from tubbing coleslaw.

'You didn't like none of 'em much.'

That's a relief, although his choice of the past tense is slightly depressing. As though I no longer exist. Well, he's right, the person he knew doesn't exist now. Four years I'd worked there, a couple of evenings each week, apparently. I must have been part of the place when he joined, shown him the ropes, joked with him, maybe shouted at him. Now I don't even know his name.

'I'm Tim.' He's blushing, as though my whispered enquiry is a rather pathetic joke. As though I'm pretending. I want to say, Did I like you? but he seems to be having enough difficulty with our conversation. I feel faintly protective of him. Not much to show for a four-year relationship, but it will have to do.

Jim Wiseman is letting me 'sit in' because Monday nights are never busy. Tim's been covering for me, mostly, and claims to be pleased about having the extra hours. If it gets busy Mrs Wiseman emerges from the flat above the kitchen to 'do the honours'. 'A lot of our regulars ease off a bit on the carbohydrates for the summer,' Jim says. 'We'll be slack now till September.'

The Pizza Parlour isn't what I expected. The front of the building has black and white beams and bow-fronted windows, one on each side of the doorway. Inside, in total contrast, there's a big room lit by red and blue lightbulbs and furnished only with machines all round the walls. One of these is a soft-drinks vending machine and the rest are PlayStations with amazingly film-like graphics. There's a street-fighting scene, and a shoot-'em-up one, and a driving game that looks practically like a real racing car.

Jim may have seen my expression of confusion at the incongruity because he says, almost apologetically, 'Got to keep the front like that because the building's listed.' He takes me through the back to the kitchen and I perch on a stool by the scrubbed worktop and watch the work. It seems very little more complicated than the video hire shop, and even has a small telly flickering high in the corner. The dough is already made and weighed into lumps. When the phone rings, Tim takes the order and Jim selects the right-sized lumps and turns them into flat bases. Then Tim tips on the toppings, barely taking his eyes from the little telly, and Jim scribbles the bill while they cook. Then an extremely good-looking bloke in black leathers emerges from the machines room and removes the pile of cartons. I can hear the throaty growl of his bike outside as he scorches off and the noise of his wheels on the spitting gravel later on when he roars back.

During the evening a few local boys come in to play the machines – you can tell because of occasional laughter or swearing – and the noise of the games intensifies. It's constant even when there's no one in there. The games all seem to be playing themselves; the pizza-making goes on through bursts of gunfire and screeches of brakes followed by a splintering crash. It's almost surreal.

At the end of this instructive evening, Tim clingfilms the leftover toppings and Jim puts the remaining dough-lumps in the deep freeze. Then we all have a cup of coffee and Tim walks me home.

Clyde is waiting in the hallway just behind the door as though I'm a little girl late back from a party. He waves thanks to Tim and scoops me in. I'm deeply embarrassed.

'You look tired,' he says, accusingly.

'I'm not,' I say crossly. But I am, actually.

He follows me to the bedroom. 'Did you talk to Jim about when you might go back?'

'No. I got the impression he'd probably keep it open till September.'

Clyde digests this, in his usual gloomy unspeaking way. His negativity makes me want to get really enthusiastic and insist on going back to work right away, this week, tomorrow! – but actually I don't feel I can face it.

'Have I worked there since it started?' I say casually, trying not to make it sound like the question it is really – *why?*

He nods. 'It was a sort of bistro when Jim opened but he didn't get the trade. You stayed on when he went take-out because, you said, you don't like being stuck at home every night.'

I digest this. I can't work out whether the justification is intrinsically selfish or whether Clyde is deliberately making it seem so in his slightly cruel, slightly toneless quotation of my words.

Next morning Janey gets me up to help her find some puzzle she wants to take to school because it's the last few days of term and all they do is play, she says. Clyde, who usually gets her ready for school, has given up on this one. I locate the missing puzzle under her bed. She can't have looked properly because it was easy to find, although I don't know why she's chosen this one – most of the pieces have been twisted up and torn. She doesn't answer when I ask why she wants it, just marches through to the kitchen with the box and puts it in her bag.

Clyde's bending over the worktop making his lunch-box and on an impulse I say what's on my mind. 'Do we need me to keep that pizza job, financially?'

'Of course we don't,' he says, looking quite unnecessarily offended. 'We can manage OK with my overtime.'

'You don't mind if I don't do it any more, then?'

'Of course not. It was you who wanted . . . I always said . . .' And he tails away looking doleful. It's a look that irritates me because it seems so self-pitying, but he surprises me now by concluding, very gently, 'Whatever you want is OK. I hate to see you unhappy.'

Me unhappy? Well, yes, but . . . I hadn't actually taken in that this sad-bear look he puts on was on my behalf. Something else to worry about.

Helen is coming round today. Soon after Janey has gone off to school I see her car glide up. She checks I've got my kit and I wonder for an absurd moment if she's going to examine it for the correct name-tag. But she doesn't. She drives us off to the gym for a workout.

The gym is much better than I expected. It's actually quite fun. It's full of amazing machines with digital readouts but the people there aren't all muscle-freaks. Helen puts weights on the equipment for me and keys in different levels and it seems straightforward but I don't think I remember, I think it's just a common-sense sort of thing.

The whole room is mirrored so we can watch ourselves working out and the music videos on the TV screen are good. A lot of these artists I know. Bob Marley, Madonna – Dire Straits, even. Sometimes I recognise the name but not the songs. And some of them look totally different – Elton John, for instance, quite extraordinary, like his own secret love-child.

The pizza-delivery man is in the corner lying on his back, slowly lifting silvered arm weights. The mirrors on the wall in front of him and close beside him make it look as though the whole room is a rippling sea of pizza-delivery men, all rhythmically lifting their glittering prizes. Helen has selected a seated piece of equipment for me and I'm repeating slow twists that turn me round so I can watch him. Now I see him close he isn't as young as I thought – he must be around thirty. His lovely mane is tied behind his neck in a slim band and he is wet with sweat.

He gets up and puts the weights back in the rack then nods to me with an almost imperceptible smile. He's obviously noticed me staring. Feeling a little bit voyeurish, I say, 'I would have said hi, but I didn't want to distract you in case you dropped one of those things on your chest.'

'Right. I'm not so easily distracted.' He has a slow, thoughtful voice, and he makes the lingering riposte sound extraordinarily provocative. Its the combination of that slight smile, which might be routine acknowledgement and might be the secret tip of something much more, and the impassive tone of his speech. The sweat is turning into juicy, glistening droplets and he pulls a long band of paper towelling from the dispenser and wipes around his neck, and under his armpits. The vest is a faded greyish black with a damp stain of jet black centrally on his chest where it has been pressed to the exertions of his body.

I turn, as Helen has shown me, and refix my equipment so I'm twisting to the other side. In the mirrored wall at the far end I can see him move to another of the machines and lie on his back with his knees pulled up. He begins to push slowly against a weighted board at his feet. Slowly, rhythmically, he pushes out and then draws back. The big TV screen puts up the name

Nirvana and starts thumping out a gritty, hard, sad-sounding music that's new to me. I like it.

'You can get a drink of water whenever you want,' says Helen, and she shows me a dispenser. The water is icy cold. I dabble my fingers in my cone cup and splash them on my forehead and chest.

'Good?' she says, and I agree. Exercise is certainly energising. It's making me feel a lot better.

As we're leaving, a tiny, fit-looking blonde with a clipboard passes us in the hallway and says to me, 'Have you thought any more about that instructor's course?'

'Oh, not yet.' That's true, anyway. She says, 'You should do it, you'd be good and we often want relief part-timers.'

Helen leads the way to the car without comment so I decide not to ask any more about this, yet, in case there's a bit of rivalry here. But it occurs to me that Kirsten's life was not without its possibilities.

Lunch is at a wholefood café in a craft centre, cottage cheese in a rather worthy brown bap with decaff filter coffee. Helen becomes more animated. She nibbles her cress garnish and confides, 'Jeremy and I had quite a sticky patch recently. I suppose you don't remember?'

'Sorry.' It must be disappointing, if she's divulged their strains and stresses to me for weeks, maybe months, to find I've lost the lot. *Your marital traumas? I put them somewhere, sorry, just can't find them at all.*

'You're OK now, though?' I say encouragingly. She nods demurely. 'Well, that's OK,' I say, nodding too. I hope that's enough.

It occurs to me that this might be a chance to find out about my own marriage stability. Maybe Helen is giving me a hint that we shared such secrets. I could say, 'Of course, marriages do have their ups and downs,' and give her a look that would be permission to spill my invisible beans there and then on the ethno-chic table. But I don't. I'm not sure why, a kind of squeamishness maybe, or a feeling that I'm not ready. Helen is nice enough but she seems to expect to have me pretty well in her pocket. I want to make up my own mind about Clyde.

Helen sips and leaves a batik tangerine kiss on her oatmeal mug, which she wipes with her napkin as she changes the subject from her problems to mine. 'Have you thought of reholding the wedding?' she enquires. 'As a therapy, I mean. It might jog your memory.'

Jesus. What a thought. I contemplate getting replicas of the ivory plunge-neck dresses, maybe stuffing a cushion up the skirt to re-create an embryonic Janey, persuading Suzy to re-don that fuel-injected blue. Sending out invitations. *Your presence is requested at a time-warp wedding, wearing your oldest outfit, preferably with a name-tag on the lapel so the bride can recognise you.* Vicar, any idea what advice you gave to newlyweds a decade ago?

'Hm,' I say, trying to look thoughtful.

'Hymn?' she queries, and I have to blow my nose busily on my napkin. Luckily she devises her own reply. 'Well, I suppose that might be a problem, if you don't remember which hymns you chose. Because men never do, do they? They just don't seem to care about the little details. But what about it? You'd make a lovely bride.'

I say cautiously, 'I've always thought wedding-day conventions are a bit . . .' Ridiculous is the word that's hovering. I compromise. '. . . unnecessary. All that dressing up and ritual.'

Helen looks surprised. 'I'd love to have mine all over again,' she says. 'In fact Jeremy and I have been talking about renewing our vows next year. On a beach in the Caribbean, probably.'

'That sounds warmer than my wedding day,' I say. Clyde's told me it was February.

She lets the idea drop then, and moves on to less terrifying subjects, like how Britain is doing in the Olympics and how the newspapers are being so mean to Princess Di and Fergie about their holiday in Provence.

Helen talks with such relish that I realise she's enjoying this opportunity for a rerun of all the salacious details. 'And, of course, Fergie is divorced too. Affairs, again. She was snapped on holiday with her financial adviser, and he was sucking her toes!'

This is hilarious. Although not really. 'What about the children?' I ask. Helen doesn't quite get my point, though she answers quickly enough. 'Well, they're too young to be tabloid targets yet, of course. Ethics, you know. But as soon as they start to go clubbing I expect we'll get the pix – papparazzi being what they are!'

But you lap it all up, I want to say, though I don't, because I'm blushingly conscious that Kirsten must have done that too. Instead I say carefully, 'Maybe we shouldn't buy the tabloids that use the pictures.'

'Oh, you and your theories,' says Helen, by way of reply. 'Never quite with us, are you?' She gives this extraordinary little laugh. It appears that my comments sound as uncomfortable to her as they feel to me. I silently pledge not to talk to any more friends until I know this new world better.

I let her gossip on without further interruption, and there's a kind of peacefulness about this mindless chatter. It's a relief, after trying to be alert to every altered nuance of this brave new world I'm catapulted into, to discover there are some things I really don't give a toss about.

'Good trip?' Clyde says, in his usual laconic way, when he gets back from work and finds the living room full of carrier-bags. Janey starts posing in the summer outfit I got her this afternoon, a patterned T-shirt and plain Lycra shorts in those fizzy lime and orange colours she likes so much.

'Fine. Helen wants us to have supper with them this weekend. Saturday – no, Sunday night, something to do with our babysitter.' He nods and tells me Emma doesn't do Saturday because she goes clubbing.

Clyde seems pleased I've kept the things I got in their carriers to show him, as though he doesn't usually get such previews. But I like showing and telling; it's part of the fun of shopping. Debs and I would never even tear off a price-tag without a second opinion from each other. It's another of those little glimpses of Kirsten's joylessness that really bring me down.

While I'm putting my things away in our room I hear a muffled sort of conversation in the passage outside Janey's room. Clyde is saying 'We've got to look after Mummy.' I've heard him say that before. 'We've got to look after Mummy. It's not her fault.'

It sounds like Janey is saying, 'Whose fault is it, then?' I stop rustling so I can listen to his reply. I hear him say, 'Janey, some things are no one's fault. Like the weather. It's not anyone's fault when it rains, is it?'

'But this isn't rain . . .' and then Janey mumbles something I can't catch.

I stand totally still, not breathing. Clyde is almost whispering: 'She's trying to remember.'

'She should try harder.'

I sit down on the bed. How could I con myself after a single day out that I'm beginning to make a new start? I stay there for a long time, detesting everybody. Outside the window it's bright and calm and sunny. I think about going for a long, long walk. I think about walking away and never coming back. The day ends like every other day, closing around me like a cloth around a creature in a cage.

The next day Clyde is getting ready to go to work when this horrible news item comes on the radio – a little boy, only four years old, found under the bushes in Bournemouth. He'd been there all night. All the police can get from him is that he was on holiday and his mum left him. They found her and she'd had some sort of breakdown and forgotten him. I find I've twiddled the volume up yelling out, '*Clyde, Clyde!*' before I've even thought about it, and he comes plodding in from the bathroom with his toothbrush sticking out of his mouth like he's chewing a straw.

He listens to the end of the news item. I say, 'Imagine what might have happened to Janey that day at the river if you hadn't been there,' and then I start to cry.

'It's not the same,' he says. 'I was there. Anyway, that child was a hundred miles from his home.'

'But whatever it was that happened to me could have happened anywhere.' Janey would have been crying and pleading, and I would have simply turned my back on her. The thought scares the shit out of me. He looks at me myopically without his glasses and tries to hug me into his damp chest but I need to go and check Janey, just to be sure.

It's the first day of no school and she's in her nightie packing her new outfit in her backpack. She stops when she sees me standing in her doorway and gives me that long-lashed look of hers.

I go in and sit on the bed so I can hold her properly. I push her thick hair aside, smell her warm neck.

'I'm looking for my swimming things,' she says. 'We always go to the river on the first day of the holiday.'

Clyde hears her. He arrives in the doorway, leans against it on his arm. He's so tall his hand touches the top of the door easily. I've noticed he often stands like this.

'Not today, Janey. I don't want your mother going there without me.'

I think about those photos, with the sunlight shining through slim reeds and the children standing in the shallow water with their big shady hats and shrimping nets.

'I'd be all right.'

'No.'

Janey sits on the bed holding her frilly swimming costume and stares at the floor wordlessly. I feel a strong impulse to argue with Clyde.

'Well, what about if I ask Helen and Sam to come too?'

'No.'

Actually I'm relieved. I do want to go to the river, but the knowledge that this is the place where I hit my head and lost my memory gives me goosebumps. But it seems unfair on Janey to refuse. I add my sullen frown to her dejected shoulder-droop and Clyde yields. 'You can go this afternoon,' he says. 'I'm taking half days for my holiday, anyway. I'll come home at lunchtime, and we'll all go.'

'We always take a picnic,' says Janey stubbornly.

He throws his lunch-box on to the bed. 'All right. You and Mummy make a picnic and we'll all eat when we get there.'

When Clyde gets back it's after one and he pulls a crust from the end of the loaf and stuffs it in his mouth as soon as he walks into the kitchen. He must be starving. 'Ready?' he says.

Janey is, of course, and wants to leave that second, before he's even washed and changed. 'Let your dad have a cup of tea first,' I say. They both look at me.

'Are you having second thoughts about this?' says Clyde.

'No,' I say. And I'm not.

We walk down the lanes to the river. It takes about ten minutes. Janey is already wearing her costume – she's been in it all morning. Clyde has made her put on lashings of white sun-lotion. I'm in my swimsuit too – turquoise blue with a really low back – with the wrap-around skirt I bought yesterday. It's indigo with tiny white flowers, light cotton and ankle-length. Clyde carries the coolbox with our picnic and a basket of towels and stuff.

I think Clyde has given up hoping that each 'special' highlight moment will be the one to jumpstart my drained mind. At least, he doesn't look at me with any particular intensity as we reach the gate, which opens into a field with a well-worn path.

Janey says, 'Paddle-place or swim-place?'

He says, 'Swim-place is nearest, Janey. Let's eat for Chrissake. My stomach thinks my throat's been cut.'

She dances down the path towards the dense bushes and trees that must hide the river.

I hear it before I can see it. That wonderful lyrical sound of constant falling water. Then I see the flickering of sunlight on dark water, glittering through the bushes. Then we reach the curving bank and there's an open place where the long grass is worn away into a kind of landing-stage, where you can step from the bank on to flat boulders at the river's edge, with a few inches' covering of clear water. Immediately beyond these natural steps the river darkens into a deep brown pool of breathtaking beauty. Yellow water-lilies float at the far side, and buttercups thickly fringe the bank.

I can see, too, where the tumbling water sound comes from. At the other side of this submerged natural platform of stone is a sheer drop of four or five feet, and here the river turns into a white foaming waterfall. I gasp with surprise: the children on the flat stones are jumping into the pool with absolute indifference to the drop close behind them. A little boy paddling a red and white lilo hails Janey. An older boy runs past a young child, skirting the edge by inches.

'What about if Janey slips?' I say to Clyde, as he puts our stuff on the long grass nearby.

'Nothing much. She forgets who she is, that's all.'

It takes me a moment to grasp the irony of Clyde's reply. I feel a moment of utter hatred as he says, heavily, 'Only joking.'

'That's where I fell?' I'm staring down the frothy white water, trying to see under the surface of the river below.

'There's only mud down there.'

Possibly Clyde is trying to be reassuring but he does seem incredibly blasé, considering what happened to me. First he won't talk about it, and then when I keep looking he says, 'People do slip, sometimes, obviously. It has been known.'

'I don't want Janey slipping,' I snap, and I tell her she's not to swim here, we'll go to the paddle-place after lunch. She doesn't argue; she's too busy putting out our little picnic on the rug.

I don't feel like eating much, and Clyde suggests I have a swim while he and Janey finish their sandwiches. It's certainly tempting.

You sit on the edge and it's so deliciously cool; you can feel exactly where the water is creeping up to touch your ankles – calves – knees – thighs – then a little bit further, you're inching in, a little bit further, and suddenly you're standing, then moving through the water, swimming. Clyde says you don't notice the cold when you're in and it's true, your body adjusts amazingly quickly and now it feels neither cold nor warm just sensational.

This is idyllic. The sun on my face and shoulders is scorching, the sky a dense hot blue. All around there are sounds of splashing and squealing laughter. The little boy who was on the red and white plastic lilo has climbed up a tree on the far bank and drops into the pool with a long, happy yell. Clyde is standing waist deep in the water, lifting Janey on to the plastic lilo.

I swim across, cross and splashy.

'I said I don't want her in this deep bit.'

'I'll be with her,' he says calmly. He doesn't argue, or try to convince me. He just does as he damn well pleases. How incredibly insensitive can anyone be?

I turn and swim away. I have never felt so aggrieved in my life. He has absolutely no respect for my feelings.

Why am I here? There is no way I could ever have loved this dour, pompous man. Hanging around in his house will make me feel like a whore. Not exactly, though, because a whore fucks for her keep. Maybe that's what I used to do, but I'm not doing it now. Clyde said he loves me but if I don't love him it doesn't matter who's screwing or who's paying, it's still a stupid mess. I keep assuming I have to find out how I got here before I can leave but I don't. I could leave right now.

A damsel-fly, very close, is flickering its rainbow-web wings. I'm floating past the yellow water-lilies, with the long grass high above me.

When I climb out Janey is out too, squatting on the bank with her hair all rats' tails and a towel round her shoulders.

'She's shivering,' I say.

He says, 'Janey, get your clothes on if you aren't going in again,' and then, while she's peeling off the cossie like a little water-baby he turns his back to her and says to me placatingly, 'It's like remounting a horse when you've fallen, sweetie. You have to do it.'

'It's not in the slightest like that. A river that has rocks in the mud is obviously dangerous, and you completely disregarded my perfectly sensible request just to try and score a point.'

He gives me a look of curious contempt. Then he says, 'This place isn't jinxed, whatever you think. And you enjoyed your swim, didn't you?'

I can't really deny that so I dry myself crossly. He says, 'So now I'll have my swim. That's if you don't mind watching that Janey doesn't suddenly slide ten feet and fall off the edge, and get carried away on a one-mile-an-hour current.'

As bloody sarcastic as that. His quick-change from nice to beastly takes me by surprise and before I can think of a really spiteful reply he's dived into the river. Just taken a flying leap, still wearing his shorts, from the bank where we're sitting into the deep brown pool of the river where the branches reflect black and silver on the water.

I have to admit that was quite impressive. But I shan't admit it to him.

It's around seven that night when I hear a thunk in the hallway and go to look. A large brown envelope, unsealed, is lying on the floor by the door. From the boxy shape it's obviously got a video inside. I pick it up. On the envelope is scrawled: 'Dear Clyde' — endearment underlined — 'I understand what you mean about gradual contact, but do you think this might help? It's got some of Kirsten's birthday (last year), the skittles night, and other things. Just keep it till you think best. All love' — more under-linings — 'from both of us. Amanda.'

I take the envelope into the living room, where Clyde is watching the Olympics on the telly and reading the paper at the same time.

'Who's Amanda?'

He looks up. 'Geoff's wife. Geoff works at the garage.'

'Your friends?'

'Our friends.'

I hand over the envelope. I refrain from saying, Have you told Our Friends I no longer understand English and have no human feeling, so patronising will be fine? Instead I say, a bit snappily, 'So you've been telling everyone I have to be kept hidden away, like the mad wife in *Jane Eyre*?'

'No, I haven't,' he says. 'I've been telling them that you aren't ready yet for a lot of different faces. Or so you say.'

He looks sullen, like if I want a quarrel he's ready.

I don't know if I do or not. He's picking at the envelope edge, as if he fears opening it might infuriate me. Then he says, 'For Chrissake, Kirsten, what do you think I do these afternoons when I take you up to the clinic for your tests? Sit in the car and twiddle my thumbs? I see people too, and they talk to me about how to cope with all this. Keeping a network of friends is important to me. I mustn't close down just because you have. I need support too, you know.'

This is an unusually long speech for Clyde and I recognise bits of Jemima-speak. I can feel myself blushing. I had never thought what he was doing — had never pictured him in a room somewhere being comforted by strangers because his wife refuses to know him.

His moodiness agitates me. I don't want to get sucked in and start having feelings on his behalf. I've got enough to do finding out about my own. I say, caustically, 'What about Janey, then? Does she have a support group too?'

'Janey doesn't need counselling because she doesn't understand. She knows you've forgotten a lot of things, but she thinks that's just the bang on the head, making you confused. She can't grasp that you're saying you don't know who she is! For Chrissake, Kirsten, what would that do to her? She can't be expected to take in that you've wiped her out of your life.'

I'm getting angry. I understand he's trying to tell me something important but I don't like the way my name appears to have now become ForChrissakeKirsten. 'So at least you haven't discussed your coping strategies with Janey. Just with Amanda and all *your* friends. Who used to be *our* friends.'

Sarcasm, of course, he recognises. He puts the sound down on the telly remote and starts to wheedle. 'Don't be spiteful, sweetie.' I wince. Sweetie is worse.

'Your "support" sounds like conspiracy to me.'

He says, 'Well, there is a group we could go to together. That head-injured support group.'

I'm shaking my head as he speaks. I carry on slowly, feeling my hair swinging across my shoulders. 'I haven't got a head injury,' I say at last. 'You go if you want to.'

He stares at me, looking exasperated. 'It's a family group,' he says, stubbornly. 'We'll both go when you're ready.'

I've seen the people going into those groups. They are not families, they are 'carers' and 'disabled'. The head-injured are not like me. They don't walk, they shuffle, or they are pushed in wheelchairs. The carers lean over them, fidget with them, whisper, then they straighten up and smile at the other carers. A world divided into two sorts of suffering. Does Clyde want to say we are like that? I can't believe him. 'And what would you tell Janey about that?'

'Janey doesn't need to know every detail of your treatment. She knows enough.'

'Well, then, that's two of us.' I'm still trying to sound waspish but the anger's washed away and I feel so tired. I want to say something savage about how he seems to think he knows best but I can't find the words. Maybe he doesn't think that. Maybe he is in a black labyrinth too, only a different one.

We use the pretext of the Olympics to ignore the Trojan-horse video for the evening, but by next day I'm getting curious. I've been dozing in the garden most of the afternoon while Janey and Alice set up a nature trail in the back field. When Alice has gone and Janey is in the kitchen I decide to fetch the envelope and take the video out.

The cassette is labelled 'Events with Friends (2)'. I rewind to the beginning and sit down to watch. Janey appears with a mouthful of tuna sandwich (she's made this herself; it was a time-consuming and mayonnaisey process).

'Can I bring my tea in and watch too?' she asks.

'I don't see why not.'

Janey's face, a moment ago serenely innocent, flicks immediately to dark suspicion. 'I won't make a mess,' she says, uncertainly.

'Good.'

'So can I?'

'I already said so.'

She darts off and reappears with her plate and a can of Coke from the fridge.

The first pictures on the video are so obscure I think there's something wrong with the tape until suddenly a firework shoots across the dark screen, then another and another. Lots of ooh-aahs. A male voice comes clearly, obviously close to the mike, saying, 'Don't poke it, Tony. Tony, stop poking, it will all collapse.' Then a child's voice insists, 'You've got to check for hedgehogs.' A kinder adult voice says, 'That's leaves, dear, not planks,' while the poking-reprover says, 'Well, if you find a baked hedgehog we can share it.' Squeals of revulsion. The fire takes hold. Close shots of carbon-blackened wood and orange flames licking around the bonfire bones, long shots of faces in firelight. There's the handsome pizza-delivery man, lighting a Catherine wheel. There's me, I think, and Janey. Clyde's handing her a sparkler. The camera pans. It lingers on a small boy jabbing his sparkler close to a toddler's face. The picture abruptly adjusts, and now the same small boy is some distance away, looking chastened and holding a new sparkler stiffly erect.

Snow, the fizzy video sort. Suddenly it's Christmas, and the child who must be Tony is on the floor tearing at wrappings as a voice says, 'Geoff, that's the wrong tape.' Snow. The unwrapping ceremony must have been captured elsewhere; this one continues with a New Year party. It's very lively. Male conversations are laced with comments like 'For fuck's sake, Geoff, switch that thing off.' Females suddenly leap on laps, showing shimmering black thighs and knees. Then abruptly it's summer. Here's the far end of our back garden – I recognise the views across the field. Children are playing around a paddling-pool. Water is arcing from a hosepipe, long silver needles dropping against a low sun. Adults are drifting around with glasses. Here's my back view, talking earnestly to someone I don't recognise. Somebody says, 'Kate,' and for some reason I turn round. Then unseen voices, very loud: 'Have you seen what Tony's doing?'

'Ssh I'm filming.'

A woman brings out a cake and everyone sings, 'Happy birthday, dear Kirsten, happy birthday to you.' The camera is panning round these faces, the faces of my friends.

Children squeal suddenly. The arching stream of water from the hose lands on the cake. There is a massed cry of 'Tony!'

Snow.

Clyde comes in and I switch off. I don't know why, I just feel like I've been doing something private.

Clyde says to Janey, 'Didn't you get a glass?'

'Mummy said I didn't have to.'

He looks at me interrogatively. I feel strong solidarity with Janey, I didn't use those precise words, but I knew what she was trying with complete sincerity to convey: *Mummy didn't give a shit about me drinking from the can.*

I say, 'Well, all kids do. They see it on the adverts.'

'We're trying to bring her up with manners,' he says.

'She's got manners. She's got very good manners.'

I quite surprise myself when I say that and Janey goes pink with pleasure. Clyde says, 'Well, as long as you don't do it at Granny Vee's.' But he sits and puts an arm round her so he doesn't sound as grumpy as his words.

She squiggles in between his legs and he holds her clamped in his knees, arms round her in a big bear-hug, rocking her slowly. He buries his head against her and goes *blurrrgh* with his mouth into her neck so she giggles shrilly and hunches her shoulders. 'Tickles!'

Yet he won't bathe her, won't sit on her bed reading her a story – in fact, he hardly even goes in her room, and doesn't like her coming into ours.

My dad always told us stories and cuddled up to us in bed. I remember when Mum was having my sister in hospital he let me sleep with him all night, clinging to his chest with my arms round his neck. And when I was a bit older but little enough to get tired walking he would lift me up on his shoulders and hold my legs tight. He was everything a father should be, tactile, loving, firm.

Clyde is so different from my idea of a dad. There's often a kind of formality about their contact. She has to stay in her bedroom till she's dressed and she never sees him unclothed. I hope he won't make her inhibited and give her hangups in the future. My father let me and Suzy run around the house without any clothes on and thought nothing of walking round naked himself. I think that kind of open-mindedness is healthier. Although I don't want to discourage Clyde's useful modesty for my own sake, when I see him waiting for Janey to finish cleaning her teeth so he can have a pee I can't resist commenting, 'Isn't that being a bit prudish?'

'If you say so,' he says heavily. He's obviously offended.

When she's in bed and I'm sitting down to watch the rest of Amanda's video he comes back. 'Cleveland was in the news before the summer of 1987', he says. He's obviously gone off to look it up somewhere. 'The child-abuse scandal, remember?'

I hate the slow way he says *'remember?'* like a clumsy taunt.

Of course I remember. All those parents accused and their children taken away, no one believing their protests. 'That was awful. But it couldn't happen again, Clyde, not now we know the doctors were wrong.'

'It could happen anywhere, anytime,' he says, and his voice is simply sad now, not pompous or sarcastic or even irritated. 'Attitudes have changed, Kirsten. You can't even take snaps of a kid in the bath now. Child abuse scares us even more than Aids. It's not just paedophiles snatching children and killing them, everyone's got to watch their own back. You can lose your child, your job, your home. I've seen it happen. Someone gets unhappy with their life, they can turn round and accuse a parent – even years after they're grown up – and take them to court and make it stick.'

He puts his hands over mine like I'm a butterfly he's caught and won't release. His words upset me. I don't think he means them to. I say, 'If a secret is destroying someone's life, don't you think they should speak out?'

He takes his hands away. 'I'm only saying it's gone too far. No one wants to be responsible for their own problems any more.'

This sounds so slick and cynical I really want to argue with him but I don't know how. 'You want children to be safe, don't you' I say stubbornly.

'Janey's safe, I make sure of that. And me as well.'

I feel obscurely rebuked. I put the video back on and look concentratingly at the screen.

Skittles is free of the ubiquitous Tony and looks like it was fun. There isn't quite enough light in this indoor room for clear images, as a muttered voice near the mike keeps remarking, but I can make out some details and recognise faces. Mine, Clyde's. It's a summer evening and we're in T-shirts and shorts. I've got a tight white top, which shows my midriff, and my hair is styled on one side like something off a naff TV mini-series. That is definitely the pizza-delivery man, with his long hair loose on his brown shoulders and a skimpy leather waistcoat over his bare chest. His upper arm has a chain design encircling it, which I can see on the closeups is a tattoo. 'Who's that?' I ask Clyde, casually. 'I saw him at the pizza place.'

'Harvey.'

I'm trying to work out if the delicious Harvey is with anyone but the way the teams are drawn it's impossible to tell who's with whom. There's a big cheer when Clyde crashes the wooden balls down noisily and sends all the skittles flying. In between each heavy thrust he looks across to the watching group as if he's seeking a face, as if he's checking for my attention and approval. But every time I get a glimpse of me I'm talking and not looking at him at all.

Polly has asked me to tea today. Janey, who's been there playing with Alice's guinea-pigs, comes home to fetch me. She acts as my escort along the village streets and I encourage her to brief me for this encounter.

'What's Alice's mum's house like?'

'Oh, it's lovely,' says Janey vaguely.

And it is. It's a big old house decorated with hangings and throws and general cheerful disorder. Polly leads me through into a hexagonal conservatory, heavily overhung with scented clematis. She wears a flowing Indian dress and flowing grey hair and talks about collecting clothes for a jumble sale she's organising. She does these regularly, she tells me, and instead of paying cash you use a sort of barter scheme. Polly seems to use this for everything, even the carob brownies the girls are feasting on underneath the willow tree. It's a really interesting scheme, and she spends most of the afternoon explaining it. 'I suppose you've told me all this before,' I suggest, and she doesn't deny it.

She says, 'It's my pleasure,' picks up a small amethyst and asks if I can feel the spirit energy of it. For some reason, perhaps the rippling dress and tresses, Polly framed under her purple clematis reminds me of Titania in a flowery dell, powerful and impulsive. I imagine her face painted all over with blue flowers, like Janey's in the photo after the fête.

'Something else that may interest you again,' she says placidly. 'Leylines. Lines of subtle energy beneath the land. Here, we are on a direct leyline to Glastonbury Tor.' I'm about to tell her I've been near the tor once, because I went to the festival, and then I remember the picture card over the mirror with the scrawled message about our perfect day, which means she knows exactly how near I've been.

Then Polly asks if I'd like her to do my runes.

Runes turn out to be pebbles with little scratch marks on them. Polly keeps them in a silk cloth, about thirty of them. This is an ancient way of accessing the wisdom of the mind to uncover the future, she explains. I take hold of the silky bundle and it clinks mysteriously. She taps on the tiled floor and tells me to lay three stones down.

The first one has a slash across. Polly taps that delicately, like touching a wound.

'That's the ice stone. Something at the heart of you is frozen. You must wait with patience for what will come. You are a skater on deep ice, you cannot hurry the thaw. Look deep into yourself to discover where the blockage occurs.' Her voice has taken on a kind of chanting resonance, like an impartial oracle. She doesn't look at me as she speaks and seems quite serious about this game.

The next stone has a similar slash with two more marks to make a triangle against the line. 'This is the gateway. You have come a long way, to the brink of a new life. You are on the threshold but cannot yet step through. The gateway is reversed. Patience, again, is required.'

When she turns over the final stone the other side is blank too. Even though the scars on the others were obscure it gives me an ominous feeling to see this one completely unmarked. Polly, absolutely impassive, continues in her sonorous tone: 'You have selected the sign of Odin the unknowable, the most powerful rune of all. Nothing here is certain. You must leap into your destiny without assurance or safeguard. Trust in yourself and your future. All is in your own hands, but is not to be known at this time.'

'Is that it?' I say eventually, as her voice finally fades.

She nods and collects up the stones into their silk cloth. 'Another mango tea?' she says, in her ordinary voice. 'Have you got time?'

But I haven't because Clyde is at the door, waiting to take us home. He didn't even ask if I wanted a lift, and it's only a few minutes' walk, I feel mortified.

'Did you think I'd forget where to go?' I say, bright and breezy, as I get in the car. I try not to sound annoyed, because of Janey.

He doesn't even answer. I think of a more subtle way to rile him. 'Polly has been uncovering my deepest secrets by casting runes.'

'Oh, yes?'

'D'you think it's mumbo-jumbo?'

I don't know what I want him to say. I expect him to say yes. I can feel my hot annoyance beginning already. But he says, 'I dunno. Hospital hasn't done much for you. Why not give something else a try?'

That dumb-ox act again. I wait till Janey has stepped out of the car and run up the path before I hiss at him, 'Well, tough, because the runes say they can reveal nothing about me. Nothing at all.'

On Sunday night it's our dinner date with Helen and Jeremy.

There's just us four, and we all seem nervous. Helen's in a vivid green dress with lavish gold embroidery all around the hem, which decreases up the skirt to a few glinty swirls at the top. She's wearing gold sandals and a three-tier golden bead necklace and her arms are a lovely sort of butterscotch colour. Jeremy's shoulders are bronzy too, very visible in his black vest tucked into black Levi's. Clyde looks boyish and gauche by comparison, in his navy chinos and blue and white short-sleeved shirt. I'm wearing a white button-through dress cut quite low at the front and even lower at the back. My skin looks a dark honey colour through the appliqué lace and I can tell Clyde approves. I chose it deliberately because it probably came from Helen's catalogue, but it's soft cotton and a simpler style than most of that stuff. I'm wearing high-heeled sandals, and my moonstone. Janey helped me choose. I felt really odd about leaving her with a babysitter, actually. Emma turned out to be a teenager with cropped hair and thick boots. I was dubious but Janey greeted her like an old friend and rummaged through her shoulder-bag for magazines so I suppose that's OK.

Helen and Jeremy have a very elegant garden with those feather-red maples and a palm tree. There's a pond, more sophisticated than ours, with irises and water slowly trickling over a big stone, and lights concealed discreetly below overhanging leaves.

A CD speaker inside the patio door is playing something mellow.

We sit beside the pond. The men are talking about cars and the price of petrol. Helen and I have kept to the social calendar of the younger royals. I'm curious to know how my life's interests became reduced to this.

Amnesia seems to scare this couple. Maybe they think it's catching. Helen's husband Jeremy is having difficulty making eye-contact. He has nice eyes, though. He reminds me of someone I know, or someone I used to know. He has the sort of looks I really like. Most women like them too, I suspect. He seems like a guy who knows he turns heads.

He brings out a bottle of white wine. He pours slowly. The glasses are chilled: they cloud slightly, mistily, as the wine slips in. His hand shakes very slightly as he pours mine. A drip slides slowly down the side from the rim to the stem. He checks it, gently, sucks his wine-damp finger discreetly. My heart melts a little.

Helen wafts off to fiddle with things in the kitchen – I'm not allowed to come and help – and returns with bowls of pistachios and olives. We have dips and crudités, which Helen shrugs and says are 'so simple to prepare, as you know'. I don't know. I eat a little bit of everything, hoping no one will tell me my preferences and make me feel more unreal than I already do. Nobody does. The men have done cars; now they talk about sport for a bit. We drink the wine, very quickly. Jeremy gets another bottle. When he comes back, Helen takes hold of his hands and says, addressing me, 'We've decided, Kirsten, that we won't attempt to force you into remembering anything. I mean, we won't keep trying to jog your memory. We want to start from here. Begin afresh. We think it's best.'

I feel quite touched. I think, This must be painful for Helen too, losing our friendship at a stroke. But she's actually thinking about how it feels to be me, floundering clumsily, every moment a trip-wire to fresh failure. I'm about to thank her when she tugs her husband's hand and says, 'Don't we, Jeremy?'

Jeremy says, 'Yes,' and my words of gratitude turn to pebbles in my mouth because this is not for me, it is for them. I don't know how I know this, I just do. They have decided to slice that other Kirsten out of their life. They want her to stay away. They don't want me to sit here saying, Did I like that song? Is this my favourite taste? More, they don't care whether I find out these things or not.

I must have hurt them somehow. Is it the forgetting that upsets them so much, or something else? I wish I knew.

Up till now I've mostly just been wishing I was Kirsty again, wishing this whole 1996 thing would go away. Now I find I'm desperately wishing that I knew why it had all happened. I wish I knew why I became Kirsten, and why I gave up on her and went back to being me. I want to know what Kirsten did that made me push her out of my head like that. And why Helen and Jeremy don't want her back.

Dusk fades slowly to dark, and midges are swarming around the light above the pond. We move inside, to an immaculate dining room. How does a carpet this pale survive a small son? The walls are elegantly matt and minimal, lights discreetly placed about in corners and bare apart from a huge reproduction of a print by Toulouse-Lautrec. Here's another house with a phobia about clutter and no sign of pulse or heartbeat.

Helen sees me eyeing the starkness around me. I improvise quickly. 'D'you have any books? I mean, I'd like to borrow something to read, at home. If you don't mind.'

She leads me into a kind of antechamber off the hallway and spreads out her hands. '*Voilà.*'

And they do. The room is shelved on three walls and practically full of boxed videos and books, mostly very new-looking, some still with transparent wrappers sheathing them like shrink-wrapped cling-film.

'Our book club,' says Helen smugly. 'All quality titles. Take your pick, there's quite a variety.'

And there is. 'How do you choose?' I say, bemused by all these wide-ranging interests.

'Oh, they choose for us. I mean, they know what's hot, so we go with their recommendation. Discount prices, of course.'

'I see. And the videos, too?'

She nods.

Helen the Catalogue Queen. Queen Mail-Order of all the Mail-ordering People. Still, at least you know she's not one of those designer-label freaks, faking a passion for esoteric art and literature. Helen gets everything from her Bumper Books of Bargains.

I reach out randomly and pick a slim book from the shelf. It's full of coloured pictures of people in cowboy boots. 'Wow. Line-dancing. That looks . . . um, interesting.'

She takes it gently from me and puts it back. 'Kirsten, I invited you to come with me when I started attending the beginners' class and you said you'd rather learn to goose-step.'

I feel a spark of sudden kinship with Kirsten but I mumble, 'Sorry, I expect I was just kidding.'

Helen recovers her let's-not-mention-the-past mode when we go back to join the others, which is a relief. I've chosen to borrow a book called *Primary Colours* but only because it says the writer is Anonymous. 'I'm trying this,' I say, and I hold it up hoping someone will appreciate my little joke. I don't think they do.

Over the rest of dinner I concentrate on finding out about my new friends. Helen works part-time at the box office of the local theatre. Jeremy is a freelance designer, she tells me, and I'm impressed, but it appears that the freelance part was compulsory when he became redundant from a firm in Bath. I wonder politely if there are any projects on the horizon but he's evasive. Helen, speaking for him, says he had a contract in Wales but turned it down, 'At the last minute,' she says. 'You would just be starting now, wouldn't you, dear, if you hadn't decided against it?'

'What made you change your mind?'

'It's so far away. He decided to stay at home, after all,' Helen is still speaking for him. I think, If Wales is so impossibly far away why take the offer in the first place? But Jeremy doesn't seem interested in discussing this slipped opportunity. I suspect Helen talked him out of it, and it's still a sore point.

Clyde and Jeremy are talking about the athletics, about whether Linford Christie should have been given a chance to defend his title, even after getting disqualified for false starts. Jeremy becomes very animated when he talks. He leans forward and his slim fingers press slightly on the edge of his chair. He has dark hair which is longer than Clyde's and curls beautifully against his collar. Clyde is stolid by comparison, scrubbed up and dressed in clean clothes like a child on an outing, with none of Jeremy's easy elegance.

Helen and I talk about the school sports day – at least, she does. I listen. By dessert we've got on to more general issues, like the Child Support Agency which is, according to both men, weighted against fathers. 'How many suicides will it take to change that?' Jeremy wonders, and Clyde nods and says, 'It's gone too far.' I excuse myself to go to the bathroom and discover Sam in his bedroom so I stay for a while watching him play some fighting game with such amazing graphics, even better than the PlayStations, that I thought at first it was a cartoon on the telly.

When I go downstairs the men have progressed to the kind of battle-of-the-sexes conversation I thought went out with bear-baiting. They're talking about this case in the newspaper of a policeman who was charged with indecent assault at work. It's not enough for them that he got off, they're complaining about the protests from women's groups. It's Jeremy who is saying,

'They won't stop till the law is reversed and men are all guilty until proved innocent.'

Clyde is nodding. 'It's all gone too far,' he says again. I think, Jesus, tattoo that on your tongue and save yourself the trouble of talking. I peer through the hatch and locate Helen in the kitchen stacking crockery in a dish-washer. She's obviously been listening to them. 'What do you think of this sexist rubbish?' I demand, pushing the tiramisu bowl through to her, wiping up the last dollop on my finger and licking it.

She comes back in with a tray of coffee and, surprisingly, adds her vote to the ayes. 'Feminism was a good idea, once, and I was all for it,' she says. 'But not now. A lot of these harassment charges are simply ridiculous. Vindictive women who don't seem to understand they're attacking other women too – the wives and the mothers. Don't forget, Kirsten, I have a son, and I fear for him the way society is going. He could ask a girl on a date, she could go willingly back to his room and take off her clothes and get into bed with him, but if he so much as touched her she could bring a charge and he'd be put in prison.'

Helen's interpretation of the law seems ludicrously flaky to me but the men are both nodding now and I don't like to argue. I sip my coffee and eat a thin mint. Jeremy puts on another CD: the air is suddenly filled with sad, plangent chords and a raw voice that's almost a whisper. I say, 'That's nice,' and Jeremy starts to say something but Helen, who can't have heard me, rejoins us at that moment and tells him to change it. 'Something a bit more cheerful, darling! Everyone's looking so glum.'

Clyde says, 'Not at all, we've had a wonderful evening,' and I murmur assent.

'Jeremy is looking dreadfully glum,' she insists. 'Don't you think so, Kirsten? Tell him to cheer up. Say, "Cheer up, it may never happen!"'

I smile feebly, this being the sort of thing I wouldn't consent to say under threat of torture, and thank them both very much for a lovely evening. She sees us out and Clyde goes through the usual formalities – must do it again, you must come to ours – while Jeremy stays at the table draining the dregs of his Drambuie. He does look a bit dejected, actually. I wonder if their sticky patch had anything to do with Helen's dinner-party manner, which would be rather trying even for a devoted spouse.

On the way home I say to Clyde, 'Did you ask Helen to cut out the memory-jogging for tonight? Because if you did, thanks. It made it easier, feeling I wasn't on trial.'

'I'm sure it did,' Clyde says. We walk on in silence.

'Maybe we should try that at home,' I say, after a while.

What I'm trying to say is, maybe we could have a future together, after all. And I think that's a giant step. I mean, for a month I've been refusing to believe I have to stay in this life. I've been longing to escape, using all my energy in trying to get away. Now I'm saying, I might learn to accept that you are my husband; I might be able to accept this life. That's what he wants, isn't it? I thought his eyes would light up and he'd stop in the street to hug me and claim another of those tentative soft-lipped kisses. Perhaps not a full orchestra playing but certainly a nightingale's song.

He doesn't alter his stride. 'Fine,' he says. 'If that's the way you want to play it.'

Something unexpected explodes in me. I think it's a ball of hate. My hand shoots out and I find I've scratched his arm. I would have clawed his face if it had been turned towards me. '*Play?*' I say. 'What does that mean? I'm not forgetting on purpose, you cunt.'

'The doctor seemed to think you might be. Blocking, she said.'

'Blocking isn't the same as deliberately bloody-minded. It means I can't help it.'

'If you say so.'

I scream. I open my mouth and scream as loudly and

obscenely as I can. He puts his big hand over my mouth. 'Jesus,' is all he says. He sounds scared. He holds my arms down, too, so my hitting, scratching hands can't reach him. He's tense and angry but not violent. I have to admit that. I have to say even as he pinions me that I don't feel afraid of him hitting me.

We're close to a street-light. There's a lilac tree, heavily scented, close by and the light is shining through the branches making it whirl in crazy circular web-lines. They're spinning a bit. I must be drunk. For a moment this reminds me of something else, and I stagger. He shakes me upright. I sober up a little. I think how stupid we must look, a man and a woman struggling in the street. Who screamed? I wonder. Kirsty or Kirsten? Am I already becoming her? Why does Clyde despise her? Clearly he loves and wants her too. Why is he so brutal to me?

I push his hand away from my mouth. He lets me. 'Clyde, tell me what's going on. Why do you think I'm playing games? Are you so stupid you don't understand what I'm going through, or is there a reason why you don't believe me? Because there has to be something you're not telling me.'

He's walking on now. He doesn't seem to care if I keep up with him or not. I hate the bastard. I think, I could scream again, then that thought scares me too. I don't know whose thought it is – I don't know who I am any more. At the beginning of this evening I was still Kirsty, still hoping that somehow all this stuff I call my 'forgetting' life will somehow dissolve like a bad dream and I'll wake up in my real life again. But these wild feelings belong to now, not to the times I remember. Forgetting and remembering are beginning to melt into each other and I don't know who I am any more.

I catch up with him. 'Please, Clyde,' I say. 'Help me. Please.' I'm crying, struggling with that sobless weeping again. He takes off his jacket, puts it round my shoulders. *Is he saying sorry? Am I? Is that what Kirsten does, cringes to him like that? Attacks and then cries? Why don't I know?*

He says, 'Look on the Amstrad, Kirsten, if you really want to know.'

I'm bewildered. There's a word-processor in the small study but I've never even switched it on. I start to say, 'I don't know how to,' then stop. If Kirsten knows. I'll have to find out.

The Sixth Week

Next day I didn't get up until Clyde had gone to work and then as soon as Janey went off to play with Alice I switched on the word-processor. Then I didn't know what to do. I was scared I might do something wrong so after a while I switched it off. I wandered around the bungalow.

I know the whole place now. I know what's behind every door. I could close my eyes and recite, left to right, right to left, every visible detail. What is still missing is the way all these things came together.

The bungalow is much newer than the neighbouring terrace and we bought it off the man who built it, Clyde has told me. The entire place is carpeted with a kind of grey-brown mossy stuff, wall to wall, apart from the tiled kitchen and a little corner of the passage by Janey's room where there's a triangle of frayed webbing because the cat tried irrationally to burrow through the metal stop. Clyde and Kirsten's décor manages to avoid any tonal rapport with the floor. The junk room is the closest, but the dinginess of its beige anaglypta probably predates our arrival. We have made our mark on the rest of the house, and a rainbow of a mark it is too. Marigold yellow in the kitchen, green for our ablutions. The main bedroom, ours, is done out in pinks with alabaster-white fitted furniture. The living room is those splodgy blues. It's split, or rather opened up, by an arch so there is a long area with the telly and seating at one end and the dark oval table and four matching upright chairs at the other. It must have been really poky when it was two rooms. The patio goes across the back here, with big picture-window doors in the dining bit and just a small window, the original one, I suppose, in the television part.

You know how when you go on holiday, for the first day or two, everything about your room is new and unknowable and full of surprises, and you look at every little detail? Then after a while you get used to it, and the specialness goes as you start to move around the space pragmatically, going automatically to the right places. I have been trying to hold on to that first state, because I don't want what I know and what I ought to know to get blurred. But at the same time I need to learn this house so I can somehow recover control over my experiences.

Jemima suggested I make notes about the items in each room but I haven't got round to that yet. Giving these things a history will make them more real, and that's too much like commitment. The Aborigines in Australia made their own ancestry by simply walking about. I was afraid of making song-lines.

I read once that architects sometimes don't put paths in new estates until they've watched the way people move around. They wait to see where the grass gets worn and put the paths there. These routes, while they are deciding, are called 'lines of desire'.

I get a pad and pen and make a rough map of the bungalow. I've decided to draw my lines of desire.

I start in the kitchen, where I'm standing now. I pick up a pink pencil of Janey's — she keeps her crayons sharpened and neatly organised in their wallet — and I draw a line on my map. It goes along the hall and out of the front door. I use a blue pencil to draw another line. It follows the first. I work through all the twelve colours in the pack and each time my line of desire takes me straight out of the door into the street. No further, because there's not room on my page for a complete escape.

My page is now patterned with a spray of multi-coloured streaks, like a broken spider's web.

I make a mug of coffee. I've taken to using the one with the blue stripes.

I switch on the radio. I've found a local station I quite like and tuned the radio to it. It plays quite a few songs I know. It's playing one now – that Genesis track about how everything's wrong and nothing seems right. I think, tell me about it.

The sun slides across the kitchen table and along the ochre tiles on the floor. It occurs to me that I haven't cleaned the floor since I came back from hospital. I fill the sink with hot water and soda crystals and use a cloth to wash over the tiles. They come up really nicely.

I feel calmer today. I think about the feeling, and identify it with the Amstrad upstairs and the sense of purpose it has given me. I am going to find out something about Kirsten.

I go back to my picture. Kirsty's picture. Kirsty is still hell bent on escape. I wonder what Kirsten might feel. I use the biro this time to draw a line for her.

It feels OK to move the pen around the kitchen. Then I'm not so sure; my hand falters, then quickly jumps down the hallway to Janey's room. I doodle circles there.

Where else did Kirsten feel happy? I can't think of any more lines to draw so, still holding the pad, I follow the route of the line. I go and stand in Janey's room.

Janey's room, more than anywhere else in the bungalow, does have a distinctive personal theme about it: animals. The duvet cover has alphabet animals, the shelves are full of ornamental animals, and there's a big pink-rimmed poster of a Persian kitten with a sentimental caption and the handwritten addition 'Love from Granny V'. This is an animal sanctuary. There are animal books and animal bags; ugly bug-eyed animals and cute big-eyed animals. I used to have a My-Little-Pony, but nothing like this menagerie. Janey doesn't even diversify, unless you count the single spindly doll, which I think must have been inherited from Suzy. This usually lies nude in the corner bent down like half-opened scissors proffering its candy-pink butt. Janey's tender impulses are confined to her bestiary. She's quite obsessive about them, especially that lion which she keeps reminding me is not Sinbad but Simba. That's from some cartoon we saw on her birthday, Clyde says, though I don't think she's mentioned that. They all have names, of course, but I haven't bothered trying to memorise them all because Janey has a useful habit of constant reintroduction. 'You know Bluebell,' she says, producing a miniature plaster kitten with a smug expression and a ball stuck to its paw, or 'Mr Zed', or 'Montgomery', or whoever, and then she burbles on for a bit and I only have to smile vaguely. Sometimes, I don't know why, she suddenly throws down these creatures and storms away.

I tweak Janey's quilt and straighten a few of the animals crouching softly on her bed and continue slowly with my self-guided tour.

The bathroom shows a lot of careful attention to detail, like green towels and shower curtain to tone with the avocado suite and antique-looking taps. In our bedroom it's the same: flowery curtains, white on pink, which are the same as the wallpaper but the other way round – pink on white. All the white furniture had porcelain flower-patterned handles and knobs. Someone has made a real effort here, too.

It occurs to me that these rooms were not actually chosen *by* a woman, they were chosen *for* one. They are a man's idea of what women like. Maybe that's why I find it so hard to recognise Kirsten's taste. It's not really hers at all. Clyde has done this for her, he has made this place a palace for her. Everything was chosen because he thought she would like it. It won't give me the clues I need to find the real Kirsten.

There are clues, though, in that machine upstairs. Clyde has told me so.

Janey comes home around three. I've put out a drink of milk and a couple of cookies. It's the first time she hasn't prompted me about this favoured afternoon ritual but she munches without comment, talking with her mouth full about a butterfly picture she's done today at Alice's on a big piece of sugar paper – one of those blot things where you pour the paint and then fold the page. You're supposed to see your preoccupations and fantasies in these things. I look and look but whatever way I turn it I can only see Janey's butterfly.

I clip the picture to the fridge, using a couple of those little magnet letters, which swarm like bees across the door. Janey seems quite pleased.

'Janey,' I say, checking my watch – in ten minutes *The Famous Five* is on and she will become selectively deaf – 'do you know how to write on the Amstrad?'

'Course I do.' A fine spray of Hobnob. 'I did my project on it.'

'Will you show me?'

She does. It doesn't take long. By the time the final strains of the *Scooby-doo* tune are ending and Janey has flitted back to the living room to watch her programme, I know what to do.

I move the mouse the way she has shown me. I put away the project (A Day in the Life of a Town Fox) and I start searching through the files, clicking on everything, opening it up, looking, putting it away.

It seems Kirsten used the Amstrad for all her correspondence. Queries over consumer goods, some standard-format letters of protest about environmental things – drilling in Antarctica, road developments. I'm glad she minded about some things. The video-tapes are logged, which explains why they all have anonymous-looking code numbers on them, and I'm pleased to see she has all the *Fawlty Towers* series. Also, interestingly, some

Open University programmes on learning Spanish. There's a file called Accounts, and inside among the documents there is another file and this one is called X.

That easy. No wonder Clyde found it. I wonder if he felt like I do now, a rush of guilty excitement at lifting the lid off Kirsten's secret. X marks the spot.

Click.

I open the file and find a set of documents, unnamed, simply numbered.

Pick a number at random. Seven, of course.

I click on document seven.

My darling, it's a whole hour since we were together and I'm missing you so much. I close my eyes and relive your strong arms and hot kisses. I'm burning all over, every part of my body you touched is wanting you again, oh, darling, you were so wonderful . . . When you look at me like that and you pull me down on you and push into me like that, I know we can't be wrong. When you said, 'Why not just go with the flow?' all those weeks ago, I never realised how those words would change my life. I faint inside, my darling, every time I think of your flushed face and the touch of your fingers, your beautiful face, and chin dripping with my juices . . .

Yes, there is more, but I've got the gist.

I'm feeling extremely agitated. It's more than embarrassment, this burning sensation like a hot douche inside my head. It is pain. To be reading these fragments at Clyde's clumsy direction hurts like an entirely new wound. I don't know what is the worse pain, this shocking evidence that Clyde wants to rub in my face, or the unremembered loss, showing me so cruelly I wasn't always this pallid ghost-woman, that once I loved ardently and sensually. *Strong arms and hot kisses.* My tranquilised nerve-ends begin to stir and I can almost imagine those demanding caresses. Tiny red-hot darts of longing shoot through my ice-flow mind.

I realise, of course, that the strong arms were not Clyde's, and that this means my 'convalescence' is no longer that of an injured innocent. This evidence of betrayal means my quest for Kirsten is altered for ever. A bad dream tightens inexorably into nightmare.

Kirsten knew whose hot kisses they were. Perhaps Clyde did too.

I don't have to believe that these letters were ever sent, of course. There might be a good reason why Kirsten chose a word-processor – perhaps so the recipient didn't have a series of handwritten epistles to explain away when the post arrived – but why save them to be found and read? They might simply represent a private fantasy.

I open all the letters, in numbered order.

1 I don't think we can go back to being 'just friends' now. Did I surprise you? Your passion surprised me. Your hunger even matches mine. I know this is important – but it feels a little bit crazy. Darling, don't contact me again unless you are sure. If I don't hear from you I shall be wild with disappointment and grief – but I will survive. I mean it. Don't say anything unless you want more. Much, much more.

2 Can't eat can't sleep can't think of anything but you. Darling darling darling are you *sure*?

3 How can you accuse me of playing games? I'm risking everything for you. If you can't believe my words then believe my body. I believe your passion, why don't you believe mine?

4 Darling, oh, my darling. Now I know what perfection is. I'm dizzy with happiness. Now I know you trust me. Please

can every time be like that, no tears no fears for the future. Our love knows no barriers now.

Five and six are so erotic I burned crimson to read them. By seven, something seems to have been pledged somehow – *I never realised how those words would change my life*. Letter eight is frantic, nine red-hot. Ten is full of angst, eleven full of hope. Twelve seems determined, committed.

I can't produce any consistent image for the recipient of these letters. I think about the beautiful pizza-delivery man I met at work, his dense ringlets and brown shoulders, and I try to imagine clinging to his bronzed body, arching up as he kneels and presses urgently into me. The idea is exciting, but it's not a memory. There is something surreal about pure passion without an imaginable partner. It's like a juicer is squeezing out pungent juice without any fruit, it's like finding a map of where fireworks have been exploding. I can't describe what it's like. But there's a frantic incompleteness about the narrative that makes me sure these letters are not a fantasy. Somewhere, out there in time, are the sensational embraces and urgent declarations that are the missing pieces of this particular mosaic. And somewhere within me there is a tiny spark of recognition, as thin as honey drizzled on cool yoghurt, dissolving a thread of sweetness into smoothness, like a tear on a metal cheek.

Not Clyde, and not invented. I'm trying to make my body remember a lover's body, a man's name. My body insists on ignorance. I'm flinching from the implications of my infidelity. My mind insists on innocence.

I close down the screen and sit at the desk, thinking. I think about Miles and the first time we made love, how he said, 'Are you nervous? I am,' and how I loved him for it, because he sounded so full of longing. I think about long before that, the first time I ever made love, in a heap of coats at a sixth-form party with someone rattling the door and me saying, 'I think we ought to stop now,' not really knowing why the boy wouldn't and thinking I must be irresistible because he couldn't, not even minding the blood smears all down my legs because of the thrill of it. I think about how I felt the next day, walking proudly, wondering if every man could see at a glimpse that I'd done it and I was different now, and how I thought I was so sophisticated until some boy I hardly knew came right up to me and whispered, 'What's another slice off the loaf to you?' I think about every man who's ever felt me, fingered me, frigged me, fucked me, and the thing I don't think about any more, because I can't, is who these letters were for.

Finally I think about Clyde. I think about him fumbling through the computer files until he found my secret letters, maybe tracking them like the paw-prints of a limping hare, hunting for the one name he needed to know for the snare. But Kirsten knew about secrets. She has not told us that.

I switch off the machine, go downstairs and have a coffee.

So, Kirsten had a lover. Well. Clyde must have driven her to it – he certainly knows about it. So that's two of them. Clyde and my lover.

Not three. Not me.

I take a sip then chuck the coffee away, mug and all. I don't know what to do and it's freaking me out. I shouldn't even be here in this stupid place with this stupid man, and he's trying to make me think I've done something wrong.

Well, fuck him. I'm me, not the person he thinks. I hate that person – I won't be her. I've had enough of this stupid conspiracy. I won't stay here. I'd rather go back to hospital.

'Why not?'

For some reason Jemima, who has been my friend till now, simply won't agree. I've called her up on the emergency mobile number she gave me but I can't make her understand how important it is that I leave, right now. 'I don't belong here,' I wail.

'Well, you certainly don't belong in a hospital,' she says, 'even if it was possible.'

'Stick me in a loony-bin, then. I don't care.'

'The psychiatric hospital won't take you, dear. It's all care in the community now, and you are very well looked after here. Your husband sees to that.'

I don't know how to argue. I just say. 'I want to go home. I don't know why my mother doesn't want me.'

'You do know why,' Jemima tells me. 'She wants you to recover.'

'For fuck's sake!'

There's an encouraging cluck at the other end of the phone. 'You have a lovely house, dear, and a very caring husband who is doing everything possible for you.'

So I'm lucky, she's saying. But I don't want to be here, I don't want any of it. I am afraid of the secrets hidden in this lovely house. I am afraid of the unknown space between my caring husband and me, and afraid of the closeness too, and I start to cry. I cry and cry and cry. 'Please ask the hospital to take me in.'

She will not. She waits until I've cried myself into silence, then says, 'Good girl,' and hangs up.

It's almost dusk outside. My eyes are drenched with sobbing and I can hardly see. It seems like there is someone in the doorway but it's only Clyde, watching me. I hate him.

I won't talk to Clyde all evening. Once Janey has gone to bed I stay outside in the garden, watching the pale orange sun huge and glutinous over the horizon, watching it droop till it tangles with the distant trees. I watch the moths come out and flicker in the light above the patio as twilight deepens into dark. I stare at Janey's bicycle, lying on its side where she's left it by the back door, noticing the place where the stabilisers used to be. I *will* myself with absolute intensity to remember the day we took them off, but I can't. I think about the passionate illicit arms that are not Clyde's arms, and I can't remember them.

At around ten o'clock I go inside. Clyde is hunched over a bottle of whisky. His shirt is off and his big shoulders look drooped and vulnerable.

'You've got to tell me,' I say.

'What?'

I hate him. He knows what I mean. I won't say it. I choose something that will hurt him more than me. 'Janey. Whose child is Janey?'

He slugs back his drink. Suddenly I realise I really need to know. 'Please, Clyde.'

'You never said.'

'What?'

'Maybe you didn't know.'

'Kirsten didn't know?'

'For Chrissake. You are Kirsten. She is you. You don't know, so what? I don't know either. Before we married, you told me you didn't know how you fell for Janey and I promised you I would never ask again.'

I'm dreaming. There's a woman flying towards me, no, swimming, so this must be water. She is coming fast, diving low towards me, but I can't see her face because of the light and the streaming water. As she reaches me she starts to break up and her limbs fall slowly through the clear water glinting like silver fish, like metal, until every fractured fragment of her is lying in the sand. Her aluminium face stares up at me, and soft sand is settling already in the scored channel on her cheek from the acid tears shed when she was a woman. The fine pale sand swirls and drizzles down, and the water around me is warm.

I wake thinking about the letters with an enormous feeling of relief. I don't know why I didn't realise it straight away: the letters are a plant. Kirsten never wrote them. It's obvious, all this anonymous *darling*. And why would real love letters be kept on a computer? Clearly the reason I feel innocent is because I am innocent. Clyde has made the whole thing up.

I get up quickly, without waking him, pull on the big check shirt I've been using as a robe, and go quietly into the kitchen. The dawn is only just breaking over the long fields, picking through the treeline with threads of pink and gold. I fill the kettle and plug it in, but decide against switching it on after all. I don't want to wake anyone. I want to be on my own.

I've decided to delete the X files from the word-processor, but I feel superstitious about looking there again. There's a story I read years ago called 'The Mezzotint', about a picture of a house with a crawling figure in the garden, which comes closer and closer to the door until he finally gets inside. I have this weird feeling the letters will get increasingly incriminating every time I look at them.

The sky is light now and the birdsong in the garden is tremendous. It's going to be a hot day. I creep back to bed and slide into the shaped space beside Clyde's back. I'm trying to breathe really quietly. I'm so wide awake I can't believe the energy of my anger isn't tremendous enough to rouse him immediately but he sleeps on. Then I hear his trilling little alarm, quickly stifled, and feel the bed lighten as he steps out. I don't turn round.

I lie thinking about the letters, and slowly my feelings are infiltrated with a different kind of heat, not fury, not embarrassment but pure longing. I'm longing to feel that erotic yearning again. That hot feeling that's like sizzling on ice. Strong arms around me, a hungry mouth seeking. My finger is sticky and I lie imagining it, that breathless hush, smelling, touching, caressing, stroking (oh oh yes) whispering words like whipped cream, the scent of wanting, that sticky sweet smell of need, and the ragged scramble to unzip, unbelt, unfasten, unbuckle, to press flesh on succulent flesh and trying to be quiet, trying to scream, oh oh oh, in silence, the long, shuddering gasp and the pulsing sweetness.

And then he comes in with a cup of tea and that sombre hang-dog look and I can't keep up my comforting delusion any longer. I know absolutely that Clyde did not write erotica on the computer. I slide under the duvet and cry, because he's taken away my innocence. He waits, for a while. I can hear his breathing. Then I hear quiet disappearing steps and then Janey's chattering voice above the radio in the kitchen, and it is safe to sit up and drink my tea along with the bitter dregs of self-contempt he has left me.

I'm clinging to my damaged self-esteem and I want, very much, to blame him. After all, I know nothing about Clyde as a husband. Janey doesn't ever flinch from him, it's true, but there could be secrets between us about which she knows nothing. Maybe he did bully me and batter me, maybe he's holding back now out of cunning because of the doctor's supervision. I could ask a few more questions at the hospital about what might have damaged my memory – if I might have been hit first and then dumped in the water. It won't do any harm to let them know I'm wondering about that sort of thing.

But then I think about the struggle in the street, and Clyde's frightened, frantic hands restraining me, and I know he is not a wife-beater.

After breakfast I search through all the photo albums and the old cards, and even the box of Janey's drawings and school books, just in case there's a clue I've overlooked.

'What are you looking for?' Clyde says, when he comes home. He may have guessed that I've found the letters but he doesn't know for certain, or even that I've looked for them. I'm not going to say anything unless he does.

I say, 'You said we might have pictures of Leila, and the place where I lived when you met me.'

'I looked. I couldn't find them,' he says.

'Well, tell me about Leila, then.'

He's hopeless at describing her. Probably about my age, he supposes; he couldn't really say. He can't remember her surname. He doesn't know if she still works at the printer's. He doesn't know if she still lives there.

'Tell me about the house. What did it look like outside?'

'I'll take you there and you can see it for yourself,' he says.

'When?'

'Now, if you want. I've taken the afternoon off.'

As easy as that. Why didn't he offer that before? Actually, it's possible that he did. I haven't had much energy for tracing the irrevocable route from then to now: I've been intent mostly on escaping it.

I call Janey in from the garden and we all set off. This feels like an enormous expedition, but in fact the drive takes no longer than our usual trip to the supermarket, which is on the far edge of the same local town. I feel almost cheated.

Clyde pulls up outside a pebble-dashed pre-war corner house too close to the road to have any front garden. Beside the black-painted door is a line of bells with plastic name-slots made illegible by rain. I ring each bell in turn. Bing-bong. Bing-bong. Bing-bong. Bing-bong. No one answers.

I go back to the car. Clyde jumps out and opens the door like a chauffeur. He's not even looking quizzical, but I want to pass on my disappointment so I answer his unspoken question anyway. 'It means nothing.'

'I'm not surprised,' he concedes. 'It's been done up quite a bit. It never looked like that when you and Leila lived there.' He slips the car into gear and drives to the end of the road and after a couple of turns stops again. 'There's the factory. Why don't you call in?'

The printing factory is a sprawling set of buildings with a car park on one side and a lorry bay on the other. A rather kitsch plastic sign where Clyde is pointing says 'Reception' so I go in.

Inside it's slightly more upmarket than I expected. There's a coffee table with a few glossy books on it, a Cona coffee machine, and a desk opposite the door where a woman is tapping on a keyboard. She has ashy hair and an emerald blouse with a floppy tie at the neck. She swivels around from the screen as I mumble about how I used to work here and am trying to track an old colleague. After wagging her head from side to side a bit she decides that she does remember me. 'Must be ten years, at least,' she says.

'Nearly.' I try to smile ingratiatingly. 'I know you're really busy but . . .'

'Never forget a face,' she boasts, sounding more confident now.

'D'you think you might have anything on file? About my friend Leila, I mean.'

She shakes her head. 'Paperless office,' she explains. 'Everything's in here, now.' She taps the screen. 'But we wouldn't have any up-to-date address for her. Why don't you phone her at the bank?'

'Oh. She's still there, then?'

'Oh, yes. Well, I think so. I met her at the cheese show last year and we had a quick chat, and she was then. She was on the look-out for a transfer, I think, but there was another promotion coming up at her branch.'

'So, you think if I just phone her branch of . . . ?'

'Lloyds, yes. On that road that goes up from the Pump Rooms in Bath.'

She asks how 'the family' is — so she does remember a bit about me — and she tells me how much the place has changed with all the new equipment. I linger looking interested and eventually she suggests I pop in. 'I haven't the time to go with you,' she says, 'but I'm sure it would be all right for you to say hello to a few familiar faces.'

The phone rings and she flickers her fingers at me in farewell as she smiles into the receiver. As long as the faces say hello first, I think, as I step through the inner door.

The place is Tardis-vast inside, with hangar-like vaults stacked with machinery and a faint mist of paper dust blurring the air, swirling in the harsh fluorescent lights. I pick my route uncertainly past pallets and stacks, round vast bales of paper, beneath noisy metal archways, along slowly moving lines of raw pages, which curve like curious baggage carousels. The men watch impassively and continue their work. The constant crushing sound of the machinery is muted like a deep purring, or perhaps the distant sound of water. I keep saying 'Hi, just revisiting!' but I can't tell if anyone recognises me. I'm looking for the colour suite where I worked with Leila, checking that each overlapping image matched perfectly so that yellow, magenta and cyan images coincided into a flawless finish.

The rooms are all labelled. I find one that says 'Photolithography'. Two men are sitting at what looks like a big computer screen. They look up, and one of them says with a strong Welsh accent, 'Well, well, if it isn't my Blondie. Long time no see!' and the other watches me curiously.

'Ten years nearly,' I say, and then, brazening it out, 'Nothing changes, then.'

'Hasn't it just,' he says, as though agreeing with some predictable irony of mine. 'It was the old red-window system, in those days. I remember showing you how to mask up the negatives on the light box. Four or more of us, wasn't it, to get the copy ready. Sheets a metre wide – all that equipment, remember, over there?'

'Uhuh,' I say, but he is shaking he head nostalgically and doesn't mind me. 'Big job losses, big. Direct from disc to plate, see – all we do is monitor the readings. Marvellous thing, progress, isn't it?' He turns to the other man, who chews slowly as he sits staring at me. 'Blondie here was on the colour plates before we got all the new equipment. Her and her chum. Two women, we had in those days. Imagine that. Two women!'

The other man laughs and says, still staring. 'Man's job, printing.'

'Printing is still a sexist industry,' agrees my ex-mentor boastfully. I wonder whether he is using Blondie as a temporary expedient or whether it was my usual name to him. I'm no longer surprised Kirsten abandoned her career here. Quite apart from the rampant sexism, this doesn't look very much different from making pizza.

'I haven't seen any women here today,' I manage to agree noncommitally.

'Well, you won't. Not even on the packing lines now. Can't have women taking up a place when there's so many men out of work.'

'I'd better go now, actually,' I say, as I can't think of any reply. 'I only popped in to see . . . the changes.'

The chewing man says, ''Bye, then, Blondie,' too and they turn their attention back to the screens.

I finish my route at the far end of the factory where a man deftly clipping a stack of gold-embossed covers into a pallet whistles as I leave. I have no idea if I know him.

Clyde is still parked in the same place outside. His big arm lolls outside the car window, hanging down the door, fingers lightly drumming. Janey is leaning against the back seat with her eyes closed, mouthing to muted radio music.

'I'm sorry I was so long,' I say, as I get in.

'No problem,' he says. 'Well?'

I shake my head. He slips the car into gear and we drive away.

*

My next plan, which I confide to Jemima first, is to contact Leila and arrange a visit. I half hope Jemima will say, 'Oh, you shouldn't go out on your own, not yet,' but she doesn't. She says, 'How will you explain what you need?'

Good question. 'Can you get me a little plastic wallet-card saying, "No need to raise your voice, I still won't remember"?'

She nods, presumably because she recognises my point rather than being able to provide the item, and says, 'Denial is a very frequent reaction.'

'Tell me about it,' I say, and she does.

'It's inevitable, really. Denial is the first part of the grieving process and to those around you this is a kind of bereavement. With death, of course, there is an eventual hard-edged finality, but with h-hm . . .' She hesitates.

I look at her without interrupting. We both know I'm waiting pitilessly to see if she will trip out that awful phrase *head injury*.

'. . . with any change in which no physical alteration is apparent, such as amnesia,' she continues seamlessly, 'there is likely to be prolonged difficulty in taking on board the full extent of the damage.'

'You mean, people think I'm faking it.'

'It's not that they don't believe you. It's that they find it diffi-cult to make the necessary adjustments on a consistent basis. So they may start out understanding that you don't remember someone or somewhere, and end up talking as if you know exactly what they mean. That is, if their own framework of reference is not sufficiently flexible to adapt, which probably includes most people. They will relate to their own memories of shared time, not yours. You look the same – they find it hard to realise that you can't talk their language any more.'

'Perhaps if I have a badge saying "My body has been taken over by aliens"?'

She smiles fleetingly. Jemima is a very serious young woman, which makes me want to be flippant but I like talking with her.

She gets really worked up with her sentences, rolling her eyes and clasping the words from the air as if they will slide back into a vast invisible textbook if she doesn't move quick. And it's good to talk to someone with whom I have no past history, because of course I never knew her before the accident.

I just did it, I just used that phrase. *The accident.* I will not do that. I will not empower that moment of my life any further. I won't define myself as damaged. I am not head-injured. I have forgotten some things, that's all. I am not a victim.

'What I think you should do,' Jemima decides, 'is find a phrase you feel comfortable with, that you can repeat if anyone talks about things you don't know. That way, if you are comfortable, they will be too. Something like "I'm afraid I don't remember. Could you remind me?"'

I tell Clyde about my plan on the way home. He looks intently ahead at the traffic and makes no comment. I've made it sound almost more Jemima's idea than mine, and his non-reaction irritates me.

'And I'd like to take the car and drive over myself to meet her near her work,' I add on impulse. 'That's if you trust me, and don't think I'm going off with a lover.' He doesn't smile and doesn't answer. This is the closest I've got to asking him what he really knows about the hidden love letters. It's obvious he doesn't want to talk about them. Should I be grateful for that? How can I know?

Phoning Leila is easy. I simply call the bank, and they put me through. Leila says she's glad to hear my voice, it must be ages, doesn't time fly? and suggests lunch tomorrow. I'm afraid she's going to say, 'The usual place?' which would give me difficulties before I'm quite ready, but she says, 'What about the café at the Photographers' Gallery? They've reopened it now.'

'Fine,' I say, then just before I ring off, 'Will you look out for me? I'll explain when I see you, but I might miss you. I'll be wearing dark glasses.'

'Hay-fever, is it?' she says. 'My mum's practically blind when the pollen count's high.'

'Something like that.'

Clyde has shown me where the place is on a map of the city. It was easy to find, and I thought I'd be there early but Bath is very distracting. It's like a foreign city. It is, of course, foreign to me since I don't know it, but it's excitingly foreign. It's crowded and buzzing with continental voices, and at every turn there's music in the streets, like a festival: men with painted faces dancing as they play their instruments, a man playing tunes on a saw, three young girls piping. And then about half a dozen times people in bright costumes, some with dogs, try to sell me the same magazine, saying 'Help the Homeless'.

The restaurant belongs to a gallery and it's very classy, with jazz playing, tiny lights and tiny tables, all looking new. A youngish woman in a smart dark suit waves as soon as I go in. She's quite pudgy and her clothes are tight, as if she's poured herself into them and hasn't quite gelled yet. But she seems nice: her dark eyes are lively and she's very friendly. The first thing she says is, 'Wow! You're looking great. Like the new look – heroin chic?' which sounds bloody rude to me but she obviously thinks it's a compliment so I just smile.

And I needn't have worried about starting a conversation.

'Hasn't this place changed since we were here last?' she demands, then, 'It must be over a year, I don't know where the time goes. You don't look a minute older.' I'm alert to hear what name she calls me but she doesn't call me anything.

A girl with a ponytail arrives and stands beside us licking a pencil. Leila orders soup and a roll, for both of us, with the merest turn of her head towards me. I nod passively. I think I must be Kirsten to Leila.

Leila is easy company. She pauses intermittently in her chat but I don't have to think up any replies because she's off again about herself, her career and her clubbing. The conflicting claims of both are making her exhausted. I'm beginning to feel tired too, but I think that's the anxiety of always expecting some tiny trigger may flick the switch in my memory – her mannerisms, her Bristol accent, or the way she goes pouf! at the end of her sentences for emphasis so her fringe lifts gently then resettles. None of it is familiar.

The soup comes with bread and butter and a glass of water with lemon in.

'That's enough about me,' Leila decides. 'What's your news?'

I've brought newspaper cuttings to help me. The local paper features a picture of the riverbank looking idyllic, with the caption SAFETY FEARS AFTER PICNIC DRAMA. The piece reads:

> Fears were expressed after a family picnic nearly ended in tragedy last week. The river pool, a popular spot for summer swimming, has always been considered safe until last Friday when a local woman hit her head on the bank and suffered mild concussion. Friends rushed her to hospital and Kirsten Villiers was detained over the weekend. 'There was never any question of drowning,' her husband told our reporter. 'Kirsten was a little bit shaken so they kept her in.' Mrs Villiers has now made a full recovery but has been advised to take things easy for a few weeks.

That's what I asked Clyde to say. But a nurse, or maybe a porter, must have contacted one of those downmarket weeklies that does the true-life stuff, and I suppose I'm lucky they didn't make more of it. My other cutting is titled SLEEPING BEAUTY, with a picture of a woman in a bra holding her hands to her cheeks, captioned POSED BY MODELS, and the text reads:

> The patient woke drowsily and saw the screens and drips all around her. 'Who am I?' she whispered. 'Don't you mean, where am I?' said the nurse, taking her pulse. But lovely

26-year-old Karen Villiers DID mean what she said. Karen, who is now a wife and mum, had FORGOTTEN her family. She DIDN'T REMEMBER her cosy home or her job. She DOESN'T KNOW — WHO took over from Mrs Thatcher — WHAT Black Monday was — WHEN the Berlin Wall came down — WHY she can't go to Yugoslavia for a cheap summer holiday any more! 'I feel like I'm still dreaming,' quipped blonde Karen, as she met her husband and daughter for what seemed to her like the FIRST time. Readers: Who or what would YOU most like to forget in the last ten years? Write and tell us, and we'll print the wackiest.

'Wow,' says Leila. 'Is that true?'

'Well, yes, apart from the name and the age and the drip and the quotes,' I say. 'Seriously, though, I have forgotten a whole chunk of stuff, and I want to track it down. One of the things . . .' I'm talking carefully here: I don't want to actually lie '. . . I don't remember, is that summer, when I worked at the printing factory. I've visited there and had a look round but I don't remember it at all. The house we lived in doesn't ring any bells either. Though it's changed a lot, apparently. I'd really like you to talk to me about those days.'

Leila starts looking every so sympathetic and also horribly excited. I imagine she's already planning how she'll be telling her mates at work this afternoon. She says, 'Oh, that flat!' and rolls her eyes. 'We were wild, weren't we?' She sounds pleased.

'How wild?' I try to smile, not to sound too anxious.

'Well, we knew how to have fun. We couldn't afford to go clubbing in those days, and didn't have wheels anyway. So every weekend was party time.' She leans back, happy to reminisce. 'D'you remember my boyfriend, Earl?'

No. Leila. No, I bloody fucking well do not. What have I just tried to tell you, you dozy birdbrain?

'Sorry, I'm afraid I don't remember. Could you remind me?'

'Wish I could forget him too! I'd dumped him, right, but he'd left a stash of grass in the kitchen and when he got picked up,' she leans forward now, confidentially, 'the sod went and gave our flat as his address. So these two hulking policemen come pounding on the door in the middle of the night and when we let them in they want to search the place. You went round with them, all big eyes and ever so helpful, showing them every little hidey-place. I made them a pot of tea. And, of course, that's where Earl had stashed the stuff, I don't know why they never thought of that. They stayed ages and got ever so mellow. When they left one of them was giving me a brotherly lecture on choosing my boyfriends more carefully and the other was trying to write down our phone number so he could ask you out on a date. God, we laughed when they'd gone. I often wonder what the sergeant said to them when they got back to the station.'

I'm quite sad to have lost the full memory of this, though it does nothing to help me understand why Clyde selected me for his bride.

'Couldn't they tell from the taste it wasn't tea?'

'One of them thought it was a bit funny, but I said it was Darjeeling, and the other one said, "Oh, yes, my mum has that."'

'Did I go out with him? The one who asked me?'

She shrugs. 'I don't remember. You had a lot of dates.'

'Anyone special? Apart from Clyde, I mean.'

'Oh, loads. But no, no one special.'

There's a bit of a pause while I think about this before Leila says, casually, a bit like someone with no interest in children who's been trying to think of the name of her friend's child, 'How is the little girl? She looked such a poppet in that picture you sent me last Christmas. No, wait — come to think of it, it was the Christmas before.'

Now's the time.

'Did I tell you who was the father?'

'Well, I knew it wasn't Clyde's. So did he, of course. I don't think anyone else did.'

'Did I tell you whose, though?'

'We absolutely never talked about it. You wouldn't tell me a thing about your college days. Honestly, it's the one thing you were really vehement about. I got the impression . . .'

'What?'

'Well, just that you were really disillusioned with that university scene. And none of our friends had got, you know, degrees or anything. I think you wanted to make sure you were part of the crowd. You know, be like one of the gang, and not stand-offish.'

'But didn't I say anything about how I got pregnant, even to you?' This is a weird conversation. I'm sure that lady in the taupe suit at the next table has just given me a sharp look. I'm feeling ridiculous as well as agitated and Leila is looking uncomfortable but I carry on, though quieter. 'Surely I must have known? I mean, I know who my boyfriend was at the start of that summer. Did I tell you why didn't I contact him?'

'No, you never said anything to me. Perhaps it wasn't his. Or perhaps you had a bust-up. Either way, you didn't contact anyone. You didn't really talk about it all. You sort of ignored the whole thing for months – you just wanted to go on having a good time.'

That phrase really grates.

'But . . . why Clyde.'

'Well, he adored you. And he was a gentleman – I mean, a bit different from most of the guys we messed about with. And he must have been an improvement on the immature students you used to hang around with when you were at the college.'

Leila seems markedly unenthusiastic about undergraduates. I can see why I might have kept this aspect of my experience largely under wraps while living with her. I'd like to ask about her training, to see how she ended up with this chip on her shoulder, but I don't want to offend her. I say, 'I was a student, too, when we first met, Leila.'

Leila shrugs. 'Well, yes, but you were never a typical student, were you?'

I fuss with some crumbs on the table top. None of this is really what I came to hear. 'I suppose I was on the fringe of things, a bit. A lot of people on the course were older than me, and living outside the city meant I didn't always join in . . .'

'Exactly. Living at home – that's not a typical student, is it? That flat of ours was the first time you'd ever been away from your parents for more than a weekend. Not that I'm saying you were a mouse, far from it. We had a bloody good time. But I've lost touch with that crowd now. You can only live like that for so long. I was getting itchy for change – a job with a future. Mind you, even banking's not secure these days.

We seem to be talking about Leila again. I say, determinedly, 'But about Clyde. What did you make of him?'

'Well, he could be quite funny, you know. Not telling-jokes funny, but a lovely dry sort of humour. Droll.'

Droll. 'Oh,' I say. *But was he a good screw?* No, of course I don't. I don't know Leila well enough to ask her crucial questions like that over the carrot and coriander soup. And, besides, that's telling her I don't know. She'll wonder why I can't find out for myself. So I just say, 'But why marriage?'

'You were going to go it alone at first, but you got so sick as the pregnancy went on, and the firm said they wouldn't keep the job open for you, and then I got this post in Bath and moved here instead of renewing the lease on the flat . . . It was everything together, I suppose. I think you just gave in.'

'So I never loved him.' I feel really sad. I'm willing her to contradict me, but she only shrugs.

'You were determined to make a go of it.'

'Not the same, is it?'

The waitress has cleared away our bowls and plates and Leila is looking in her bag for a purse. 'On me,' she says, waving away my proffered note, and she makes a little pile of coins on the saucer. I look up at the black-and-white photographs on the walls high above our table.

Leila follows my gaze. 'I've still got those baby-belly pictures you gave me,' she says. 'In fact one of them is up in my flat, framed. Everyone loves it.'

I look at her hopefully, and after a few moments say, 'I'm afraid I don't remember. Could you remind me?'

'Oh. Sorry. You did some pictures of your bulge, in the mirror. They're lovely, so natural and sort of fecund. Almost like landscapes. I don't know how you did it. When I try to take a picture in the mirror all I get is reflections of the flash.'

I'm keen to tell her because this is one thing at least that I do know. 'It's reflective angles,' I say instantly, 'and probably natural light with a slow shutter-speed. Are they soft – like, not very sharply focused?'

She shakes her head, shrugging. 'They're beautiful. Everyone says so.'

'Black-and-white?'

This time she nods. So I was still doing some photography that summer. I must have had access to a darkroom. I start to feel excited, like a sleuth finding a button with a torn thread twisted round it.

'Did I go back to college to print them?'

'Oh, no. You said you were never going back, once you found out about the baby. Your tutor phoned and everything. In fact, your tutor came to see you. I think he got your prints done and sent them to you, hoping you'd change your mind. But you didn't.

'Evidently.'

'And when you moved out, you were going to throw them away. I said, "You can't do that!" So you said I could have them, and I did.'

She gets up and edges out of the slim space between her chair and the table. I get up too. 'Any plans? Shopping?' she says.

'Not really. Maybe. Is there anything special on? Is it a Rag Day, or something? There were lots of people begging.'

'Don't think so. Just the usual homeless.'

After Leila has gone I wonder if I should have found the courage to ask her about the other part of the puzzle. I suppose I could have tried: *OK, Leila, skip the paternity, just tell me who's my current lover? No clues, no conferring, any reasonable suggestion considered.* But I don't think there was much point.

I take a closer look at the pictures along the passageway leading to the gallery upstairs. Names I know. Cartier-Bresson, Steele-Perkins. I pay at the desk and go into the exhibition.

It's about the Amerasians in Vietnam, abandoned children of the soldiers. The information sheet tells me this lost generation is around my age, twenty to thirty – both my ages, in fact. They are called *bui doi*, the dust of life; 'Forced together into comradeship by scorn,' says the caption. The American families will never accept them. 'The rejected return to the same life but without their dreams.'

My eyes are stinging. I peer at the captions, trying to find a woman who is my age – my age now, I mean. Here's one, with her child. She looks older; her eyes are sad but her face is smiling. Maybe comradeship does that. 'Unified by scorn' is still united. Not like me. I am utterly alone.

I sit down on the plump leather circular seating in the centre of the gallery room. I'm starting to panic. I know nothing of why I forgot my life. What if it all happens again? What if I go outside and the world has changed again, once again it's ten years older, or even more? I would cry out, '*I was young a moment ago,*' but they'd deny it and tell me I've been old for years. Perhaps a stony-faced woman would step up to say, 'I'm Janey, Clyde is dead, now go back to your nursing home.'

My heart is pounding and I'm sweating with fear. If I can get outside and find the street the way I left it I'll be safe, comparatively safe, in this new time I am beginning to learn. But the roaring of the air-conditioner sounds like the rushing of water and I'm surrounded by these images of dust children with their dark expressive eyes; I'm paralysed.

I was crazy to think I could get myself back to the bungalow on my own. I don't even remember the roads. I pull out Clyde's map. It's carefully drawn and shows the one-ways and the road signs to look out for, and I feel a little bit calmer. At least I'll be able to show it to someone and get help. He said, as he gave it to me, 'I've put the number at work too, so you can call me up if you have a problem.' I look at the phone number and see that below it he's printed 'IF THIS WOMAN SEEMS CONFUSED PLEASE PHONE URGENTLY.'

Bastard, I think. Telling the world I'm mad or sick or both. I'm trembling with anger now. I get up and walk quickly out of the building. Then I find I'm calming down, just as quickly. If Clyde wrote that, he must believe me. Perhaps he'll stop the hints and the sneers. Perhaps we will be forced into comradeship – or, at least, a kind of truce.

I've walked a few yards before I recall my panic about another time-slide. The notion seems a bit stupid now. I'm feeling more confident again and I've got a couple more hours on my parking ticket. I decide to look around.

On the corner there's a hairdressing salon with a picture in the window of a girl who looks a bit like I used to when my hair was straight. I go in and ask for a cut. A young man who looks like an Italian waiter starts to discuss styles. He pulls my hair out to the side like an injured bird's wing and lets it fall. I tell him to do what he wants and I close my eyes and lie back, listening to the soft rush of water around my ears, feeling the calm controlling warmth of it relax me.

Clyde believes me. At last he really does believe me. But he doesn't trust me, does he? It's not even because of those letters he won't talk about, it's the person I am now that he mistrusts. I tell him I'll be fine driving a few miles, and he thinks I won't. I say I'll find my way around and he thinks I can't. Basically, he thinks I'm not safe out of his sight.

I'm starting to seethe with irritation but then I remember that my dad was like that and I feel almost nostalgic.

I don't know why Dad was so possessive, since he did such a lot and went to so many places when he was young himself. 'That's precisely why,' he used to joke. 'I don't want you running into men like me.' But under the jokes he meant it, he didn't trust me to be on my own. Why else didn't he let me go to Exeter and share a flat with Debs? Money wasn't the issue. My help in the shop wasn't necessary. It was just a man thing – it was about keeping me at home. And if I had gone away then my life would have been a little bit different, every step of the way. Maybe I wouldn't be here today. I start feeling emotional again, a kind of wretched weepy frustration and wanting . . . wanting . . .

'Coffee?' enquires the Italian-waiter man, wrapping my head deftly in a warm white towel. I find I'm in another seat, being combed out. The Italian-waiter man starts work, curling my wet hair into his fingers and pulling it round my cheekbones, nestling his own lovely chin close to my face so we can confront the mirror together at the same eye-level. I'm tugged back into my reverie. Why did I go along with my father's rules? Why did I accept the same role as my mother, placid and obedient. And cheerful. *Come on, where's your smile? Let's have a smile, then.* Routine requests. Formative fragments. Even now as I see a man in the mirror looking at me, automatically I have adjusted my face into a pleasant, tranquil smile.

The Italian-waiter man puts the blow-dryer down and we peruse his efforts together. My hair is straight and sleek now, and slicing off the candy-floss layers has lost the silvery highlights too. Now it's a darker blonde, a sort of toffee-mallow gold. My real colour. I turn my head slowly from side to side, liking what I see.

'Takes ten years off you,' says the girl at the till, as I'm searching for one of Kirsten's cards to pay. My pulse gives a little wooden bump. But that's what people say to a woman of my age, isn't it? It's not a key to unlock the secret path home. Only the way hairdressers say *Have a Nice Day*.

'You made it, then,' says Clyde, when I hand him back the car keys.

I plan to say, 'Of course!' but the achievement seems so enormous I can't be that blasé, even to cover up.

While I'm formulating a noncommittal reply he says, 'I like your hair.'

'Do you?'

'It looks fantastic. You look fantastic.'

'Do I?' One step nearer the night when he will push his face over mine and say, 'That's long enough, Kirsten. I've waited long enough.'

I wake early, remembering my dream. I was at Newton Abbot racecourse and I was waiting for the others to collect me in the car. Debs and Paul and Miles were watching the horses racing but I was walking along the back of the stands because I was going to the loo. People kept turning to look at me and staring because I was wearing a tiny little baby-doll nightie and I knew, though I couldn't see, I had my face made up as a doll. My hair was in two plaits, sticking out of the top of my head like a puppet. I knew there was some reason I was dressed up like that so I brazened out their stares. I also thought I looked good and most of the men were looking lustful in spite of the sniggers, which turned me on. I found the loo and it was full of shit. I mean, absolutely. There was a bath in there too and that was full of shit, the walls were covered in shit; most of it was crusted with green and grey mould and the noise of flies buzzing was as bad as the stench. I stopped in the doorway, appalled, and said aloud, 'This place hasn't been cleaned for years.' A woman came out of the toilet and said, 'Well, it's all your shit.' I looked at her in horror and I saw she was Kirsten. Outside the gusts of laughter came again and I realise that it's true, and everyone knows.

Clyde's still asleep. He's lying on his back with his hair ruffled and a kind of shininess around his nose where he's been sweating in the hot night. I can't stop thinking about those letters. They've gone now, for ever, but not-being somehow seems as strong as being. They still exist in my mind, half remembered, incomplete but unalterable. They have no context – no past, no future. Just abandoned letters to an absent lover.

Who was he? I keep thinking. Who is he? And why? Perhaps who and why are linked. Perhaps Janey's father wasn't Miles, perhaps he was an impulsive one-night stand and he never knew he had a daughter. Then he discovered the truth and followed me here, to persuade me our destiny lay together.

So where is he now?

That's the trouble. Every potent answer to the question Why leaves me with another and more dreadful question – so why not any more?

I've been looking around in obscure places in case there's a cache of replies to the letters on the word-processor. I'm not really expecting to find anything. The more I think about it the more sure I feel that those letters had no written answers in between them. They were impulsive responses to encounters, not the chronicle of a carefully managed long-standing affair. Something happened, then escalated, then something became decided. I wish I knew what.

But I keep looking, just in case. I remember reading some-where that a plastic bag in the cistern is a classic place to hide secrets. Clyde catches me in the loo looking under the lid and I feel really stupid. 'I'm cleaning,' I say.

He's been in the study and he's holding a printout from the Amstrad. I find myself blushing. Has he been prying again? Is there something else he wants me to find?

'I've been looking at our accounts, actually,' he says, with an inscrutable expression. 'I don't want our credit-card repayments escalating.' I think about the haircut in Bath and the new clothes and start to feel like Imelda Marcos. Maybe this is why Kirsten stuck to catalogue repayments.

'You said it was all right.'

'It is all right. We are all right – I'm just keeping an eye on things.'

'You said we didn't even need me to work.'

'We don't. But . . .'

'But what?' It's like whipping a snail, trying to get Clyde to explain.

He stands there blinking at me. 'We may need a bit extra later on, if Janey wants to go to college.'

Later on. I shudder, as if an icy spider is running across my shoulders. I say, 'She'll get a grant, won't she?'

'Probably not. There'll be fees, too.'

Fees? 'Will we have to pay those?'

'Probably. Education costs, these days. Everything costs.'

Bumpy edges are intruding through the misty unreality of this life. I'm still skating over frozen years but ordinariness is closing round. Janey's growing up, providing for the future . . . Mundane realities, rocks that enclosed Kirsten's life. I'm fearful that life is caging me in. Perhaps that's what life does.

At the end of the week a curious thing occurs. Mrs Crabbe accosts me in the supermarket. She starts off with a chat to Janey, then sends her off to fetch some Comfort, and immediately lowers her voice to me. 'I missed you at the end of term. I was hoping to talk.'

I edge nearer the cereals. There's a determined look in Mrs Crabbe's eye that I don't like. I've psyched myself up for shopping, not this.

'About Janey?' I suggest needlessly, popping a sample-sized Shreddies pack into my trolley.

I notice Mrs Crabbe has meringue nests in her trolley, and a vast bottle of Frascati. I imagine her sharing these items with Mr Crabbe in a small dinette. Or perhaps there is no Mr Crabbe and she sits solitary among red setters, sipping forlornly from a bubbled glass.

She's nodding. 'Frankly, I've been worried. She's become so withdrawn.'

'She's a quiet child,' I say. I've noticed that. And this is really not a supermarket sort of conversation, is it.

'Well, no. That's it. Usually she's quite a little chatter-box,' says Mrs Crabbe.

I digest this. I pick up a packet of tea-bags, discover a ghastly miniature attached, and replace it on the shelf. Mrs Crabbe is asking if I have noticed any other signs of tension. Other signs? What does she mean? Janey plays with her food a bit. Don't all kids?

'Has she started bed-wetting?'

'No,' I say quickly. But I don't really know for certain. I've never thought about it, never looked. If she has, and she's not saying, does that mean she's been sleeping all week on a wet patch? I stare stonily at Mrs Crabbe, willing her to stop this inquisition. She's talking now about how fond she is of Janey, how fond they all are, as though that makes it all right to confront me among the preserves and push these accusations at me. I can't comprehend how anyone who seemed so nice can do this.

When I get home I go straight to Janey's room and put my hand under her duvet, feeling gingerly down the length of the bed. It's full of soft toys but perfectly dry.

At tea-time I watch Janey. There's nothing wrong with her,

and I'm increasingly incensed by Mrs Crabbe. I wonder what good she could possibly think she was doing by raising my anxiety about the child so unnecessarily. All right, her schoolwork flagged a bit, but it's holiday time now, what business has a teacher got to interfere? I'm fuming, and I can't wait to complain to Clyde when he comes home.

But before he arrives I notice something. It's the way Janey rubs at her arms – she does it a lot. And there are tiny little marks, all the way from her elbows to her wrists. Little pinch marks, where her small nails have dug into the flesh deep enough to gouge, to leave tiny red weals where the skin has broken. Hundreds of them.

The Seventh Week

Clyde has nearly finished making the rabbit hutch. I've been lying here on the lounger listening as he ponderously describes each stage to Janey. 'The wire netting has to cover the whole of the pen, including the box, so the rabbit can't dig its way out. Which is what they want to do.'

He wraps the wire netting methodically around the sawn struts. 'It's got to be galvanised netting, see. Two and a half metres – call it three.' She's nodding judiciously.

I've made a bit of an effort over lunch today. That is, I've opened a packet of mixed lettuce and a tub of supermarket houmous and put some pitta bread in the oven to warm up. I thought it might encourage Janey if I showed a bit more interest in motherly sorts of things like meals.

Janey comes in, looking grubby. I say, 'Teeth and hands, Janey.'

'I know,' she says, in a singsong voice.

Clyde has followed her in. I catch his expression.

'What?'

'That's what you used to say.' His voice is grating.

I feel a curious tightening around my chest, as if some of the excess galvanised netting from the rabbit hutch is suddenly pressing heavily on to me, as if an invisible mesh is tightening.

'I expect so. My mother always said it to me when I was young,' I say, as nonchalantly as I can. I desperately don't want him to make anything of it. Janey isn't, why should he?

Which makes me start thinking about Janey in the bathroom soaping her little hands. I get this horrible picture of her pinching and pinching the soft flesh above the wrist. I chuck down the salad servers and barge down the corridor to the bathroom.

She looks up at me, startled. The hot tap is dribbling where she hasn't turned it off properly and the basin is frothy with scummy water. She bursts into tears. 'I'm cleaning up, I am!'

I'm crying too. I've got a big towel, for some reason, and I'm trying to wipe her all over, not just her damp hands and her face but her frock and her hair, I'm burying her entirely in this fluffy shroud, and holding her and rocking her from side to side.

And after a while we both stop sobbing and Janey gives a nervous giggle. And I sit on the side of the bath and pull a jokey face, and we go quietly back to the kitchen.

I hope she won't say anything about it to Clyde, and she doesn't.

And then in the afternoon she's in the garden, playing with Alice as usual, and for the first time I listen in to the long rigmarole of her game instructions as Alice looks dumbly back. My daughter is saying, 'Let's pretend we don't know each other and you're a stranger. Hello, hello, how do you do? I don't know whether I like you, do I?'

I can't bear to stand and watch her poignant masquerade. 'What about a walk to the river and a paddle?' I say. They immediately abandon their activities and scurry over. I put a towel and some fruit in a carrier-bag and we set off.

It's a hot afternoon. There are kids' bikes flopped on the grass by the riverbank, and children swimming by the frothing weir but I steer the girls to the shallow paddling-place further down. Here there is only one child, a little boy in long shorts with a pale, grubby torso and a jar full of murky water.

'Hello, Janeysmum,' says Daniel.

He shows us his catch and the girls squat so low to examine the treasures of the stream that they get their bottoms soaked but they don't seem to mind. Daniel is alone and appears used to his own company. We stay for around an hour and as we're leaving I say to him on impulse, 'Come round and play in our garden sometime, if you want to,' but he makes no reply.

The girls are engrossed in their own conversations as we stroll back along the quiet cow-parsley lane from the river. I'm watching them, but my thoughts slide into dreamy reverie. What do I know, after nearly two months? I know this sunny village street I'm walking, the crumbly ochre wall with its blistering pink valerium. What do I know about Kirsten Villiers? How did she fill her days? She got up, she tidied the house and maybe the garden. Some days she helped at the school, some days she went to the gym. Some evenings she went to the Pizza Parlour and some evenings she watched the dazzling sun drop over the long fields beyond the fence. And secretly she made illicit love.

About her thoughts I still know nothing. I know nothing of the empty spaces between each separate activity. But this is where Kirsten's real life lay. All the passion and the energy of longing and lust and love, her emotional chaos, the blacks and golds of her life. She must have walked docilely along this street, like I am today, with her mind in turmoil. Poor Kirsten, waiting for her prince to wake her from inertia.

Somehow I've got to fuse Kirsty and her together into one identity, so that I can say, 'This is me.' But first I've got to want to.

Later, when Polly comes to collect Alice I offer her a cup of tea and a biscuit. 'I don't suppose you worry about your shape,' I say, and then wonder if she'll be offended.

But she laughs and agrees she's past caring. 'One of the joys of advancing age,' she says cheerfully. 'I used to long for someone to invent a pill so that eating would use more energy than the calories in the food. You could eat, eat, eat all day, and the more you ate the more the layers of flesh would roll off. With all the pills on the market, don't you think someone could do a simple little thing like that? But when I hit forty I realised that you can't eat the years away, even with a magic pill.'

Polly is smiling but that doesn't sound like a joy to me. 'I don't look outside any more for solutions,' she explains. 'You have to go within.' She helps herself to another coconut macaroon and says nonchalantly, 'What do you do? To keep your shape, I mean.'

I don't know what I do. Well, I know what I do, which is nothing much, but I don't know what Kirsten does. 'I don't really bother about it,' I say.

A third voice joins our debate. Old Mrs Thing from next door, who has been mumbling in the corner of her garden, comes over saying something that sounds like 'mingling, fingering'. She reaches the fence nearest us and straightens up, fixes me with an uncannily steady gaze and recites:

> 'The moving finger writes, and having writ moves on.
> Nor all your piety nor wit can lure it back to cancel half a line,
> Nor all your tears wash out a word of it.'

I'm impressed. I have heard this before, actually, or at least the first part, but I didn't realise it was so sad and strong. Especially when you're me, watching those tears washing down the words and no earthly idea what's been written. I'll have to learn Braille, I think. Then I can finger the pockmarks of time and learn what I did with my life.

Polly's standing with her hands on her hips, shaking her head, as we watch the old lady wander off down her garden path. 'Losing your mind must be the worst thing that can happen to anyone,' she says. Then she puts a hasty hand out to my arm and says, 'Oh, I didn't mean — oh. How tactless.' And she giggles guiltily. I find this quite endearing. I mean, if it was someone else and not me, I'd be tempted to see a funny side. Not funny-hilarious, but there are moments of ironic levity in the absurdity of my plight. If I've thought of that, I'm sure other people have. Which is all part of why re-meeting them without remembering them seems so difficult. But I feel safe with Polly. I don't mind a bit of tactless giggling.

'I don't think it is, actually,' I say. 'I mean, I don't think losing your mind is the worst thing. The worst thing would be realising you'd lost it. If it stayed lost all the time, you'd be all right. It's very egotistical to think we must know who we are.'

'Egotistical,' says Polly thoughtfully. 'Ye-es.'

So I go on, warming to my theory. 'Not knowing doesn't hurt. It's knowing that you ought to know, that everyone around insists you must know, that's what makes you feel . . . char-grilled.' I was going to say, 'like charred stubble in a burnt-out field,' but I thought that would sound too morbid. I haven't talked like that to anyone, except maybe Jemima. Polly doesn't seem to mind me getting heavy, and before she takes Alice home she gives me a really nice hug.

Next day Clyde comes up with this idea that the three of us go shopping in Bath. He wants to buy me a photographic book, which is quite touching although I suspect it may be a bit of Amanda-therapy, which limits my enthusiasm. We go into Waterstone's and after much attempted consultation he chooses a big how-to book with a cover showing sunflowers. By now Janey has come whizzing back from the children's section about eighty times, like some small bibliophilic boomerang, wanting us to see

— i.e. buy — some book she says Alice has, which comes with a kit of beads and threads. 'So you can make friendship bracelets.' She eyes my naked wrist as she says this. I recall, uncomfortably, the wristband thing I pulled off that night in the hospital. 'Well, let's get it and then you can make me another!' I suggest cheerily. I don't quite have the presence of mind — or the effrontery — to invent a lie about its loss. But this seems enough: Janey beams like a maniac and marches back to the children's section pulling Clyde's hand. I'm just about to follow when I see Helen's Jeremy.

He's looking at the man-stuff magazines. He really is nice-looking, I do think Helen is lucky. He's got that kind of supple, long-boned look that makes me think of jaguars slinking through night landscapes.

I go over and say, 'Hi', and, since I can't see Sam or Helen, I add, 'Are you on your own?'

He gives me a look of such quizzical intensity I almost wonder if he doesn't recognise me now that I've liberated myself from his wife's supervision of my dress and hair. I'm about to back away when a man with a baby in a canvas infant-carrier on his chest suddenly reaches towards the woodwork magazines. The baby is asleep, his lolling little face all fudgy and his chubby arms slightly damp. As the father moves I turn aside quickly so's not to be brushed by them and disturb him, and find I've swayed into Jeremy. My breast touches his arm. There's a tiny frisson, like static electricity, and then the man with the baby steps away and we move apart.

Jeremy has to say something now. He can't really avoid it, though he's not looking at me. 'It's good to see you're so much better,' he tells his magazine, rolling it into a narrow trumpet then smoothing it out again. He has lovely hands. His voice is husky, too, but his absolute inability to deal with this meeting makes me feel embarrassed and slightly angry. 'Well, see you around,' I say coolly, and he nods.

I see Clyde and Janey in the other queue and go over to join them. 'Jeremy's over there,' I say, and Clyde nods nonchalantly across to his friend. 'He's really uncomfortable about my amnesia,' I say, as we leave the shop, 'even worse than Helen.' I think about poor old Mrs Thing next door and vow not to back off in future when she begins her eccentric confidings. 'I don't know why other people get so uptight. It's my problem not theirs.'

Clyde doesn't comment. He's keen for me to take my book and exclaim how much I love it, like Janey is with hers. Janey is already planning patterns and colours to plait and who to give them to. She says, magnanimously, 'You can make one too, Mummy.' I just smile. Who would I give a friendship bracelet to?

Now we're back in the car Clyde's gone all glum and edgy again. To please him I say, 'I really do like the book – especially the way you really chose it for me, not off one of Helen's catalogues on the art of living.'

He's not amused. 'You never used to be so snobby.'

Uh-oh. And Janey's listening in the back. Time for the breezy, jokey voice, I think. I search for it. 'Clyde, I'm trying to relocate a missing identity here. This is not about snobbery, it's about trying to find a taste that isn't so bland you could use it as a dip for chilli tacos.'

He doesn't laugh at that either. He says, 'If you're fed up with Helen, why don't you try seeing one of your other friends?'

Good question. I try to explain how unconfident I feel, especially since seeing that gang's-all-here video and knowing Clyde has talked to them about me. I say miserably, 'But didn't you see how Jeremy looked at me in the bookshop? If that's how our best friends react, you can't be surprised I don't want to confide in the rest.'

For a long time he drives in silence. Then he says, 'What about Pol?'

What about Pol? She's friendly, and quite interesting to talk to. She doesn't worry about the percentage grey of her hair, but she's not boringly complacent. To be honest, I didn't expect to feel comfortable with a woman of that age – I suppose that sounds naïve but I've become a bit sensitive about getting older. Perhaps I was afraid it was catching, and I might lose another decade overnight if I hung around too long with Polly.

But Polly has been nice to me and when we get home I'm actually considering giving her a ring until Clyde disappears into the spare room and comes out with a couple of well-thumbed charity catalogues full of unbleached towels and organic pulses and elephants carved in green jade. 'You're happy enough to use these at Christmas,' he says. 'Mail order is only another way of buying things, it's not a crime for the style police.' He's obviously been pondering my catalogue comments for the last half-hour and this is his notion of rapier-fast wit. I give him a watery smile. Maybe this encourages him, because he goes on, 'These days, people buy whatever way suits them best – off the TV, off the computer, even.'

'Wow, we could do our shopping on the Amstrad?' I make my eyes wide and show by my voice how sceptical I am of this sci-fi scenario and he concedes, reluctantly, 'Not right now. But when we get an attachment, and maybe a different computer . . .'

I stop listening. Not just because I don't want to talk, or even think, about what can be done on the bloody Amstrad, but because I don't like this argumentative shift to Clyde's strategy. I don't like Clyde playing time games with me. And he was. *These days*, he said, all superior because I'm some kind of anachronism, some kind of savage child from the forests of the past. If he thinks he can teach me his rules for *these days*, he's wrong. I'll find out on my own what Kirsten knew, I won't be manipulated by him or anyone else who thinks they know what I should be like.

Which takes me back to thinking about Polly and what she

asked me yesterday when we were having our keep-young-and-beautiful conversation. *I don't really bother*, I'd said, but Kirsten bothered, didn't she? There's enough clues. Walking around the lanes, going swimming. And the gym, and the nutritious recipe cards – Helen's influence, I'd thought. Those weird tapes, which I'd put down to something Polly might have lent her. Kirsten was seeking something, and maybe not magic pills.

But if Kirsten did make decisions and choices for herself, this doesn't help me lose those flaky feelings of uneasiness. Because if she was active, not docile, in her life, then maybe the way she left it was her decision too. She's chosen to leave me here, an un-rehearsed understudy in her world. What part does she want me to play? What on earth does she expect me to do?

I need to find someone who understood Kirsten but will accept me, not want me to be her. I need someone who will be honest with me without condemning. And the last thing I need is a strange and unsympathetic mother-in-law choosing this night to arrive without warning.

Clyde's mother is a kind of compressed version of him. She's small but sturdy with thick glasses, and she has his colouring, the light skin and reddish hair. That, more than the sparse photos in the albums, is how I know who this is when the doorbell goes and she's standing there, looking belligerent and holding a big brown grip. 'My bus home is the day after tomorrow,' she announces, by way of a greeting, as she steps into the bungalow.

Clyde gives her a perfunctory embrace that is more like a pat on the arm, takes the grip from her, and says, 'Well, you'll have to be on the put-you-up in Janey's room. I don't want Kirsten put out.' He sounds very definite about it, like I'm a pedigree queen that's coming in season.

His mother gives an enormous sniff. She says, 'In My Day, if you were sick you went to Hospital.'

'You never went to hospital in your life,' says Clyde calmly. 'And, anyway, Kirsten is not sick. She's just a bit forgetful.

You don't need a sickbed to help you remember things.'

She's still looking at me through her pebbly glasses. They make her eyes look huge, like beetles with curious glazed patterning. 'Doctors should do something,' she says.

I smile feebly. 'I'm still going for tests,' I say, ingratiatingly.

'Don't waste your breath,' Clyde advises me, audibly, and then he says, 'I don't want any upsetting, Ma.'

I decide to be very civil. I'm getting some useful insights here, I think, into why Clyde is not overly communicative.

'Do you want any tea?'

'I ate on the bus,' she tells Clyde, even though it was me who asked her. 'I brought my own. It's all morello and smelly Brie in those packages. You never get a proper cheese and chutney sandwich, these days.'

Clyde's mother's idea of sick-visiting is not too arduous once I get used to her habit of looking straight past me. It involves basically watching TV all evening and making unrelated comments from time to time. Janey seems pleased to see her, surprisingly, when she comes back from Alice's as Clyde is putting the bed up. She goes into her rabbit conversation, interrogating her grandmother's opinions on the best sort to acquire for fluffiness and temperament. 'I really love lop-ears, but some of them need so much grooming,' Janey is explaining.

'You'll get wasps around that plum tree, I suppose,' says my mother-in-law.

Her grandmother's general manner must make it more difficult for Janey to be certain that she isn't listening; she seems to suss it straight away with me.

When they're both settled down and we've gone into our bedroom too I say to Clyde, 'Was she always like that? I mean, when you were little?'

He goes all defensive now. 'It was difficult for her,' he says. 'Bringing up a child on her own was difficult.' He looks at me stuffily, like that's something I've never had to know. 'She was widowed, you know, while I was still a baby. And then losing one of her children.'

Yes, I think. Difficult, and sad. And I find I'm thinking about Clyde, orphaned while he was still a baby, brotherless while he was still a child. Brought up by a mother who doesn't touch, or smile, or even look at you much.

So why did he pick me? Because I was different, or because I was the same?

I wake early to a strange noise in the kitchen. A stealthy scraping sort of noise, like someone dragging a knife across ice chunks. It's Clyde's mother defrosting the freezer compartment above the fridge. She's got a bowl of hot water inside it and she's dabbing round the sides with a J-cloth. Little scraps of yellow stripy cloth stick to the frosty edges. I haven't taken much interest in kitchen matters up to now but my proprietorial instinct immediately goes into overdrive as I see the sodden pile of packets on the draining board: a green-bean bag sweating icy droplets, packs of baps weeping, the ice-cream carton sagging forlornly with dribbling corners. 'That fridge has an automatic defrost function,' I say, as coldly as I can in the thawing kitchen, 'You only have to empty the tray.'

Clyde's mother completely ignores this. 'Things want doing,' she intones, into the perspiring cavern of my freezer compartment.

I stamp back to the bedroom. Clyde is sitting on the side of the bed looking apprehensive. 'We'll have to throw most of that stuff away,' I tell him, at the conclusion of my terse summary. He holds my hands unspeakingly then hugs me. It feels a bit like comfort but I'm not sure which of us in being consoled.

By the time I calm down and get up, Clyde's mother is out in the garden toeing a moss patch on the grass. Clyde, just about to leave for work, joins me at the kitchen window as I watch her navy court shoe prod disparagingly at our neat lawn. He strokes my shoulder.

'We're not going to use weed killer on that garden,' I say.

'I know,' he says, and then, 'It's only for a day. She goes back tomorrow, first thing.'

I turn away as she bends to scowl at a daisy. 'I don't think I'll last a day.'

'Take her to the market.'

'The cattle market?' I have a wild image of trading his mother in for a handful of coloured beans. Clyde says, no, the market hall beside the river in town. She loves stalls, he says.

'Will you leave the car for me, then?' I say, but he says there's no point, his mother will insist on the bus anyway.

So when she comes in for breakfast – Clyde's mother has brought her own individual packet of All Bran – I suggest a bus trip into town. Clyde's mother nods. Janey cheers thinly and pours herself a large bowl of frosted cereal with blithe indifference to her grandmother's comments about bowels, and I sigh with relief and make some toast.

Clyde's mother has brought her own copy of our local bus timetable too, which I think shows an intriguing degree of forward planning. She tips her head back and straightens her arms to peruse it then announces, 'We'll get the nine oh-eight, and then we can come back on the three twenty-three. Eh, Janey?' Janey, who perhaps hasn't worked out that this means six hours of close company with Granny Vee, nods serenely.

The indoor market is actually a flea-market, selling just about everything that's not new. Books, postcards, maps, medals, buttons, beads, shoes, clothes, Clyde's mother patrols the stalls doggedly, looking at everything, her purse never emerging from the big brown bag she clutches. Janey's patience is thinning. 'What's that smell?' she says audibly, a few times.

'Mustiness,' I explain, as neither the stall-holder nor her grandmother are prepared to enlighten her.

At the end of the hall there are teas and little cakes with Smarties on top. Clyde's mother sits expectantly at a table so I go up to the counter and get us two teas. They have some cans of cola but only the cheap ones, not the sort Janey likes, and they're not chilled. I ask Janey if she wants anything and she shakes her head bravely. I take our two cups over to Clyde's mother, who acknowledges my arrival by reversing their position on the table and remarking, 'Can't abide weak tea.'

'I'm just going to take Janey to the library,' I say hurriedly, 'so she's got something to do while we're having our tea.' Janey leaps to the door like a loosed whippet and I follow.

The library is on the corner, literally a few yards from the market hall. I did intend to take Janey there straight away but the sun outside the frowsty indoor market is so enticing we spend a few moments loitering beside the river. Janey wants to see whether any of the spring ducklings have survived the rats. We count seven, and she's happy. A flock of pigeons from the bank takes off suddenly, whirring and circling above us, their wings tipped silver in the sunlight.

As we stroll towards the corner I notice the ice-cream van in the precinct, a local firm which makes delicious ice-cream. Janey doesn't say anything but her eyes widen hopefully so I buy us both cornets and we sit by the river to lick them. As Janey says, you can't take ices into the library.

After a while Clyde's mother emerges from the market hall and we get up quickly, guiltily. She plods across to us apparently bearing no grudge at our absconding. 'I suppose it's the pet shop now, Janey,' she says flatly, and Janey switches allegiance in an instant with a clap of her hands. She skips on the spot too. I'm tempted to tell her to stop acting like a child but at least she has an excuse for that, which is more than I have.

I follow them to the pet shop, praying to every deity I can think of that there will be no rabbits. I'm beginning to feel weak and it isn't even lunchtime.

There is a rabbit, a big black buck, but he has a label on his pen that says he is only visiting while his owners are on holiday.

Janey squats down to enthuse over him while Clyde's mother has found a macaw to marvel at. There's a note on his cage saying 'Keep Fingers Away from the Bars', and underneath it says, 'Please do not teach this bird Swear Words'.

'Isn't Blackie beautiful?' drools Janey.

'What are they feeding this parrot on?' says Clyde's mother.

'Bugger off,' says the macaw.

'Lunch,' I say firmly, so's I won't die of hysteria on an empty stomach.

I'd planned to take them to the place where Helen took me, but Clyde's mother leads us back to the precinct into a bun shop with steaming urns and tables crowded with gossiping shoppers. The room is full of cigarette smoke so I persuade her to let us take our cheese-slice sandwiches outside to eat. We sit by a pyramid of big polythene bags crammed with baps and buns all going for a pound. Clyde's mother wonders aloud so many times how they do it for the price that I don't have to think up any conversation at all.

We finish our lunch and I look at my watch in despair. It's only one o'clock. And then like an angel, hair all flowing and Indian bells jingling like distant chimes, here's Polly, hand in hand with Alice.

'We're off to buy a birthday card,' she says, 'from that shop at the top of the cobbled street with the stream running down it. Have you seen it, Mrs Villiers?'

Clyde's mother nods tersely. 'Tiring, those steep streets,' she confirms, but Polly has another angle. 'Yes, it's so hilly and picturesque the television people used it for filming there last year.' I mime blessings on her as Clyde's mother lumbers to her feet and sets off as though cameras are still rolling. Pol and I follow, exchanging smiles as Alice and Janey lag behind talking together.

As we reach the shop Polly says, 'Oh, look, here's Geoff and Amanda. Day off, Geoff?'

'Half day,' Geoff qualifies. He steps forward to shake

hands. He's a pleasant-looking bloke with sun-bleached hair, in his thirties, I suppose. He's not exactly what I'd imagined from the video. Amanda has long hair tied behind her neck and really lovely eyes. She gives me a little social street hug and a nice smile, and I realise I have seen her before, around the village. Actually, I must have glimpsed most of my friends – in a village I could hardly avoid it.

'Tony not with you?' I say, and Geoff laughs. 'We left him at home, chained up,' he says, and Amanda says, 'He's not very keen on shopping for other people's birthdays.' She dips into a silver carrier-bag and pulls green tissue aside to show a decorated mirror they've just bought. It's all so easy and amiable I wonder why I've been so determined to avoid everyone, walking around in blinkers and concealing myself like a recluse. These people are gentle and pleasant like Polly: they don't make me feel like a freak. Helen's hard-edged nervousness had convinced me I was right to hide away. But maybe I was wrong.

When we go back down the street Polly asks where I'm parked, so I explain regretfully about the three twenty-three bus. Pol says she'll give us a lift and I don't even turn round to see if that brusque intake of breath means that Clyde's mother is demurring. I say yes.

'We went to the market this morning,' I tell Clyde, when he comes home. 'We came back just after lunch. Your mother's had a nice nap in the garden.'

'I hope you were firm,' he says.

'I was.'

'She means well, you know.' I nod. I don't know how Clyde can fathom benign intentions from the Gothic expression and disjointed utterances of his mother but I don't ask. She spends the evening playing cards with Janey and we all agree on an early night.

Clyde is lying there on his back when I get into bed. He always does this if he gets in first, and then as I curl quickly on to my side, away from him, he lumbers over on his side too so that we lie there back to back, breathing in ragged rhythm, about a millimetre apart. Tonight I lie flat. I'm not quite touching, but I'm not turned away.

There's a kind of silence as though he has simply stopped breathing altogether and then I hear a heavy, sighing breath and his hand comes cautiously creeping over my belly. I concentrate on my own breathing. I think about relaxing. *This power can be used to make contact with etheric world intelligences, should you so desire.* I hope I don't start giggling, or crying.

Clyde has rolled on to his side towards me and one arm is around me while his other hand caresses me, all over. His arm has gone octopus-long, he can reach right down my calves and he's stroking everywhere. His dick is huge; it's pushing into the top of my thigh and quivering and I know we have to do it now. I have to let him, it would be too awful not to. He's kissing into my neck with his soft gobbly lips and I'm hoping I won't shudder and wondering if he would notice. It's a bit weird that he wants to do it with his mother in the house but it suits me because I've got an excuse for not responding much. It occurs to me that maybe he realised that – maybe he was even allowing me an excuse to refuse him. Maybe he was trying to make sure he didn't get too hurt if I pushed him away. Perhaps Clyde is a bit more sensitive than he seems.

His hand plunges down between my legs and I think, He'll know now, and I wonder how I can fake it without that big thing hurting me. But his fingers when he strokes around my thighs are wet and sticky. He lunges slowly over me, groaning very quietly. He guides himself in and begins to rock slowly up and down, muttering and kissing me. I don't have to do anything, only keep my eyes closed and concentrate on not turning my face away. And when he comes, he's crying – not aloud, but I know, because his face is all wet with tears. He smooths my hair away and kisses my forehead with his gentle soft lips and then lies back. When he falls asleep his arm is still around me.

In the morning he's smiling and blinking, and being so soft and tender with me, as though I'm a thousand-pound note that's come fluttering through a terrible storm and now he must find somewhere safe to place me to dry. He whispers that he's taking the day off and 'she' will think it's to get her off on the bus. 'So she'll be pleased too,' he says *sotto voce*. I had almost forgotten about *her*. She's up already, busy looking for her umbrella. I did try saying, 'I don't think you brought one,' but she scolded the empty room by way of reply, 'I'm sure it was left here last Christmas.'

Around eight thirty she goes, after consenting to a small boiled egg. She hesitates in the hallway and I wonder whether to kiss her grim cheek. But as I step forward she whips out an enamel compact and says, 'I couldn't get caked and I don't like this soft stuff,' and begins to flour herself busily while peering into the little mirror. I feel Clyde's arms circling me from behind, holding me firmly. His body is pressed close, hot and loving. He says, 'Coming to say 'bye to Granny Vee, Janey?' and they go off to the bus stop. When he comes back he looks so happy.

'Shouldn't you have taken her in the car to the coach station?' I say, but he doesn't stop smiling.

'No point,' he says. 'She likes doing it her way.'

I can think of a lot of comments on 'her way', but I abstain. I'm preoccupied, anyway, with my own plans. Clyde comes right over and hugs me. 'She said goodbye to you, in her own way. That compact, you gave her that for her last birthday.' He smiles like this is a shared secret. I give him a bit of a smile back and he starts hugging me again. I gesture towards the kettle and pull away, but slowly, and he squeezes my arms all the way down to the wrists so that even when we part we seem to be touching invisibly in the space between our hands. I fill the kettle, fuss with the mugs and tea-bags. He really seems to feel that last night flicked a switch. The self-conscious, glum holding-back is gone. He's all over me. I can smell his man-smell stronger than my own.

We stand together waiting for the kettle to boil. Janey's little singing voice comes from her bedroom where she's been planning one of her expeditions. He has put his big bear arm around my shoulder and carefully moved my hand across him, nestling into his waist. It seems to fit there.

'I met Amanda and Geoff yesterday.'

'Good.'

'Maybe you're right. Maybe I should try to socialise more.' My voice sounds prim and ungracious. He looks so pleased. 'I didn't mean right now,' I say quickly. 'It's school holidays and people are away.'

I unclip myself to make the drinks and we take our mugs to the window. It really is a glorious day. I suppose this feels quite late to Clyde – it's after nine – but I'm still sleepy and wondering how to convince him with my plan for today.

I'm not ready to give up on Kirsty and give in to Clyde entirely. I've already decided I'm going to drive down to Devon, to Newton Abbot where I used to live. I can say it now, *where I used to live*. So maybe now's the time to go back, and perhaps at last find the end of the thread I lost somewhere, when that was my home and I was me, before I became the 'her' that now I have to be for ever.

He's not convinced. It's too long a drive, he says. But it's obviously not just that: clearly he had his own plans for today.

'I was thinking,' he says, 'that we could try and track down some of the people from that summer you spent at the printing factory. Maybe have a retro party? Get them all together, ask them to bring some music and wear what they wore then – it could be good for you, Kirst.'

A bit late, isn't it, for him to start with the good ideas? He's begrudgingly left me in terrified isolation for weeks and now after one shag he wants to get out the party-poppers.

I disengage from his gentle grip. 'I don't think there's any point in that, is there? Like you said, everyone will have gone. And, anyway, that was just one of my forgotten summers. I've got to start looking before that. And believe me, Clyde, I have to do this.'

I really tried, with those last words, to get through to him, to get through that blissful myopia. Evidently I've succeeded.

The happy look drains absolutely from his face. All the softened edges harden into dourness again. 'Finished?' he says. He's staring down at my tea mug. I nod, and he takes it from me and slowly washes it up. I stand with my arms folded, watching as he stoops over the sink wiping carefully round the tannin stains with a cloth.

When he looks round he says, 'It wasn't always like this. We used to laugh, Kirst.'

I think about that. Laughter is what I'm missing, and I can't imagine Clyde laughing a lot. Also, it's irritating that he's compromising my name into Kirst. It begins to sound like a curse – a terse contraction of For Chrissake. Cursed.

I say, 'I'm Kirsty.'

He blinks, then says, 'Hi, I'm Clyde,' shakes my hand and then kisses me on the lips.

Is that the sort of thing we used to laugh at? Sad.

'I have to go to see my old house. Please let me have the car, Clyde. Just for the day.'

He talks a bit about driving being too tiring and suggests the train, but it's obvious as soon as I start talking about British Rail that the new schedules will completely confuse me. Then he wants to drive me. 'I'll wait in the car,' he says, nearly whining. I think about the footmen and the pumpkin waiting for Cinderella after the ball.

'It wouldn't work,' I say. 'I'd get anxious about you, I wouldn't be able to free up and follow my instincts.'

'Time for dead or alive', sings out the radio. Clyde reaches out and flips it off with a force that nearly cracks the plastic. Then he hands me the car keys.

I make a fuss of Janey before I go, telling her she's going to have a lovely day with Daddy and I'll bring them both a treat tonight.

'A laughy treat?' says Janey, in a singsong, careless tone.

I've sometimes wondered how much she hears while she's crouching in her bedroom playing. She's hugging the cat, which is not allowed into the bedrooms so Janey always has a perfect reason to be kneeling in a doorway, half in the passage, whenever she claims Dandy wants a cuddle. Dandy is a fairly benign creature who consents placidly to these embraces although I've never noticed it actually seek them out. Now I think about the tense way my brief rapport with Clyde in the kitchen broke down. I say, 'Did we used to be more fun? I'm sorry if I'm not laughy, these days.'

Janey releases the cat. It slides gracelessly to the floor and disappears. 'Well, this is your sad summer, Mummy. Daddy says you'll laugh again when you're better.'

The princess who couldn't laugh. Cursed Kirsten. Where's my prince, then, to dislodge the poisoned apple? Why has he left me all alone?

The drive to Exeter was straightforward, in spite of the road-works, but the city is a nightmare. I had intended to stop here and visit all my old haunts, but I got buried in a one-way system and was so relieved to see signs to Torbay and Plymouth that I came straight out of the city again. After all, there won't be anything going on in August to help me recall student life. I should postpone this piece of historical research until next term.

Having made this decision I simply turn towards the A380 and head for Newton Abbot. As soon as I'm there I park and walk up to the big Georgian square by the park, where I used to live.

While I was growing up they moved the park nearer to our road. I don't know how or why. Once upon a time when I was little and going to see the fish was a Sunday ritual, the park was quite a long walk away. Often I got carried home on Dad's shoulder – my chariot, a privilege relinquished with screaming reluctance when Suzy came along. By the time I was at big school, someone Herculean, or maybe a silent tribe under cover of night, had dragged the entire park hundreds of yards closer. It didn't seem to have suffered in transit, though it did shrink pitifully in the process. The lily lake became a pond, the long hill up to the bandstand a mere well-mown slope. And those big glittering fish the colour of sunset on the sea mottled by silver clouds, they had all been replaced by ordinary goldfish.

Now it's hardly more than a brief step away from the old house. The bandstand is still there, and the black-railed green-membrane pond, and the casual spread of bushy trees. There's a new section specially for the blind, with circular paths all made of little concrete bubbles. I close my eyes, pretending to be sightless, and trace a route around the aromatic beds. The surreal feeling of moving unseeing between invisible walls suits my mood. When I open my eyes I'm in a central circle of grass and there is nobody else around.

The roofs of the town spread densely into the gauzy blue skyline of the moors. I walk down the short connecting street to the square where I used to live. It's been painted up recently and looks smarter than I remember. I decide to walk the route that I took home from primary school every day, tracing it backwards from my house up the hill to Debs's house and then back down to the school the way we called the Hundred-steps.

Debs's surname was Adolfi. We used to have long discussions about our names, usually sitting on these steps after school, eating Twixes. At one time Debs hated her surname because it was unusual, but later she came to revel in it, inventing Italianate connections that included a contessa and an uncle with an ice-cream factory in Milan. I didn't have any violent feelings about my name either way. Middleton is . . . well, middling. Not noticeable but not completely anonymous, not overbrief or overlong. A middle-of-the-alphabet, middle-of-the-road, middle-class, Middle-England name. When Debs and I had talked about changing our names when we got married, I had decided to look for someone with a similar nebulous sort of name. Paul is Parr, which I think is roughly acceptable. Miles is Vellacott, which is rather on the dashing side. It suits him, but I'm a bit put off by the thought of all those how-do-you-spell-thats, which esoteric names always inspire.

I wonder now if Debs made it to Deborah Parr, and if she likes that any better.

I reach the top of the hill in three minutes, which surprises me. I thought it would take about twenty. I suppose we always dawdled, even when we were old enough to realise this was only a long, steep road, not a mountain. Debs's parents' house looks recently decorated, and I wonder briefly whether to ring the bell. There is a car in the drive, a Range Rover. It could possibly be theirs. But I'm feeling curiously safe in my isolation, like an unperceivable ghost. I stroll on.

The public-footpath sign is new and there's a new rail leading to the Hundred-steps but they're just the same, chipped and a bit chewed-up-looking. An old woman ahead of me is throwing a yellow ball for her dog. It goes bouncing down and disappears into the bushes at each turn of the steps, and the little dog goes flying after it. His legs are hardly longer than the depth of the steps but he manages to scrabble back to her with the ball in his teeth before she's tottered down more than a few each time. There's something about the ritual and the silent rapport between the woman and her dog that makes me want to laugh, or maybe to cry. I realise that it's the consoling timelessness that moves me. I am absolutely lost in time.

I cross the road at the bottom, which is a lot busier than I remember. Our old shop is still there, no longer a video library but a general store. It looks more like it used to when I was little than it did the last time I saw it. There's even a chalk board outside advertising 'Scrumpy 2-and-a-half Litre only £3.25'. It's obviously an off-licence now. I suppose satellite and cable TV have gobbled up the video market.

I'm just about to walk down to my old primary-school building when the most bizarre thing occurs. It's so bizarre that for a moment I don't believe my eyes, and when I do believe them I have a strong sensation that I'm not standing on the pavement at all but floating.

Debs is standing right in front of me. She has just walked out of the offy with a bottle of wine and a packet of biscuits, both of which she is trying to cram into her shoulder-bag without looking at what she's doing, and it's so typically Debs that I nearly sob aloud. I recognise the gesture before anything else.

The rest of her is different. Smart in a sloppy sort of way, with one of those linen suits that need pressing as soon as you've put it on and a blouse that begs for a classic brooch at the throat. Her hair's well cut, though, very short at the back and with a glossy long fringe all round so it looks boyish and slick. I'm taking in all this in the instant I see her, as though this second has spun out endlessly, like in a car accident.

And then she sees me. 'I don't believe it!' Her voice is the same. She says it as if a TV camera is on her, close-focusing on her amazement.

'It's me,' I say stupidly, and she says, 'I know – that's what I don't believe.'

Then we both start together. 'Why—' She stops.

I carry on. 'Why are you here?'

'I came to get some papers.' She sweeps her hand behind her, indicating down the road. 'We teachers don't get the same long hols as the kids, you know.' Now she does sound different. *We teachers* and *long hols* aren't what my friend Debs would say, not like that. Then I take in that it's our old primary she's waving towards. She grins, a flash of real Debs. 'Oh, yes, I've been there for ever! Well, since I did my teaching practice there, to save all that travelling in and out of Exeter, in my final year. They offered me a post and I've been there since. Stuck like a limpet.' She laughs. 'What about you? You're looking so good – you haven't aged a minute, you bitch.' She pulls a face. 'It must be nearly ten years!'

'Nine,' I say. Nine years and a month and a half.

We are so close now it's absurd we're not touching. And suddenly we do touch, suddenly our arms go out simultaneously and I grab at a bit of her sleeve while she's pressing her shoulder-bag awkwardly between us. She kisses the air close to my nose.

'Oh, Kirsty. I am so pleased to see you. After all this time.'

We separate and stand smiling at each other. Then she says, 'Oh, but you mustn't go, don't go yet. We must talk, How's the career? I keep looking out for your name in the Sunday supplements.'

'I gave all that up,' I say.

She gives me a look I can't quite fathom, then says, 'We must have a drink – a coffee. There's so much to catch up on.' But we're still both standing like we've taken root there on the pavement, looking at each other.

'Are you still living up the hill?' I'm remembering how when I was at school it seemed the teachers went into filing cabinets at night when we went home, and how amazing it was to see them outside doing ordinary things like waiting for a bus. In Debs' case apparently the reverse has happened. She simply stayed all her life in the shadow of the school.

But she looks scandalised and says, 'Oh, no. My parents are still there, but we've got a little cottage in Shaldon.' I'm wondering whether to ask about *we* when she says, 'Look, I'm parked near the centre anyway. Come and let me buy you a coffee in the precinct.'

She leads me into the precinct and round the corner to a coffee-house I've never seen before and orders cappuccino at the counter. Silvery saxophone tones slide through the shuttered, nearly empty room, and a fan hanging from the ceiling purrs coolly. We take the chocolate-dusted froth-filled cups over to a table and Debs slips off her jacket. 'You must find the town looks completely different,' she says. I'm happy to agree about this. I know from Mum that I never went back home much except for Christmas trips, and even those stopped after they moved to Spain. So, in an odd way, this is a perfectly normal conversation, quite unlike the sort I have in the village where I ought to know things that I don't. In this particular chat, the baseline is my understandable ignorance. Quite a novelty, as well as a big relief.

The small-talk is a relief too, but Debs herself . . . that's another thing. Because, once I've got over the shock of actually recognising someone, instead of knowing I ought-to-but-can't, the intervening years are hitting the pit of my stomach painfully. Debs has fine lines around her eyes and a kind of softness under her chin. My sharp, funny, lovely friend is nearly there but not quite, like an ink sketch that's had a pot of water tipped on it then mopped up. The outlines are not quite the same. I'm frightened I'll find that her personality's gone soggy round the edges too.

'This place is a bit different from our doughnut caff days,' she's saying. 'You don't mind, do you?' I don't at all. Totally new is a lot less unnerving than half remembered. The décor here is fine, Debs. It's you that's disorientating. Debs is talking about Key Stages and Inset and Ofsted and I can't tell whether or not she knows she's drowning me in jargon. Either way, that's not Debs' style. She would have taken the piss, once, out of this rather loudly talking woman.

She breaks off suddenly, though I think she'd finished

anyway, and presses her head into her hands with a long groan. Then she drains her coffee cup and says, 'More importantly, how about *you*?'

I'm reminded of Leila, in the restaurant. *That's enough about me – what's your news?* I wonder why I've gathered these sort of people around me through the years. Even Helen, in her artless sort of way, seems to have assumed the lead whatever we did. The thought makes me churlish. I've waited too long to confide; now I ignore the invitation and persist in questioning her.

'A cottage in Shaldon! That must be lovely – a bit out of the way, though, isn't it? Do you need two cars?

'Oh, yeah. Both got Fiats. Punto and Uno. His 'n' hers!' Clyde would probably have gleaned more insight from this information than I can. I just keep on smiling. But she's seized with the notion that I must come and see the cottage, I must, I must, because her better half will kill her if she says she met me and didn't bring me home.

'So, you're married then?' I say, in my bright-and-breezy voice, thinking that using deliberate banalities like *better half* sound totally unwitty in an adult. I hope it doesn't turn out here that Mum's given me duff information and I was her matron-of-honour, because at the moment I feel really reluctant to mention the forgetting.

She nods, and trails her teaspoon round the clinging coffee froth in the empty cup. 'College sweetheart is a tad clichéd, isn't it? But we'd stayed together, and the mothers were keen. You know mothers! Mine simply wanted an excuse to go out and buy a hat.' Then she lowers her voice. 'I wish you'd come to the do, Kirsty. I sent you an invitation through your mum, but never got any reply.'

'I was probably too jealous,' I say, rather pathetically, trying to make it sound quippy. I'm shivering a little bit as I think about Paul and how it would feel to see him again.

She's still on about the abyss that split between us when I left college and I'm beginning to think she sounds a little bit defensive, under the regretful tone.

'I tried to contact you, oh, loads of times! But you'd just dropped everything and everyone from home and college — everyone said so. So I stopped trying. It seemed to be what you wanted.'

'Yes, I think it was.' I can hear that my voice sounds not vehement but clear and certain. Being here has given me respite from fumbled recollections and I feel more confident. 'I needed the space then. But times change, and I felt this summer was the right time to do some revisiting.'

At that moment a man sticks his head in the door of the café and says, 'Why are you girls skulking in here on this bright day? You should be out in the sunshine.' Debs guffaws and, when he's gone again, she says, 'That's Tom, our deputy — he is a card!' And I realise as I smile back that this pastiche of school roles is their way of communicating. It seems to be a grown-up thing. I think about Clyde, chatting away about cars, then getting agitated when I want to talk about feelings. Is that what getting older is? Talking in a rut. Clyde and his motors, Debs and her Ofsted, me with — what? Not a career niche like the rest of the grown-ups. Only a secret lover. Maybe that's why I left those letters on the computer, as some kind of solid assertion that I exist, even if I have nothing to say.

It makes me wonder how these life-style selections happen anyway. Do we grow accidentally, randomly, into the adults we become? Or do we select, through years of watching, choosing the mannerisms that are easiest to copy, inching inexorably into our occupations and habits, our place in time. But then I had second thoughts. I wanted to change Kirsten, but I couldn't. So I lost her — or, worse, I trashed her deliberately, dumping everything she was and did, but along with the rest of her I've junked the reason why.

This is all a bit obscure for an old girls' reunion, so instead I say, 'I remember when we used to skive off, if it was a hot day, to go to the beach and take the ferry across the river to Shaldon.' In fact, I remember it as clearly as if it was only a few weeks ago, but I don't tell her that. 'It was a very smart place then. Those classy catamarans on the quayside . . .'

'Yes, it's still quite boaty,' she agrees smugly. 'We get a lot of mega-rich bods mooring, then cluttering up the local pubs. You get used to it.'

I've finished my coffee now. We look at each other, for a moment uncertain, and then Debs decides. 'You can't – you simply can *not* – go now, Kirsty,' she tells me, 'not now we've met up after all these years. Come back with me. Your car isn't a problem, I'll drop you by it, and you can follow me.'

So I may get to see Paul, after all. I feel a tiny shiver of automatic jealousy, even after all these years. What does Paul look like now, I'd wondered, four weeks ago when my dreams of college were more vivid than the waking days. Now I'm about to find out. 'The lord and master will be home by now so I hope he's got my pipe and slippers ready – or, at least, some wine chilling!' Debs says, as I get in beside her. She flicks on the CD with a remote and something violiny blitzes us until, after a moment of contrived delay, she turns it down.

As I point out my car at the end of the car park I ask, 'Are you still Debbie Adolfi?'

She smiles and pulls a face. 'No, I must admit I succumbed. I did think about it – or maybe going for hyphenated, like lots of our chums did. But that would have been such a mouthful.' Adolfi-Parr, I think. Parr-Adolfi. She pulls up beside the blue Escort. 'I'm just Deborah Vellacott,' she says.

My mouth seems to have opened into a gaping black wound around a single word. *Miles.*

Not Paul but Miles. Debs has married her college sweetheart, Miles Vellacott.

Miles. I'm turning the jigsaw round again. Another whole

section completed here, but not the way I expected. (That distant patch, not rock but densely wooded trees . . .) Debs married Miles.

'We got to be an item in our second year, after you left. After Glastonbury. You look like you don't know who I'm talking about. You must remember Miles, Kirsty, you used to go out with him, dear!'

'I know. I mean, I remember.'

'Well, we've sort of stayed together.'

'Oh. Good.'

And I mean it, I really do. Finally, after those nightmare weeks, Debs has given me a glimpse of some way I can actually find a little bit of self-esteem.

This explains everything. Janey's father is Miles. I can see, at last, why I never told anyone, as well as why I cut myself off. I must have confirmed that my missed periods were serious at about the same time I found out from one of those unanswered letters that Debs and Miles were serious, too. So I did this incredibly brave, incredibly good thing and embarked on a new life to give my friends a clear start together.

I feel so good. Kirsten was not just a bitch. Kirsten was actually a bit of a heroine. Maybe not Mother Teresa, but pretty amazingly unselfish.

I'm thinking about what all this means as I follow Debs's car along the streets and the town gives way to countryside. Sun strobes through the arched branches of the tree-hung road. I can't tell Miles he has a daughter now, after all these years, but I don't want to lie about her, so maybe it will be better to say nothing about Janey at all. But maybe Miles and Debs have children too, and she's got a little half-sister or half-brother. Then I'll have to think again. Perhaps I owe it to Janey to tell her if she has any more family.

But then again, Kirsten didn't think she owed anything here. She hasn't been in touch for years.

Thinking about Miles getting together with Debs and never knowing about his baby is mind-blowing but it does make sense. It's the first thing to make sense for weeks. It must have been such a hard secret for me to keep alone. I wonder if Clyde lied to me when he said I wouldn't tell him who the father was. Surely I would have talked with him about why I was choosing to protect my lover – and, more importantly, my friend Debs. But even if I didn't confide in him, Clyde decided to go along with my secret. He must have felt quite a hero when he married me. Maybe we were both able to admire ourselves then.

Debs drives fast but the road is quiet and I stay close. We reach the big estuary where the river Teign spreads into the sea. I can see the high cliff that shelters the smuggler's beach, where we spent that crazy, happy day, when Miles was still with me. It must have been such agony when I found out he was leaving me pregnant. I'm still overwhelmed by finding this extraordinary and unexpected nobility at the core of Kirsten's life. I'm so relieved I could almost fly into the dazzling sea and dissolve.

We're crossing the long bridge over the grey-glass river, limpid and smooth except for dark ripples left by the gliding white swans. Gradually I become aware of something swimming about in this pool of euphoria in my head. Something discordant. Janey's father is Miles. Suppose my love letters were written for Janey's father . . . *After all this time*, Debs had said. *It must be nearly ten years!* That culpability feeling again, like a stone in my throat. Is it so long since I saw Miles too, or did we meet more recently, privately, and then find it impossible to go back to being *just friends*?

Debs is signalling to turn into a little mews. I park behind her outside a bay-fronted cottage overlooking the estuary. The tide is really low and lines of expensive-looking boats are roped up on the muddy sand so the view looks more like a car park than a beach.

The door is on the latch. Debs ushers me in and I follow her into the kitchen. Miles stands with his back to us, squeezing a lemon. 'Yoohoo,' he says, without looking round. 'Nearly ready.'

'Look who's here,' says Debs. I have an agonising moment to wonder if he shares my secret, and then he turns round.

Miles seems if anything even more altered than Debs, but that's because his hair is a lot thinner than it was. Clyde only has a bit of a receding forehead compared to Miles, whose scalp is almost bare although he's had the sense to crop his hair extremely short rather than try to hide it. He's wearing baggy knee-length shorts and a T-shirt that reads FOR FOX SAKE STOP HUNTING and green Gandhi sunglasses, which he takes off as I appear.

'Strewth,' says Miles.

Then, and I do think this is quite stylish, he flings open the fridge door, pulls out a bottle of champagne and in about two seconds he's fiddled the wire off and slipped off the top and poured out a glassful while I'm still standing there saying nothing. He advances towards me with the effervescing goblet and kisses my cheek.

'Any excuse!' sings out Debs, and she takes the gloss off his gesture a bit by adding, 'It's only ersatz, mind you,' and telling him off for using the wrong sort of glass. Miles takes absolutely no notice of her comments. 'Christy! You look as edible as ever,' he says.

Debs, of course, drops on him like a ton of bricks over the name gaffe but he carries on smirking at me unfazed, and I smile back. It's clear we have not met for ages. Miles is friendly and self-assured, a nice husband and a nice host. Not someone with *strong arms and hot kisses*, whose chin dripped my juices . . . I wish I could delete the letters from my mind as easily as from the computer.

I murmur appropriate admiration of their cottage and Miles tells me about the problems of owning a listed building and the amazing cost of authentic bottle-glass panes while Debs tells me of their ambition to buy a boat. They don't have any children. She says, 'Heavens, I see enough of *kids* every day, thank you!' and pulls a face as though I've suggested time-share in an abattoir. There's something shrill about her, as if she's trying to prove to me that her world is important – like she was in the café screaming with laughter at her teaching colleague. I have a life, she seems to be trying to insist. I look across at Miles but he doesn't comment, though he can hardly see *kids* every day.

I feel a bit sad for Miles, but I'm even more determined to say nothing about Janey. I've even tucked the little snap of her on my car-key fob away in my bag so he won't get a glimpse. Suppose he were to say, 'Why, she's the image of my sister when she was young,' or something like that? As long as I can keep them talking about themselves I'm safe.

They both insist I must eat with them, and after a glass of champagne it does seem a good idea before driving home.

Miles puts on a plastic apron with big tasselled boobs. 'It's his barbecue apron,' says Debs, 'but any excuse for a flash of nipple!' and now I know that they deserve each other.

The meal he has concocted is admittedly delicious. He's done a starter, which he tells me is spinach steamed with cashews, sultanas and vinegar ('Balsamic, of course,' he says, waving a bottle) and it tastes absolutely excellent. Then pasta in some sort of sauce with black olives, with salad and a herby bread. It makes me decide to put a bit more effort into mealtimes when I go back. Maybe not go as far as playing cookery-card snap with Helen, but I could definitely be more adventurous. It will be good for Janey, too. I could teach her to cut tomatoes into rosettes, she'd love that.

Miles is in computers now, he tells me, working mostly from home. He assures me that photography is dead. He picks up a magazine from the dark leather sofa and flips through it to show me a big picture I recognise immediately as Liz Taylor. She looks exactly the way I remember her. 'Computers,' he says, 'manipulate far better than the old touch-up darkroom techniques. You can eliminate wrinkles, tighten skin tone, enlarge eyes . . . See for yourself.'

She does look a bit like a cross between a piece of chewed fudge and one of Janey's potato-head people in the inset mugshot, but if that's her now, why not?

'A magic mirror for the wicked queen,' Debs says.

'Very impressive. But why? It seems like saying it's better to be young whether you are or not. Wouldn't it be better to look like who you are?'

Debs hoots. 'Everyone wants to stop the clock, Kirsty,' she says.

Ironic, really. I turn back to Miles. 'You still need the photo to start with,' I say, but he shakes his head and says loftily, 'Digital imagery. You can do anything.'

I can't really argue, because I've packed in photography, but I keep getting the feeling that I don't really agree and I wish I knew more about why.

There's something else more urgent on my mind anyway, and all the time we're talking I'm waiting for the right moment to ask. When Miles stops talking to clear away the plates, I say, very casually, 'And what about Paul?'

Debs answers. 'Well, naturally, I didn't see much of Paul after he and Miles moved out of that room. He went to America after graduating – oh, you won't know about that, will you?' She leans back to put the salad bowl on the shelf behind her, where it inches inscrutably through the hatch into the kitchen.

'About what?'

Our messy plates retreat, replaced by a big wooden fruit bowl. Peaches on top. 'I heard, ooh, two, three years back that he drowned in a surfing accident at Long Beach.'

I actually wince, as if I've been stabbed. I feel a gutted, wiped-out kind of wretchedness, as though it's all my fault, as though I sent him there and watched him die. The arrogance of love, I think. The utter self-centredness of romantic passion. And he never even knew.

'I must admit I didn't actually lose many nights' sleep, though. We'd completely lost touch after the festival,' she's saying. 'Well, naturally. D'you remember? He sodded off and we had to telephone Miles's brother to come and collect us. Though you'd managed to scrounge a lift home on the back of your tutor's Motoguzzi. Remember that, Milo? We dropped Kirsty's stuff off and her dad went ape-shit at us.' He passes round the fruit knives and they both laugh heartily.

I can't laugh. I'm aching for Paul. The image of his lovely face and lean, lithe body are cramming my mind, much more real than this room and these people. My picture of Debs and Miles – the real ones, my friends – have become muddled by their partnership and blurred by their ageing. But Paul, sweet Paul, he is beautiful and young and clear in my head. I can't bear it that he's dead.

Debs has taken up the reminiscence theme now. 'Guess who I met at a cross-curricula meeting! Nicholas! He's a head of art now, somewhere in the Midlands. You remember Nico?'

More clearly than you might believe, Debs. I say, 'Really? Spazzo Nico?'

She flinches histrionically and then laughs. 'That's rather unreconstructed, Kirsty! He's Tourettic, of course, though we didn't realise then that his ticking was a compulsive syndrome.' She smiles at my blank face. 'All that fidgeting? Tourette's syndrome.'

'I thought he just liked juggling,' I say, and she rolls her eyes.

'You haven't been reading your Oliver Sacks!' she says, with roguish gusto, and I think, Shit, I'm going to get set extra contemporary-psychology homework by Mrs Vellacott.

Miles wipes his fingers on a navy napkin and gets up. He puts a CD on the system, taking out the one that's already in although Debs says, in her teasy-weasy voice, 'I'm sure Kirsty would prefer

Nigel Kennedy.'

Miles smiles blandly and ignores her. He seems used to doing this. 'Kirsty won't be averse to a little time-trekking,' he says suavely, and he shows me the cover of the disk he's picked, saying, 'Oysterband – the 'ninety-four remix.'

It's a song I don't know so it must be from the missing years. A sweet, sad song with muffled words that crawl like insects across my ears. *We can forget our names.* My heart's doing a slow drum-beat on my breastbone. It seems the world finds a way to betray our hidden secrets. *We can forget each other's faces.* The inexplicable enigma I'm struggling to conceal is seeping out, merging into the surround-sound of Miles's sophisticated system with optional bass enhancement and shuffle facility. Luckily Miles is explaining about this rather than listening to the song, but the subtle energy of the surrounding air knows, the room knows, the tiny spider quivering on a tremulous thread by the window knows. I'm hyperventilating. I pour the last of the fizzy water into my glass and drink. I let the curious synchronicity of the words drift around me. *Don't be afraid, don't be afraid.*

'I haven't got this album,' I say casually, and Miles decides to make me a tape of it there and then on high-speed dub so it goes into a squeaky gabble and it's a relief when he turns the sound down.

I realise that I've had two glasses of champagne and feel a bit too wobbly to drive back just yet. Debs urges coffee and promises 'a natter'. Miles is off to his caning class, which is why they ate early, Debs explains. (And yes, yes, there are the inevitable quips and ripostes to wade through before I am allowed to confirm that we are talking furniture not fetish.) I ought to telephone Clyde, really, but I'm reluctant to make contact in case I get into a conversation with Janey and then I'll have to explain her to my new friends.

It occurs to me, as we settle down on the big floor cushions, that seeing Debs was an excellent idea, and not only because her marriage to Miles explains my long vow of silence. It's the way she's so utterly altered that has jolted me out of my introspective inertia. Finding out that my parents were older only distressed me, but meeting this couple is quite different. Now, at last, I'm convinced my student days have really gone for ever. There is nothing to learn about my future here. I need to focus on a more recent past – and the other piece of the puzzle. Those letters. I can't decide anything until I understand exactly what was going on.

So when she says I must, I simply must, tell her all about me, I plunge straight in. 'You know what you said earlier, about how everyone wants to stop the clock?' While she's still nodding I tell her about what's happened to me, and how other people can only tell me superficial stuff about what I used to do because no one knows what I really used to think.

I'm building up to the crucial bit carefully but I'm not sure Debs actually gets all this, even though I'm toning it down. I don't admit how completely I've forgotten Clyde and everything about my marriage, for a start. I make it sound like there's about a year missing. Even that sounds pretty incredible when you think about it. Debs seems to be thinking about it.

The champagne is finished and she has opened a bottle of white wine, which she wags at me enquiringly. I remind her I'm driving. She nods and fills up her own glass to the brim. She kicks off her shoes and scratches her toe and she's almost looking like my Debs again. She's obviously puzzled about why I've turned up now out of the blue to tell her this unbelievable story. I explain how I'm getting fed up with saying sorry all the time because I feel like I'm letting everyone down by not remembering them, how I just wanted to see someone I actually know that I know. and as she sinks into the pouffe like a little girl at story-time, I tell her more and more. How I can't find any traces I recognise, books or anything. And then I found these hidden love letters . . .

'Love letters!' says Debs, immediately alert. This is the old

Debs. She was always nosy. So I describe how passionate they are, and as I'm telling her I realise with increasing certainty that I've got to know who this man is. Maybe he is still waiting for me, or wondering why I've stopped writing. This love affair may still be vibrant – it may yet save me. The conspiracy of silence around me had panicked me, my own powerlessness paralysed me. I feel unsure and fearful, but I can't ignore this part of my life any more. I have to find and meet my lover.

Debs is getting excited. 'Typed? You found copies of love letters from you, typed on the computer?'

'I know it sounds crazy,' I say, 'but I suppose I wanted them to look like business mail.'

'Well, you could have typed an envelope label for that,' says Debs. 'I reckon you must have set them up as files to e-mail. You don't have e-mail?' She mimes amazement. 'We've been on it for aeons – Miles couldn't work without it. So much transatlantic business, these days, is done that way. You know, downloading files and images.' And she's off. I almost start retreating into my humble time-trip shell until I remember this has nothing to do with me being alone in a long-gone world, it's simply Debs showing off about having a lot of up-to-date hi-tech stuff in her life. So I take a deep breath and say, 'Do shut up, Debs, we were talking about me,' and she does a quick mental channel-change.

'And your husband knew they were there? You've got to talk to him about this, Kirsty. He probably knows who they were for. Why don't you talk about it?'

'Don't you think that conversation might be a little bit tricky, Debs? It was difficult enough asking him to remind me where the nearest postbox is, and that's not even in the same league.'

She sweeps this aside. 'You must confront him. Kirsty, your future could be waiting out there. You're like Rapunzel imprisoned, waiting for rescue.'

'Sleeping Beauty, according to my . . . someone I met.'

Debs is definitely taken with the fairy-story notion. 'Really this is more like Snow White, because life's gone on while you're entranced. I must see what Bettelheim has to say — he's so good on the psychology of myths.' She hares over to the bookcase. 'I bet the key is something to do with your father. You know that the wicked stepmother is a projection of Snow White's jealousy of her mother, and the poisoned apple is the sexuality she fears, of course.'

What a load of crap. Debs has changed so much. That sort of pseudo-psycho analogy would have had her pissing herself when I knew her. I begin to feel sorry I said anything about forgetting, and especially the letters. I wish I hadn't started talking to Debs about finding who my secret lover is. I thought it would feel the way it used to be, when we could discuss anything together, but Debs going on like that, like a teacher, makes everything I've explained seem simply absurd.

After a few moments, during which the silence between us becomes almost tangible, Debs gives up looking on the bookshelf in favour of more wine, and plops down on her pouffe again. 'You know,' she says, 'I knew, from the minute we met, that you'd got a secret. Don't ask me how, I just knew. When you said you weren't doing journo-photography any more, I thought, is she going to say, "I've got a major book commission", or "I'm in the movies now, doing skin flix." Could be either, with Kirsty.' She waves into the air, as though Kirsty has once again become an absent third party.

'Oh, come on, Debs — me? A porn queen?'

She shrugs and slurps. 'If you'd wanted to. Devious, under that meek smile.'

Devious? Me? I get up feeling wretched, wishing I hadn't told her anything at all.

She jumps up, too. 'Oh, Kirsty, I did miss you. I didn't know — I didn't realise what a wound you left in me when you went away, it never really healed.'

I sit down again, shakily, and she sits next to me this time, not looking at me but still talking. 'I felt so guilty. No, hurt. No, both. But I think I grew up a bit, then. Because Miles was the person I talked to instead of you, so for the first time I had a proper full relationship with a bloke instead of just the sex thing. And I wanted to tell you – I tried. I poured out everything in my letters, and when you never replied I felt so hurt. I rang up your mum to check I'd got the address right and I said I was thinking of going to see you and she said, "Oh, I think she's awfully busy with her job," and I said, "At weekends too?" sort of laughing, and there was a long pause and then she laughed too and I knew, I just knew, you'd told her you didn't want me to. It was horrible.'

Debs drinks a few hectic gulps and stares down into her wine-glass.

'Mum was probably just as hurt herself,' I say. I wish I knew what the hell I was talking about. But, then, if I did I wouldn't be here. Ironic, really.

'Well, I didn't think of that,' says Debs to her glass. A small tear plops quietly into the dregs and she hurriedly drowns it in more wine. 'And Miles said Andy the History Man kept dropping hints that you were still in touch. It was so hurtful. Handy Andy, Miles always called him.'

'What sort of hints?' this I really do want to know about. Debs leans back against the cushions, closes her eyes, and her clasped glass sways perilously. I put it gently on the floor between us.

'Miles said he saw a print in the darkroom, a silhouette of naked breasts. Andy pulled it out of the tray and pegged it up and said, "You don't recognise them, Miles? Not familiar?" and he laughed. Miles was sure he meant they were your boobs.'

I remember Leila saying, 'I've still got those baby-belly pictures'. I imagine them swelling slowly up under the fix liquid in the sultry red-lit darkroom. Andy pulling out the print and pegging it up to drip, the way I'd so often seen him, wiping his hands slowly like he'd been stroking something sweet and sticky and was almost reluctant to wipe it away. 'You did some pictures of your bulge, in the mirror,' Leila had said, 'They're lovely, so natural and sort of fecund. Almost like landscapes.' I imagine my breasts swollen with pregnancy, and think about the pose I would have chosen to accentuate those curves into a body landscape.

'Andy processed some prints for me,' I say cautiously, 'because I didn't have access to a darkroom. I was still making images, though. I think maybe I was keeping my options open.'

'No darkroom! We thought you had a high-powered job as a studio assistant.'

'No. Just a lab technician, doing coffee-table books for other names.'

'Honestly? I know how secretive you can be.' Debs seems to be slowly readjusting nine years of resentment. 'Well, perhaps not secretive, but you never say exactly what you're planning, do you? You act all sly and then you wonder why people get the wrong impression.'

Debs was always a tough critic, but I don't recall her dressing up spitefulness as psychology in the old days. She delivers this hatchet job on my personality with a big familiar grin that says, '*Only joking!*' I am expected, now, to submit to the hurt or else add a charge of huffiness and lack of humour to her cutting edge. But I seem to have changed, too, in the missing years. I find I can look back at her without any apologetic answering smile.

I don't curl up and die. I don't defend myself. I say, 'I'm sorry you felt so hurt back then, Debs. But you and Miles seem happy enough now.'

She nods, and pours another millimetre of wine into her brimming glass. 'I'm being mean, aren't I? I suppose it's because I did feel awfully guilty. We both did, of course we did. We couldn't help that.' She pauses.

'But I'd left . . .' I say. I let the words linger, with a subtle note of query.

She gulps and nods. 'Oh, yes. Of course you had. And – well, be honest, Kirsty, you wouldn't have lasted together, you and Miles, would you?' It's not a question so I don't hazard an answer. 'Everything was against it, anyway. And it wasn't our fault . . .'

Now she leaves a hint of query. I say quickly, 'No, of course not.'

Debs has brightened up again now. 'Oh, Kirsty, I'm sorry – going on about my feelings, and poor you!' She pats my knee.

'I didn't come here for pity,' I say, bright-and-breezily. Fortunately, I think.

But I do feel positive still, in spite of her assault. I've really moved on today – another chunk of the jigsaw filled in, and a big decision made. I will talk to Clyde. I will ask him about the letters.

I get up to go and Debs follows me to the doorway. She says 'There's something catalytic about you, Kirsty.' I think of the white noise of confusion I'm groping through and I laugh, but she insists, 'Oh, yes. Always was. You've always brought out these intense reactions in people. Women can't resist having a go at you, men can't resist you. Always. Going round with you was a good way of getting boyfriends.' Her cheeks are very bright, those rosy triangles she gets under her eyes when she's a bit pissed.

I don't know what to say so I don't say anything. We both step forward and replicate the fumbling little hug we gave each other in the town, when we met again after all those years. But her grip is firmer now, and the warmth of her face is close to mine as we kiss.

I hug her and tell her, 'I'm really glad I came,' and it's true. Just as I'm going Debs calls out, 'Good luck with your search,' and then she adds, as if blurting out a joke she'd been holding back. 'Maybe it's not a man!'

I can't help smiling as I get in the car. I'm glad the last thing she said was a flash of the old Debs wit.

Driving home I think about everything I've learned and I feel
. . . numb, really. I suppose I sound cold. I loved Paul so much,
and he is still more real to me than this new Miles or even Clyde,
but this world I have woken into is so full of extraordinary news
that it's difficult to react appropriately. Difficult even to work
out what an appropriate reaction is. In the last two hours I've just
found out the guy I thought was my boyfriend has been married
to my best friend for years and I'm simply an old flame whose
name he half forgets. And somehow along the line he fathered
my baby.

I put the Oysterband tape in the deck and listen to that song
again. *We can leave right now* . . . I think about the myth of the reeds
that whispered to the river 'King Midas has ass's ears' and sent
the scandal drifting down to the sea. It occurs to me, absurdly,
that this would please Debs, with her love of multi-allusory
myths. *All you need to do is walk away . . . Don't be afraid.*

Debs thought I had acted really shitty to her, but I hadn't.
Think how much more pissed off she would have been to find I
was carrying Miles's baby once she'd started going with him. It
must have been so painful for me, deciding to protect them
both from knowing. But at least my silence is something I can be
proud of.

Because of the early meal at Debs' it feels later than it is. I'm
surprised the sky's only just beginning to darken as I get near
home. All the way I've been thinking about Janey being Miles'
daughter. It's logical, but it's not quite right. Miles has button-
brown eyes, which crinkle pleasantly as he smiles. Those eyes of
hers, so expressive and so blue.

And I think about Clyde, and about the letters on the word-
processor, and how Debs had been aghast when I said neither of
us had mentioned them since he told me they were there. How
she said, 'Why don't you talk about it?'

And I think, Yes, but you didn't talk to me, did you? When
I lost myself in some strange town with a dead-end job because I

was frightened of going back, you didn't talk to me. You left me, because it seemed to be what I wanted. It was easier, that's all. So don't lecture me on evasion. Deborah Adolfi-Vellacott.

But I really would have confronted Clyde the instant I got back, if he hadn't come out to meet me as soon as he heard the car drive up saying, 'Janey's run away.'

The End of the Seventh Week

I head straight for the river, running.

I've never felt OK about Clyde's blasé attitude to the river swimming-place. Quite apart from what it did to me, it's so obviously not a safe place for children. Nobody else round here seems to think that and now I'm terrified that this will be the tragedy that makes them change their minds. I haven't got any proper kind of plan, only to find Janey, and I'm about a hundred yards down the road when Clyde catches me up, panting, and pulls me to a stop.

'I think I know where she's gone – Jeremy came round. The other children say she went to the Valleys. It's where the older ones go, on their bikes. She's taken hers.'

I know where he means and it's miles away, outside the town where we go shopping. Janey, on that bicycle, on that road. Quarry lorries come along that road, squeezing close to the hedge, severing the buttercups and hawthorn branches. I can hardly breathe for terror, I can feel my heart pumping and my legs have gone ice cold and jelly-weak. A car pulls up, not Clyde's – I'm still clutching the car keys – but Jeremy's grey Peugeot. He pushes open the passenger door and I scramble in without speaking.

Jeremy is waiting for Clyde but he says, 'I'll stay, in case . . .'

His face looks bleached. He turns back down the road. I want to wind down the window and shout to him to call the police but there's no handle and before I find how to open it we've accelerated away.

Jeremy is driving fast but each turn in the road seems elongated, in slow motion, like a dream. He's murmuring, 'She'll be all right,' but he seems distracted. I don't talk at all. I watch the hedges and the tangled cow-parsley crowding along the darkening verges, knowing it all so well now, and I think about the streets of Newton Abbot where I walked a few hours ago. In seven weeks the unfamiliar has become familiar. I can't say any longer that one is home and the other is unknown.

Suddenly Jeremy swerves the car into a muddy patch in front of some kind of works access beside the woodland, and points across the road to the hills beyond the fence.

There are rabbits everywhere. Dozens, scores of them, quivering and only just visible on the dark hillside. Little dumpling bundles, softly brownish-black, their ears pale against the lingering dusk. Bunny silhouettes, unmoving apart from the nibbling motion of their heads. It's a surreal sight even without the little girl lolling over the gate silently watching. 'Alice told me,' she informs me, as she sees me coming across the road. She picks at the scabs on her arms and makes no move towards me. I want to grab her and squeeze her and shake her but I wait. I seem to have forgotten how to speak. She says, quite calmly, 'Some rabbits got out of their hutches, and had all these babies. They're half tame and half wild. You can't see them in the day, but Alice said they come out when it's getting night. See?'

I'm nodding, still unspeaking. Jeremy is sitting quietly in the car. The engine is turned off. The crashing sound of silence rolls around the sky.

'Silflay,' says Janey. Then she pinches herself. I put out my hand instinctively. 'You said you'd bring me,' says Janey. She flashes me a look with her blue dark eyes, a look I've never seen there before. Pure anger.

I find my voice. 'I forgot,' I say limply, and she answers coldly, 'You always say that.'

That's when I start crying. That's when I find I'm crouching down on the road next to the fence, holding her and sobbing. Jeremy's out of the car in a flash now, he's grabbed us both and somehow we're in the back of the car together. Janey squeals, 'My *bike*,' in an indignant but rather small voice and he says firmly, 'It's going in the boot.' And the car shakes as he swings the bike in and slams down the door. Then, just before he gets into the driving-seat, he peers in at us huddled sobbingly together, and he takes off his jacket and tucks it around us. His eyes meet mine with an expression of intense and curious helplessness.

Then he straightens up and says, 'Home time, I think,' and gets in the front and drives us home.

Helen is round at our house making coffee and Sam is sprawled on our settee watching *Bottom* on telly when we get back. Clyde decants us and Jeremy collects his family and departs. I march Janey into the bathroom and plonk her on the wicker clothes basket and turn on the bath taps. She points out the bubble-bath character she wants, but in a whisper not her usual jaunty voice. I pour it in without answering and we watch the water fizzle and stain blackberry dark.

'I can bath myself,' she says, rather worriedly, as I stay sitting on the side of the bath while she steps in.

I take the big puffy sponge and gently stroke her little body, lifting her hair so's I can soap round her neck without getting the dark locks all bedraggled. 'It's too late for a hairwash tonight,' I say. I soap down those little distressed arms and she looks at me suddenly, warily. 'No more pinches, Janey,' I say. She turns away. 'Why are you punishing yourself, when it's me you're angry with?'

'It wasn't a punishment,' she says, in a small clear matter-of-fact voice. 'It was a pinch for every forgetting.'

'Read me the rabbit book,' she says, when I get her to bed. She's using her imperious voice, the one that usually makes Clyde say, 'Janey!' in a warning way that shuts her up.

I don't feel like chiding. I say, 'Janey, don't test me. You know we'll both be upset if I fail.'

She looks stubborn for a moment, then climbs out of the bed and fetches a copy of *Watership Down* from her bookcase.

I read from the place she shows me. She lies with the quilt pulled up to her eyes watching me until her lids begin to close.

God, she looks so much like someone.

I read for ages, until I sense we've reached a kind of truce. Then I kiss her and switch out the main light and watch her shadow-lashes long on her cheeks in the dimness of the nightlight. I'm trying to decide how to show her I know why she chose that passage to help me, and to thank her. 'That reminds me of those feral rabbits we saw tonight,' I say, 'the passage about silflay.' Her eyes flick open wide and then close. She nods. A strand of dark hair is curling across her face very close against her mouth. I stoop to push it carefully away. She's breathing deeply already, near sleep. I push the corner of her mouth into a little smile the way I've seen Clyde do it. She says, 'I love you, Mummy.'

I say, 'I love you, Janey,' because, like a tiny corner of jigsaw, it seems to fit.

Don't breathe too soon, because when I come out from this touching scene Clyde is slumped back on the settee with a whisky bottle and the phone rings and it's my mother, from Spain. 'You must speak to your father. Tell him, for goodness' sake. He won't listen to me.'

'Tell him what?' But she's put him on the line, and he's in a worse state than Clyde. His voice is deep and I can't understand what he's trying to say. When I do understand, I wish I didn't. I say, 'I want to talk to Mum – put her back on!' and when I get her plaintive voice again she confirms what this call is all about.

'He's driving himself frantic. He thinks they're going to start saying he abused you when you were a little girl. He's been reading these cases about therapists using hypnosis to get women to say that awful things happened when they were children and traumatised them.'

'Of course I won't say that.' I'm embarrassed as well as shocked. And sad to think of my father talking drunkenly about stuff like that. 'It's not being young I've forgotten, is it? My child-hood memories are perfectly clear.' She makes me say that over again to him. He's getting maudlin now. 'Never laid a finger on you. Never touched you, ever.' His voice is slurred. I can hear my mother ranting in the background. Jesus, what's going on?

I'm shaking when the call's finished. Of course he touched me, and Suzy too, every day. He hugged us, bathed us, dressed us, and kissed us when he tucked us up in bed. It's grotesque that now he's pawing over these innocent memories and trying to deny them because he's afraid, for some reason, that I'm going to misconstrue our intimacy and try to blame him for everything that's gone wrong in my life.

'Did you give them that horrible idea?' I say to Clyde. He's been listening so he knows what I'm talking about.

'I said they had suggested regression hypnosis, that's all. Everyone knows the kind of things these people come up with.'

I put my hands on my hips and lock eyes with him. 'Nothing happened to me while I was living at home with my parents. I'm quite certain about that. It's since I've been living with you. If someone abused me and I'm repressing the memory, maybe it was you.'

He doesn't look away. He says, deadly quiet, 'I thought it would come to that. I thought you'd get round to pinning the blame on me. Well, I'll tell you this now, and you can believe it. I have never touched you, either you or Janey. I've never hurt you in any way, whatever the provocation. And if you want some truths, you should start with that.'

There's a crumpled dignity about him as he delivers this statement. He's looking me in the eyes and willing me to believe him. I sit down, not saying anything, thinking about what he's said. *Never touched you* – the same denial my father used. As though the word has lost its meaning and can't be used for contact that is caring or loving. *Touched* equals *abused*, these days. How bizarre, and how really sad.

There's a kind of quiet, snuffling, groaning sound, and I look at Clyde and he's crying. He's still standing there and his head is drooped and his chest is quivering with these awful stifled sobs. I don't know what to do. If I make him cry then there's no one left to turn to. I get up and go to him, wondering what I should say. But he puts his big arms across his face like a child protecting himself from being slapped. And we stand there. He's silent now and I'm just watching him as his struggling breath tightens on the stifled tears.

All the hard-edged certainties I brought home with me from my talk with Debs are mushy and unravelled now. Thinking about that awful phone call is making me feel sick. That Mum should do this to me, that Dad should think it – speak it – I'm realising with pain the rippling repercussions of my amnesia in others' lives, permeating beyond my knowing like acid spreading in a lake. How many nights of pacing anguish before Mum consented to put my distress on one side and make that phone call. I know my father wasn't perfect, and maybe I should never have tried to believe he was for so long, but he never abused me and he never deliberately hurt me. And neither did Clyde. I can't make someone else guilty just so that I can go on feeling innocent. We all need a way forward, not accusing fingers pointing back and blaming. And now Clyde sniffing like a pink-eyed rabbit, saying, 'I thought it would come to that.' Everywhere I scratch this relationship there is nothing but mistrust.

I can't talk to him.

I've still got the car keys, though, and a tank full of petrol. I've got my old friends back. I can just imagine Debs's satisfied grin as I knock on their listed front door at two in the morning. 'I knew you had a secret,' she would say. 'Oh, Kirsty, I am glad you've come back.'

I leave Clyde alone and go into the hall to take down the card from the mirror, the one with a picture of Glastonbury and a scrawled name. Pol. The P is clear and the L, but there is just the remotest tiniest most microscopic imperceptible chance that it's not an O, though. And if it's not O, couldn't it be A U?

And if . . .

Debs and Miles don't really know that Paul is dead. They heard a rumour, that's all. Debs said, 'I heard, ooh, two, three years back, that he drowned in a surfing accident at Long Beach.' She doesn't even know when she heard, never mind when he died. If he died.

And if . . .

I'd have to be pretty cool to lie to Clyde so comprehensively, if that card was from a lover, to convince him I was walking that day with my friend Polly.

But Kirsten was a liar, wasn't she? I still don't know much about her but I do know that. Kirsten had the euphoria of passionate love to blunt the painful edge of guilt, but I don't. I only have this nightmare sense of culpability to wake into day after day. I long for someone else to blame. I think of Janey and her terrified little arms, all scored with her daily anguish. Innocent Janey knows how to blame herself. Isn't it ironic?

I go to the door of Janey's room. As I listen to her breathing

I know I'm not going anywhere, not without Janey. Right through the core of all these dark and muddled emotions is this curious, sad, wonderful feeling that she's my responsibility for the whole of the rest of my life. I'll never wake up in the morning again without thinking about her and wondering if she's happy, even when she's grown up and left home. I suppose I must have had this feeling when she was a tiny baby. Then, perhaps, the wonder of it faded and ordinariness took over, the way day-to-day things do. I feel sort of privileged that I can have this special feeling all over again now.

I'm just so terribly tired. Clyde doesn't even look up when I tell him I'm going to bed.

I wake suddenly, jolted awake by Clyde's arrival beside me. His breath is fetid with whisky and his whole body stinks of sweat as he rolls nakedly on to me. He's got me pinned under his heavy leg as he lurches across me with his mouth very close to my face. 'Is this what you want?' he whispers. 'Is this it? I've never forced you, Kirst. But maybe that's what you want.' Those are the sensible words, the rest is just bleary swearing. He's pressing my shoulders back, forcing me down, pushing himself into me, thick but half flaccid, hurting with his thumbnail as he forces in and I'm horrified because it's true, I can't believe it but it's fucking true, it is what I want. I can feel my wetness flooding his pathetic drunk dick and he can feel it too and in the end he lets his prick hang there and thumps into me again and again with his fingers and thumb and I'm crying out and clinging on to him, scratching down his back and tearing at his thighs and bum and arching up each time he slumps against me so the quenching, burning pain will break into me again. And after I've screamed into silence and he's put his dripping hand over my mouth gently to muffle me and the stench fills my nose and he pushes the sticky sweetness of my cum into my lips and then, then I can feel that he must have sobered because now he's seriously hard. I roll on to my side towards him and he hauls me on top of him and holds me up like a kitten, gripping under my armpits, and I feel childlike and light and beautiful, an essential angel in his arms. My hair swings forward and when he says, 'Jesus, Jesus,' I know it. He pulls me down on to him and groans as he's going in, all the way, into my hot and swollen tender place and he keeps right on groaning until I can feel the fireworks right within going bloody hell all the way all the way up tingling my spine practically giving me a nosebleed and then I rock slower

and slower and finally sort of half lift myself, half slip, off him and beside him. I suppose I should go and wash, there's a lot of mess dribbling around, trickling down my thighs, but the snaily cold feeling is nice because I'm so hot and in the end I fall asleep there on his arm probably giving him a dead arm.

Oh, and in the night I hear him being sick in the bathroom. But that's not what I'm thinking about when I wake because I've been having a terrible dream. Jeremy was driving me and Janey along a dappled road faster and faster until the sunlit trees were whirling past the windows, and Janey started screaming thinly. I looked round and the whole road behind us was strewn with the carnage of run-over rabbits. And in the moment that I wake I had just turned back to shout at Jeremy to stop and he had turned to me slowly with that same unfathomable look he gave me last night, long and lingering.

And I think, They are Janey's eyes. But that's impossible. And, anyway, as I struggle into wakefulness I know that Janey's eyes are not quite like his. They are absolutely not like Miles'. The dream hasn't explained anything; it has just reminded me that this part of the jigsaw has been done all wrong.

The radio's on when I get up and Clyde is in the kitchen, standing by the sink with the tap running drinking water from a pint glass.

'You're not going in to work this morning,' I say, and he shakes his head, then says he wasn't due to anyway. He refills the glass, turns the tap off and takes a few more deep slugs. I'm waiting for the right moment and wondering about the right words to ask him about those letters.

Last night's interlude has left me feeling rather, well, weary – but also that there is, after all, a chance that Clyde and I might be able to communicate. I even have a wild, half-hopeful idea that the hidden letters could have been to him, that maybe it's a game we play, and he was only angry, irrationally, because I'd forgotten that too. I can't really believe that theory, though.

'We ought to talk,' says Clyde, and I think about last night, and how the unhappy violence of Clyde's passion turned extraordinarily to tenderness. 'We need to talk to Janey,' he says. 'She's got to promise never to do that again.'

I really want to talk about us, not Janey. I don't want Janey any more upset. I can't see that hassling her will do any good at all. I'm actually even wishing that Clyde's weird mother had plumped for a slightly less fleeting visit – having her around would have been a distraction. But he's got that look, the one I used to think was pompous and I know now is just worried and unsure. I suppose we'd better have a go.

Janey is in the living room watching Amanda's video. I watch her in her nightie with a bitten piece of toast in one hand and the remote control in the other, pressing fast-forward. Bits of the skittles night flash by, and then silver-speckled fizz.

'What are you looking for?'

She doesn't answer. She presses play at a bit I didn't see before, beyond the fizz. It's a group of us in the garden I recognise as Polly's. 'Limbo,' says Janey curtly, as Clyde joins me in the doorway saying, 'Janey . . .' in his warning voice. There's a song playing, it sounds like 'Ooh, Margarita', and a line of laughing people are trying to dance their way under a bar, which is a yard brush, held by me on one side and by Helen on the other. The people who are least good at this are lurching closer to my side because I'm lifting up my end to make sure they get under without collision, while Helen is being rather more strict with her side. I watch, fascinated, as Polly paddles through with her arms and legs wide and head flung back and I sneak the broom up a good six inches extra to accommodate her while cheers resound. On the video Clyde is standing behind me. Almost imperceptibly he lifts my hair and whispers, and I see myself laugh and turn my face to nuzzle briefly against his.

'What did you say to me then?' I ask the real-time Clyde, standing behind me unsmiling.

'I don't remember. Put that off, Janey. Why did you go off like that without saying, yesterday?'

It seems to me Clyde is getting this all wrong. It's obvious why Janey went off without saying – if she had said he would have stopped her. But Janey comes up with a different angle. 'Oh, I don't remember,' she says, in an affected singsong voice.

Clyde looks across at me with a you-started-that face, so I say to him quickly, 'That's what you just said.'

He looks shocked. 'What?'

'Just then. I asked what you said on the video, and you said, "I don't remember."'

Shit, now he's looking really mortified, like last night's mingling is all cancelled and even the sweet, silly glimpse of affection on the video has been slashed away. He thinks I'm blaming him. He's back on that thing about who's to blame.

And now there's further confusion. Old Mrs Thing from next door, her of the phantom washing, took a further step towards the moon last night, apparently, when she was spotted on the lawn standing naked dead-heading white roses in the darkened garden. Her daughter Eleanor has been summoned from Bridport and it's this lady who's rung our doorbell and is now sitting in our kitchen in a distressed state writing down phone numbers for emergency contact and telling us wretchedly that she knows this is only the beginning. 'She looks at me as if she doesn't even know me,' Eleanor laments. Janey seizes the opportunity to return to the kitchen and help herself to a bowl of Coco Pops, regarding Eleanor with huge inquisitive eyes. Clyde looks sympathetic and muted, which I suppose is the best he can do with a hangover. I listen and try to work out whether I've been a previous, or even regular, recipient of Eleanor's concerns. I'm very sorry for her but, without wanting to sound heartless, I don't think her mother's plight is as terrible as Eleanor seems to feel.

'It's probably much worse for you than for her,' I say eventually, topping up her teacup. 'You've got a fixed idea of how you want your ma to behave. She's more fluid about her sense of what's appropriate, these days. She's probably not so bothered.'

But Eleanor shakes her head and tells me how houseproud her mother used to be. 'Everything in its place,' she says, 'and now you should see the state of her spoons.' Eleanor has also confiscated the secateurs, she tells us.

But I've come to the conclusion that forgetting things is not so very abnormal. I think people overlook that fact. Like that moment on the video of the limbo dancing. Why should anyone remember every tiny jokey thing they ever said? And there's times when we're looking at the photo albums and Clyde has to take a snap out and check the place or date on the back because he doesn't remember. There're days when Polly phones because she's forgotten what we arranged, and often Janey forgets where she's put things. I notice them all: I notice how easy and acceptable it all is. I conclude that forgetting is all right as long as you know what you've forgotten. These omissions are small holes in a strong fabric, easily patched. It's when the fabric is all holes, like me and old Mrs Thing, that it becomes so scary to other people. Why? Maybe we're a clouded mirror showing them a land they're afraid that they will have to reach one day. What's so wrong with this place, anyway? Why does everyone assume it's so necessary to know what has happened during all our yesterdays? How can you put a value on knowing something, unless you actually do something about it?

When Eleanor's gone I say to Clyde, 'Maybe it's a good thing her ma's obliterating the pain of the past, if she remembers the things that made her happy.'

'And you think standing outside the house with nothing on is a good thing?'

'Is it a bad thing? It seems to me there's a lot worse things than forgetting, with all the horrible things that happen.'

Clyde rubs his face where it needs a shave and says tiredly, 'Yeah, but if we choose to forget about the "horrible things", they'll go on happening.'

He obviously doesn't have his heart in this discussion but I don't want him starting on at Janey again, so I carry on. 'Remembering isn't enough. Remembering the past doesn't change anything for the future, not on its own. Why does it matter that I don't remember the fall of the Soviet Union? Janey doesn't remember the Falklands war. I do, and that hasn't made any difference to either of us – or anyone else.'

Clyde says slowly, patiently, 'Knowing about events you've lived through makes you who you are. That's what makes your thoughts, and your personality.'

I say quickly, impatiently. 'And during the Falklands war we thought those battles were important and heroic. After that telly programme about Goose Green you said it was all utterly un-necessary and a total tragedy. So how does it matter what your thoughts were at the time? Why does it even matter whether you remember them or not?'

'OK,' he says. 'Look, I know you're trying to make out that what's happened to you doesn't matter, but be honest, Kirst. It makes life difficult for you and you know it.

'It makes life difficult for other people. It's other people who care – that's what I'm saying.'

Clyde shrugs his shoulders and shambles over to the kettle to make more tea. I don't know if I actually believe everything I've just said, but I want him to start thinking about me as a real person whose experience is unusual and interesting, not just a shadowy ex-person with a chunk missing. Maybe it's been good for me to think about the difference between forgetting and remembering. Perhaps if everyone suddenly woke into an unknown world we would all come to the conclusion that we don't need the past; we can start from here, today.

I try to put it in perspective for Clyde. 'I read about a man who's lost his memory totally, not a slice of the past like me. He doesn't know whether he's in the middle of eating a meal or not, or what anyone's just said to him, or even what he's just started to say. Now that does make life difficult.'

'Does it?' says Clyde, sugaring his mug and pebble-dashing the worktop at the same time. 'I'm surprised you can't come up with a case for that, too. Like, ultimate freedom.' And he grabs his tea and mooches off to the garage.

Flashes like that from Clyde surprise me. Is that something I once said? 'I don't like rows', he told me, weeks ago when I was first getting to know him. But that doesn't mean he's always placid. I find I'm almost relieved that Clyde can take a quick swipe like that, now and again. I start to think about the confrontation I've been postponing, and I'm getting all edgy about what to say. And I'm still working that one out when Helen turns up, asking if there's anything I want doing for the barbecue.

The bloody barbecue! I'd forgotten about this, a return visit planned when we left her place after the dinner party. I should have remembered when I saw Clyde rummaging around in the garage and wheeling out the equipment. However, it's not even eleven yet and all we'll need is things to grill and salady stuff and bread, surely. 'I shouldn't think so,' I tell Helen. 'I reckon a barbecue is in my sphere of capabilities, just about.'

Perhaps that doesn't sound very funny. Perhaps it isn't very funny. Helen looks at me bleakly for a moment and then says,

'You think you're so smart, don't you? Oh, yes, you do. You stand back and watch, and wait for things to happen. "Nothing to do with me," says Kirsten Villiers!'

I'm shocked. Is this merely Helen's famous premenstrual bitchiness, or am I on to something here? 'Tell me about it. I mean it, Helen, please. Honesty is what I really need.'

This admission does not spring in any way gratefully from my lips. But this sparky edge to Helen, this nearly out-of-control note in her usually creamy-silk tones, this seems like a chance too good to miss.

She droops her shoulders and blows her nose and looks wanly over her tissue. 'Well, things always seem to happen round you,' she compromises. 'We sometimes used to call you Kate Adie, actually. You know, that journalist who goes into war zones and a battle always seems to start right in front of her.'

I refuse to be distracted by Helen's analysis of media responsibility, even though it's the closest to interesting she's ever got. Something else is much more fascinating.

'We? Who? Who called me Kate?'

She won't be drawn. 'It was like a pet name, really, not being horrible or anything. And, Kirsten, we were the best of friends!' Now she's looking pleading, and a little bit weepy. It occurs to me maybe she's slightly drunk, which is odd for this hour on a Saturday morning.

'I really want to make amends,' I say, and I do. It seems terribly important to placate this woman, not just to recover from this awkward nearly-row, but for my future. Because if I stay I want her friendship and if I go I need it to be clean. I don't want Kirsten to do any more running away. I get that weird feeling again that I've been left here to do something she couldn't manage, and I don't know if it's to stay or to go, but either way I need Helen.

'It's possible, Helen, that I was mentally ill for quite a long time before I lost my memory – the hospital said.' In fact, Jemima had merely touched vaguely on clinical depression as a possible contributory factor but I have this gut feeling if I mention depression Helen will take it personally. 'Mentally ill' hits the spot. She wipes away her bleak look and puts a bangled hand on mine. 'You must have had a terrible time,' she says. 'Terrible!'

The way she says it – *tear-able* – gives me this picture of my life torn into tattered shreds, fluttering through the summer air.

'So tell me about it.'

But she won't. The moment of truth, or spite, or whatever it was, lies between us with the porcelain coffee mugs on the breakfast bar. She addresses Janey, who's dithering about in the doorway. 'Are you going to be helping Mummy tonight?'

Janey nods with a somewhat scathing expression that I feel is entirely appropriate for the fatuous tone of this question. I ask if Sam will be coming, but Helen says no, Sam is camping with the Woodcraft Folk this weekend. So I make a hasty shopping list, and as soon as she's gone we set off for the supermarket. 'We' is all of us; Clyde, despite his heavy-lidded eyes and the fact that I'm certain he's still over the limit, insists on driving.

Harvey's cruising into the car park when I come out with the trolley, not on his glossy bike but in a ratty gold Sierra with dark pink rust-seal daubs like thousand-island dressing on breaded plaice. I'm waiting at the end of the parking lane because Clyde has taken the car and Janey to the recycling bin at the far end. Harvey pulls up in the empty space next to me and says, 'Hi,' as he gets out. There are two big Alsatians in the car and one jumps up and pushes its nose through the open slit of window, which makes me laugh. I stroke the protruding bit of muzzle and she wags her tail. 'She's friendly!'

'Better than a missus,' Harvey agrees. His voice is a slow drawl. I smile vaguely, wondering if I knew he had a car. And that's about all we've had time to say when Clyde drives up far too fast and steps out looking angry. Harvey looks him up and down. I hadn't realised Clyde is actually taller than Harvey.

'When you going to let that gorgeous little wife of yours come back to work?'

Clyde says levelly, 'She does whatever she wants. I've no doubt she'll go back to you if she wants to. And if she doesn't want to, she won't.'

Harvey grins and turns away to pet the dog before striding off. Clyde slings the carriers in the boot and gets back into the car. I get in too.

'You were rude.'

'Was I?' he says, without a shred of curiosity.

Behind us Janey coughs quietly.

'Never mind,' he says, 'I'm sure you were nice enough for both of us.'

I squeeze out a laugh for Janey's benefit as if this is quite a witty joke. Actually I don't object. Clyde angry has a slight scent of dangerousness that, in some way I can't explain, seems to tauten his personality. Jealousy gives him an edge, a firmer, more exciting edge, and I quite like it.

And Clyde wants me. In spite of everything, Clyde still wants me. That's enough, isn't it? What else do I need from a man, apart from moaning with joy with my legs wide and wet? *'What else is there?'* says the voice of Debs in my head. But that Debs is long gone. She grew up into a woman who has other answers to that question – a Georgian house, matching cars, savings to buy a boat. That's the kind of list a woman of my age needs. That's what I have to do. Make a list. When I start to think like that I know the top and bottom of it is Janey.

The baseline is that I never would have contemplated leaving Janey. I just know I wouldn't. So maybe someone came back into my life – her father is my lost lover. So – where is he?

Dangerous games, I think. The phrase arcs through my mind like flash lightning through livid pre-storm skies.

Clyde knows. Clyde told me about the letters not because he

didn't know who they were written to but because he did. Clyde is waiting for the direct question that we've both been dreading and that won't be postponed any longer.

There's no easy way of asking your husband for the name of your lover. I pick a moment while we're unpacking the shopping, while I'm putting the caramel-swirl ice-cream with mocha-meringue chunks into the freezer compartment. Clyde seems to find it a lot less difficult to reply than I do to blurt out this pent-up demand. He lifts his head and looks at me like a poacher who's been crouching a long time beside a snare and he says, 'Jeremy.'

Jeremy.

Shit.

Not a temptingly unattached work colleague, not Janey's long-lost father, not a romantic stranger from my past. My best friend's husband.

Jeremy.

'And we're having them round for a barbecue tonight? That's fucking civilised, isn't it?' I slam the shopping on the worktop then push the lot of it off on to the floor.

Clyde doesn't pick it up. The kitchen seems very crowded, somehow, though there's only him and me and the mess of meat and staring fish spilling between us. Janey has melted away, into the garden somewhere.

'Why didn't you tell me before?'

He lifts his arm in a kind of wild exaggerated shrug then thumps his fist on the worktop.

I flinch.

He says, 'You didn't even know your fucking child, and you want me to talk to you about that?'

Well, I suppose I can see that. He doesn't have to get nasty, like I meant it to happen, like I wanted it all to come to this.

Then he says, quieter, 'We just wanted things to be back the way they were. Before all this.'

We? We? Who is we? I may have said this aloud because he says, 'All of us. For the children.'

I've seized the solitaire ring from its little bowl and I'm tapping rapidly on the worktop with it, mostly because I want to hear the snapping noise but also because I see from the way Clyde's watching that he's thinking symbolism. He doesn't like that. He picks up the shopping and I keep on rapping. I can feel I'm boiling over with emotions and I don't know what they are.

Jeremy.

'So *all of you* have decided, have you, to sew up the past like a kitten in a sack for drowning? My mind's wiped, you could have got away with it. Why did you start telling me things?'

'You asked,' he says grimly.

'Helen and Jeremy don't know you've broken the pact,' I say. 'That's why you can't cancel tonight and tell them to fuck off. Don't you want to?'

Again the fist comes down. That fist could smash a rabbit's brain to pulp. 'It's a small village. If we four fell out, everyone would know. Tongues would wag.'

'Tongues would wag!' I jeer back at him. I poke mine out and grimace at him as uglily as I can. I wish my tongue was a loaded gun. He looks at me, disgusted.

I wipe my mouth, which is slobbery from my anger. 'So you're happy to pretend,' I say, with clear precise contempt.

'Helen has managed to save her marriage. That's what I was trying to do.'

There's a question in there somewhere. Somewhere between his tense shoulders and the limply clenched fist a question is trapped. I don't want him to ask it because I don't know the answer. I keep thinking, Jeremy.

Jeremy, long-limbed, long-lashed, quietly absorbed with the magazines in the bookshop. Jeremy leaning forward to talk over the dinner table, animated and intent. Jeremy in the garden, leaning back in a black vest over bronzy shoulders, his eyes sultry and enigmatic, watching me arrive. I trawl back through every remembered glimpse of Jeremy's strong arms but the hot kisses aren't there.

Now Clyde's quiet again. 'I thought it was worth it,' he says, and I want to kick him. Fucking prat.

I say, 'Pretend whatever you like. But now you want me to pretend too, in this farce of a barbecue tonight. To sit with him, and her, and you, and pretend along with the rest of you that nothing ever happened.'

'Why not?' he says. 'You used to be good at it.'

Oh. I'm winded, I literally wince with the pain of it. The battle's over. Janey arrives back in with the last carrier from the boot and sits in the middle of the floor opening cat-buttons. There's nothing I can think of saying anyway. He's won.

But he hasn't won the war and I know there's a weak link in the iron-cast welding of their triumvirate. Not Jeremy, who has withdrawn from me utterly as though our passion was only ever a dream, and certainly not Clyde, who would tether me in chains to keep me here. Helen. I know how frail Helen is, and I know that even in this misty turmoil I am the stronger.

Dangerous games. This time he started it.

So I'm going to pretend. If that's what they want, I can do that.

I get all the stuff ready and start on the box of wine before I'm even changed. Clyde is plodding round watching me but he doesn't say anything more about the evening. I've already drunk about four glasses of Chardonnay by the time Janey and I are ready. She's wearing the leggings and T-shirt I got her, and I've persuaded her to wear a little white cardi to cover her arms. I've put on a long skirt, a kind of gauzy new-age patchwork, and a black crop top. 'Am I OK like this?' I say, smoothly seeing Clyde's lip droop as he stares at the place where my bare skin meets the waist of the Cinderella-raggy skirt, my body between the swell of breast and belly naked and absolutely firm.

Dangerous games . . . The phrase keeps coming into my head, like a music refrain, but it's not from one of those songs I keep hearing that resonate achingly with my life. It comes from somewhere else, I don't know where.

I've decided I'm going to get Helen drunk. I don't really know why, maybe just spite. I've got to do something to break the net of conspiracy. I'm half drunk myself, anyway, by the time they arrive.

Jeremy is looking delicious, almost edible. I think about walking straight up to him, brushing against him like that day in the bookshop, just to feel again that unmistakable frisson and saying boldly, 'Clyde's been explaining to me why we have this electric reaction. And to think I thought it was static off your shirt!'

I say, 'Hi. Take a drink, have a dip.'

'Tzaziki,' says Helen. 'Oh, I shouldn't. Is it Greek yoghurt, not low-fat?'

'Yes,' I say. I haven't the foggiest. I bought it ready-made in a sell-by dip-pot. 'Go on — sin a little! Forbidden fruit is always the best.'

Clyde looks across the smoky barbecue and says sharply to me, 'Are you going to be warm enough? It's clouding over.'

'May even rain,' says Jeremy, examining the sky. I think of Pooh Bear in the story, trying to fool the bees so he could steal their honey, and I start giggling uncontrollably. I go inside to the bathroom and splash my face with cold water. In the mirror my hair is wild and my face flushed. I look almost outrageous.

Jeremy.

Jeremy looking down at me and Janey in the car, like he would drive to hell for us if we asked him. Jeremy in the bookshop, recovering from my collision as if he's a wound and I've torn away the bandage. Jeremy putting on slow, sexy music just before we left his house after that dinner party, ignoring Helen's spiteful panic, burning in disbelief as I turned away.

I don't know how I ever doubted it.

'Outrageous, and gorgeous,' I tell my reflection in the mirror. I go back outside.

I've plugged our portable music system in and put that tape on, the one that's labelled *Everything Must Go*, because I know now where it came from.

'You've got this, haven't you?' I say triumphantly. I don't know why I'm sounding so pleased; I don't even know which of them gave it to me. I don't know if this was always a secret our-song message from Jeremy, or a copy Helen made for me back when our friendship was innocent, before I betrayed her trust.

'Let's dance,' I command. I pull Jeremy up and begin to waver about in front of him. Clyde and Helen are staring so I pull Helen up too.

I am so close I could touch his pain.

I can't stand it, I reach out –

Everything is suddenly silent. Clyde has turned it off.

'Too slow, anyway,' I say. 'Helen can show us line-dancing. You do the side kicks, Helen, and I'll do the goose-step. No? OK, let's talk. What were we talking about last time? Oh, yes, we were slagging off women. Saying how feminism's lost its way. Your whole world has lost its way, if you ask me.'

I realise I'm talking like I'm from some alien planet but I am so angry at their deceit and so frustrated at this whole sham of a party I don't care what any of them thinks. 'You want to go back to the days when women with opinions were burned as witches,' I say wildly, 'shrews to be tamed. "Such duty as the subject oweth the Prince, even such the woman oweth the husband." That's what Kate says at the end.'

I've remembered this from doing the play at school but I'm not sure I've got all the *th*s right, there seem to be rather a lot of them. While I'm enunciating this furiously and with as much dignity as I can, another quote from that play stings me unexpectedly. 'Kiss me, Kate.'

Jeremy lifts his head and looks at me. His look is brimming and blatant. Now I can believe it. I know now absolutely that this man has held me, has traced those supple hands along the contours of my body as I shuddered for him. The air between us seems to tremble like a heat-hazy summer road shimmering before a storm. There is a resin of longing seeping from the cut stillness around us, it's almost palpable and it's driving me crazy that my head won't admit what my body knows.

And then slowly it begins.

Jeremy pulling back the shower curtain, Jeremy naked, staring at me, stepping towards me, dropping to his knees so he can grasp my legs, groaning, pressing his face against me while the spraying water pours down my breasts and belly and soaks his beautiful black curling hair and oh . . . oh . . . Jeremy.

Clyde's having trouble with the sardines slipping through the grill bars. When I ask why he didn't put them on foil he says lugubriously, 'We don't usually have fish.'

'So sorry!' I say. 'My mistake. We mustn't do anything we don't *usually* do, must we? Tongues would wag.' Then I see Janey with her arms rammed up her cardigan sleeves and I feel like screaming.

Jeremy walking towards me through the woods like a figure in a dream, Jeremy holding me, gripping me tightly, whispering bitingly. Can't sleep can't eat can't think of anything but you, the smell of you the taste of you the touch of you. I can't breathe without you. You're so lovely, so delicious, let me be wherever you are, let me be the oil in your bathwater, let me be the mud under your boots, don't laugh, oh, laugh and I'll be the crease in the secret corner of your mouth, oh, please, please, Kate darling, please —

What?

— come away with me.

Instead of screaming at Janey I go and help myself to more wine. I stand in the kitchen poking at the cardboard tag on the second wine box and there's a sound behind me. I jump about three feet.

Jeremy, seizing me from behind, be careful, be careful, I don't care, don't you know I burn for you? Every moment apart is agony —

No. It's Clyde. He reaches across my shoulders and puts his arm across me and kisses me hard on the neck.

'You look beautiful,' he says huskily.

'You're crushing my tits,' I say.

This is not such an elegant event as Helen's dinner party. There is less orderly conversation. Basically, we're all getting drunk, extremely quickly. Janey has eaten five sausages and retired to the living room to watch some vet programme. There are a few charred chops left on the grill and the sardines, salvaged and grimy, drape limply above the embers. I tell Clyde to throw them for the cat and he says, 'You should have cut the heads off.'

'They don't in Spain.'

How do I know that? My mother must have told me.

Jeremy in the car, that first time, when he gave me a lift to the lodge after the fête and I watched him obliquely, his long-lashed eyes intent on the road and every pore of his skin plangent with unmistakable wanting, and as the car slowed down I put my hand out to him, on him, and whispered, 'Drive', and he unspeakingly accelerated again, out of the car park, into the pinewoods, out of sight of everyone in the grounds. Jeremy, stopping the car and turning to me his eyes heavy-lidded and his mouth dry and taut, and I unclipped my seatbelt and leaned across his lap. Jeremy pressing his hands through my hair and shuddering with pleasure and quietly groaning. And afterwards when we went, late, to collect our face-painted children he said, 'Don't try to phone. Write to me.'

Now Helen is saying we should clear up, take the things inside, because it's raining. I'm fascinated by this information, until I discover it's true: I'm soaked. My floating skirt is trailing, clinging to my legs, completely transparent.

'Get her inside,' Clyde says to Helen. I start to laugh. I dance away from her. I won't go in. I'm dancing in the rain, whirling around, and the lights of the garden torches are whirling around me. I say, 'Was it like this on our picnic? We went in the river, didn't we? All of us soaked to the skin.' Jeremy steps forward and Clyde's voice comes loudly, 'Leave her.'

Jeremy at the studio with my first letter tucked in his Filo, and I said, 'Helen knows my handwriting at a glance, don't leave it there.' And he insisted, 'I want your words with me, I need to touch them, I need my fix of you.' I said, 'I'll type next time – but don't write back, our post arrives before Clyde goes.' And he said, 'keep a copy then, read them and think about me reading them. Because every time you think of me I'll be thinking about you.'

They have all gone away inside. There's only me, dancing on the lawn in the garden with needles of rain golden in the torchlight and Helen in the porch watching. The wetness all around is soaking me. With that powerful sense of isolation comes sudden absolute conviction. I stop still, giddy, fighting not to retch. I walk carefully over to Helen. 'You don't need to tell me anything else, but just tell me this. Who hit me?'

'It was an accident,' says Helen. 'Truly, Kirsten, nobody hit you.'

'So how did this happen to me?' I'm screaming at her, stabbing at my head as though it's broken and bleeding. 'Who did this to me? Did I try to kill myself? I want to know. Did I jump in the river?'

Helen is crying. Her words come out like moans, sliding on the dribble of her sobs. She's saying, 'I never meant it. I never meant that.'

I stop still. She's saying, 'I only pushed you a little bit – you never hurt your head or anything. You were only under the water for a moment.'

'You pushed me?'

Helen is crumpling. She's staggered against the wall and I have to grab her to hold her up, to stop her from sliding to the ground as she cries.

'You wanted everything! You were taking Jeremy away from me, away from Sam. How could you do that to a little boy? If you had no loyalty to me, how could you do that to a child?'

I can't maintain the terrific effort it takes to keep either of us upright and we both slither slowly down the wall together, grabbing each other for futile support. Helen is still doing her moany little sobs. I try to sound calm, swallowing my desperate urgency, wishing I was less drunk. 'Tell me the rest.'

'That job. He never told me about it, and he was going to accept it. And you were going with him. Clyde found out, Clyde told me, on the way to the picnic. We didn't know what to do, we went on pretending that we didn't know, but I couldn't bear it.'

Clyde the great pretender. I can see him in the doorway of the darkened patio, watching like a brooding bear. Jeremy is a frail shadow behind him. Now I wish I was drunker, in fact I wish I was unconscious. Helen keeps whining, 'I only wanted to stop you.' She flinches from me when I put my arm out to her, but I'm only trying to make her listen because I need to explain something terribly important.

'I didn't want Jeremy. It wasn't Jeremy I wanted. It was Paul.'

Because now I know what happened nine years ago. I know why I never went back to college, why I never contacted Debs again or Miles or Paul. I know why I stopped taking photographs and tried to start a new life. I know what happened and I know whose child Janey is. Because now I remember.

This is what I remember.

Wet. The air was saturated and the grass was drenched. There were kites flying and paper banners fluttering all around with the sun shining through. The sound of drums vibrated distantly.

I was sitting on an oil drum outside the Tiny Tea Tent with Debs, hugging my hot mug with chilled fingers and thinking about Paul's beautiful body, imagining him panting, collapsed, in the tent; wanting to run back and lick him all over and push my hand slowly and gently into his crotch to hear him groan with wanting.

And Debs said, 'Oh, fuck, Kirsty – why don't we swap?'

The thought made me tingle. She said, 'He's gone off me, it's obvious,' and then, grinning, 'We should swap guys.'

I listened to the thrumming of the drummers squatting on the wooden benches behind the Tiny Tea Tent, and I remembered last night and the thrill of dancing around to the Oysterband, thinking about Paul and Miles watching. And how every time I looked round Miles was nodding to the music with his eyes closed and Paul was staring at us. Especially at me.

'OK,' I said.

Debs laughed and then said, 'Seriously? Suppose they say no?'

'We won't ask them,' I said calmly. If you don't think you're going to like the answer, don't ask the question, my dad always says. 'But I know how we could do it. If we stay together for most of the day, all of us, then separate in the evening into twosomes. A me-some and a you-some. You and Miles, me and Paul. Go with the flow . . . then tell them afterwards, when it's *fait accompli*, that it wasn't actually accidental after all.'

'Like, me seduce Miles first and then tell him afterwards you said it would be OK? No way! He's got scruples, your Miles.'

'OK, not actually afterwards. But not beforehand, because they might argue. It'll have to be during.'

'During?'

'During.'

We were both laughing hard by now, as if this was a hilarious unlikely joke that we could brush away later as fantasy. But I was hungry for Paul, and when we went back to the tent it felt as if somehow, at some level, he must have sensed what we were planning. He was really sweet and flirty with me, and it was easy to keep close with him as we went round the Circus Field. We watched some fire jugglers but the weather was beginning to get stormy and the high trapeze act was stopped.

Then we went right down to the end of the Green Field looking for the drummer Debs and I had danced to last night. We didn't find him but there were other people in the Sacred Space with didgerydoos, which sounded great. Some little kids with hair like dandelion clocks were running around with nothing on. A guy ten feet tall in silver armour came clanking by. Then these theatre people showed up with an enormous beach-ball patterned like a globe. They were rolling it over the grass and letting children crawl on top. I love this place! It's the way the world ought to be, all colours and music and craziness. I was nearly going to buy a hat like a medieval clown, all velvety points and jingling bells, when Debs pointed out that (a) I couldn't afford it and (b) I looked utterly stupid.

So we danced around at the stone circle for a while, until Miles and Paul wanted to go back to the markets to get some food at the Japanese noodle bar.

The rain was setting in again and some of the stalls were putting their stuff away. Bedraggled coloured scarves dripped and the baskets of blankets were sodden. Our programme was un-readable papier-mâché so we just headed for the Theatre marquee for a bit of shelter – us and a few thousand others. It was difficult not to get separated but I stuck to Paul like fluff on a toffee apple. There was a brilliant woman comic on who was raunchy and vulgar, and what with that and the wine box and Debs's lascivious nudges I felt really elated. I felt like I could fly.

When we had finished the wine I offered to go back to the tent for the other box. It seemed a good way to make sure the guys didn't wander off.

'It's pissing down,' Miles said, but I said I didn't care, and I set off into the rain.

The path across the fields, which had been stony and well trodden, was slowly churning into liquid mud. Fag ends unravelled, gushing their entrails like fibrous leeches. Polystyrene beer-glasses floated down rivulets and shipwrecked themselves in mud. All the stuff in our tent was damp. I got out the last wine box and set off back when I was hailed by a guy in a black leather jacket.

'It's the delicious Kirsty!' said Andy Gray. His eyes were dilated and his face, even in the rain, looked greasy. 'Let me buy you a beer.' He was actually offering a half-smoked spliff as he said this and I took a generous suck. So did he. I started to laugh and he smiled at me benignly.

'Why have you got a teabag on your toe, Andy?'

He laughed too as if I was being really witty, and then when he saw I was pointing at his Doc Martens he looked down and became quite intrigued.

'Hey!' he said, and then, 'Hey, hey! I really have got a teabag on my toe.' He seemed pleased about this. 'I must've put it there for later,' he said.

'It won't be much use later. It will be all washed out,' I said, and he nodded wisely.

'Better stick to this,' he suggested, and gave me another drag.

It seemed funny to me to find my tutor off his head in a wet field. I kept giggling about this until I realised he had his arm around me and was breathing extremely close to me. I disentangled myself. He didn't seem surprised, although he sighed deeply. 'Kirsty, Kirsty. Do you know you have given me wet dreams all year?'

It wasn't a point we'd ever discussed in tutorial. I said this but he didn't laugh. He was groaning and twiddling bits of my hair in his fingers. 'At this moment,' he said, 'you look exactly like an undine. Do you know what an undine is, Kirsty Middleton? Of course you don't. You are determined to squander your extraordinary loveliness on undeserving students.'

At this point I remembered that I was deeply in love with Paul and stepped away from Andy's pawing fingers. He sighed a bit more and his eyes rolled up to show the whites.

'What is an undine, then?' I asked as he carried on staring at me when he had got his eyes focused again.

'An utterly gorgeous unattainable creature who drives men mad with lust,' he said.

'Oh. I thought that was a siren.' It felt good to be talking hard like this with my tutor. It made me long for tonight and the exciting unfamiliarity of Paul's embrace – it made me feel powerful and certain I could make it with him.

'You're right,' Andy conceded gallantly. 'But an undine is gorgeous too. An undine is a female watersprite. She gains her soul by marrying a mortal man and having a child. Would you consider sleeping with me, Kirsty Middleton? To gain a soul?'

It didn't seem fair to smoke any more of his joint once I'd said no, so I made my way back to the others.

It was getting dusky when I got back to the theatre marquee. Flares and lanterns glowed in the damp twilit air. I was glowing inside from the wine and the thrill of our plan and being soaked through didn't bother me at all. Miles wanted to go up to the main stage for Elvis Costello, so when Paul said he wanted to hear the African group in the bottom field I said I fancied doing that, too. Debs said she was for Elvis Costello, and suggested she and he should head off to get a place at the front. And in a few moments Paul and I were on our own.

We'd drunk most of the wine and I wasn't taking in the music much, apart from the insistent underlying beat that made me want to dance. Paul was moving about to the rhythm, like everyone, and I was swaying around making sure I touched him a lot. He seemed to like it. When the African group finished playing we started making our way back to the camping field, at first a big group of us and then, as people turned off to find their own tents, we were suddenly alone.

The sky was black now and we stopped to look up at ̤̤
infinity of stars. Open fires like little flares glimmered in ̤̤
camping field. The space around us was scented with the heady,
herbal, indefinably exciting smell of festival.

A burst of fireworks cut across the sky. That sound of
distant drumming pulsing in my head all day suddenly became
louder on the wind. I was clinging to Paul and he was laughing
and suddenly I pulled him towards me and kissed him passionately on the lips.

'Wow,' said Paul, in a voice like melting chocolate, 'what's
going on here? What about Miles?'

My plan was so sharp and clear in my mind I'd almost
forgotten Paul didn't know. Miles was miles away. I giggled
aloud. 'Never mind Miles,' I whispered.

'If you say so,' Paul said, and he stuck his tongue in my
mouth and kissed me while his hands dug deep under my jacket.
He didn't mention Debs as his grip tightened and I thought,
Maybe he knows, maybe he guesses, or maybe he wants me so
much that he just doesn't care. My breasts felt clammy under all
the damp fabric but I could feel my nipples hardening as he
touched them. I kissed him some more, long and warm and
lingering. He moved his hands lower and pushed them into the
top of my jeans and said my name close into my hair. His voice
was throaty and suggestive and I felt a frisson of incredible
happiness. I was right to go with my longing – his responsive-
ness was proving it. Paul loved me too. He was groaning
gently in that luscious, yearning way that turns me on so much,
I could feel him pressing against me. I whispered, 'Touch me.' I
knew he was wild to, and suddenly it seemed really important to
explain to him that everything was truly beautiful.

I said, 'It's all right, Paul. Debs knows.'

He pulled away from me as if he'd been shot.
'Whaddayamean?'

We were on a path beside a hedge when we'd stopped and now he staggered and practically fell into the bushes. He swore and righted himself. 'Where's Debs?'

I put out my hand to him again. I tried to laugh, I said, 'With Miles.'

'You planned this,' he said, and his face was a mask of hating. 'I've been dumped.'

He started howling, quietly, like a lost dog, and then he shook his head dizzily and began to run towards the top field. I grabbed hold of his sleeve to stop him. 'It's not like that,' I pleaded. He turned. 'It's not like that,' I said again. 'I love you.'

'Slag,' he said. 'Bitch.' And just when I thought he was going to pull away again he fell on his knees and sobbed on the wet path. I tried to hold him but he pushed me away. 'I've been dumped,' he muttered, over and over. I felt panic building up in me. Partly it was the fear of his anger and distress, mostly it was from an aching sense of terrible rejection. He couldn't take in how beautiful and neat it was. I wanted so much to stop it all going wrong.

Which is why, I suppose, I followed him when he dragged himself to his feet and stumbled back to where we were camped. Which is why I pushed my way into the tent after him and flung myself down beside him, trying to console him, trying to embrace him, trying to make him love me.

'You always were a prick-tease,' he said, and then he grabbed my shoulders and pushed me down. 'Dangerous games, Kirsty.'

He rolled on top of me as my head hit the hard earth. I was so desperate for him to desire and love me I was still trying to stroke and kiss him and for the first few minutes I didn't notice the pain. He was hitting me violently, in the shoulders, in the stomach, in the crotch. 'Is this it? Is this what you want, Kirsty?'

I managed to whisper, 'You're hurting me,' and I tried to restrain his punching hand but he dragged it away and pressed

my face sideways into the mud. 'Please . . . please,' I was w..
pering, 'not like this, Paul,' but he said viciously, 'Like what? It's
a hole, isn't it? A greedy bitch of a hole, and it wants plugging
up.' He had forced my jeans down and was scrabbling with his
hand outside the tent flap and now I could feel with retching
horror that he was filling me with mud, pushing the cold slime
into me with one hand as he held me down and swore abuse at
me. I pissed myself, I could feel the hot stream trickling out over
my legs, my jeans, over him, and I knew that he was unzipping
now, that finally he was going to do it.

He fucked me. He passed out. I pulled up my soaking, stained
clothes and crawled away. Drowned campfires glowed feebly
among the tents. Firecrackers were sparking from the Dragon
Field. The sound of distant drumming thrummed faintly. I
crawled away towards the lights.

I remember now. The welfare people gave me a blanket and
kept me there that night, and took me back down to the meeting
point on Sunday morning because I kept saying that I couldn't
go back to my tent and I wanted to go home. That's where Andy
found me. It was Andy who realised something unrecoverable had
happened, took me home, got me the summer job.

And I'd forgotten it all. I'd forgotten that I tried to take Paul
and he refused me. I'd wiped out of my mind that it was his anger
not his love that made Janey. All these years later I'd found Jeremy
and tried once again to swap what I didn't value for what I wanted
so much. Only this time something else stopped me.

Helen has gone. Everyone's gone. I don't know how long I've
been out here. It's still raining and the garden is whirling more
slowly now, steadying around me.

Clyde's trying to take hold of me. I struggle within his grip.

'I have to tell Janey. Her father is dead – I have to tell her. I
loved him but he died.'

'For Chrissake, Kirsty! Not now, she's asleep – you'll terrify her.'

I don't want to frighten Janey. I stop struggling and he leads me inside and over to the kitchen table. There's black coffee there and he's pulling at my wet skirt. I won't let him. I need to talk, and I keep telling him.

'Well, talk to me.'

He's there. He'll do.

'I know. I know everything that matters now. I know why I stopped taking photographs.'

'And that's what matters? What about me?'

He doesn't seem to understand how absolutely important this is. He's staring at me, whining, 'Don't you remember about us?'

Now I remember why Clyde won't do at all. Clyde is one of my betrayers. I jump up: coffee splatters and scalds.

'You knew she pushed me.'

He sits there glaring. 'D'you blame her?'

And I'm supposed to be the confused one -- the one not facing up to my feelings. What about Clyde, defending me and witness for the prosecution too.

'Did you want her to kill me, then? Why don't you kill me now, Clyde?'

'You're hysterical,' he says.

Hysteria would be quite reasonable, really. This is more of a snowstorm feeling, as though my head is full of shuddering flakes that whirl and won't settle. I tried to escape from here but Helen stopped me. Or maybe I stopped myself.

Escape. Jeremy was the wrong way. His wanting me confused me, the way men's wanting always does. Clyde's bolted the door to the back garden so I run through the hall and escape out of the front door.

I'm standing at the gate watching the sleety rain drizzle golden on the dark road. Gradually the street-light stops whirling and the supernova sycamore leaves settle. A figure like a moon goddess stands before me, wringing her hands, dripping wet and naked.

It is not a naked moon goddess, it is old Mrs Thing from next door.

Her body is curiously beautiful for an old lady's, bulky but lissome, with smooth pearl-white skin. Her grey hair streams like that of an undine in the saturating rain.

I approach her.

She anticipates my curiosity. 'I'm waiting, dear.'

'For your washing?' This seems funny and I start to giggle.

'For my silkie,' she says serenely, without reproach or rancour, and she suddenly starts to sing.

> *'An earthly nurse she sits and sings, and aye she sings by lily wheen*
> *It's little ken I my bairn's father, still less the land that he dwells in.'*

I know this ballad. I heard it years ago, when I was at college, at a folk club. All songs seem to have something to say in a fuzzy-thinking way, but this is special.

'Is it a song for me?'

She tuts.

'It's a song for a silkie,' she says. 'But he neglects to come.' And then she puts her hand over her mouth like she's told a secret that should never be spoken, and she starts to sob 'Oh – oh – oh –'

It's a bit upsetting, this wild crying. Maybe it's not so nice to be Mrs Thing. I decide to take her back indoors before she catches her death out there. As I'm precariously climbing the little fence between our gardens the throaty roar of a motorbike dissects the darkness and I catch a glimpse of Harvey's pizza-bike hacking down the road. I clutch at the top of the fence and hear my skirt rip.

Mrs Thing lets me lead her back inside. I'm stumbling a bit

but sobering slightly. The kitchen stinks of bleach from Eleanor's cleaning. No wonder she went out in the fresh air.

She trots off and fetches a towel without my asking and we have a bit of a tussle, with her trying to mop my hair and me trying to wrap her up. I start giggling again and get hiccups, and she gives in gracefully. Now she looks so frail and like a little bird and I don't know what to do with her.

'Have you got a nightie?' I manage, between hics.

But she shakes her head and says sadly, 'All gone away with the washing,' and she cries, and I cry too.

Clyde's here now, in a bloody big oilskin like a lighthouse keeper. He looks about seven feet tall. 'You are big,' I tell him, admiringly.

'Go home,' he says. 'Eleanor's coming.'

'You didn't need to phone Eleanor at this hour, she's OK now. I can look after her.' I have to say this in little spurts between the hiccups.

'And you'd know all about care, wouldn't you?'

God, I am so sick of his snide comments. I'm looking round for something to really hurt him with but Eleanor's done a quite excessive tidy-up and there's nothing with an edge on it visible anywhere.

'I can get her to bed,' I insist.

'She needs proper attention. She's bleeding.'

'It's only scratches from the roses.'

'Go home. You're not fit to be here.'

And then we have this extraordinary fight, in the middle of Mrs Thing's antiseptic kitchen. He's in his wet oilskin and I'm in my torn, drenched skirt, and there's nothing around us to grab to hit each other with and I don't want to scream or even swear because of poor Mrs Thing sitting wrapped in her towel with her mouth open in a big dark O of horror. So we just grip each other and rock and struggle in breathy silence. He's pinching my arm agonisingly to stop me squeezing at his throat and I manage to stab my knee up into his groin and hear a stifled, gasping groan. I'm squeezing on his neck now trying to kill him and he's stifling me, crushing the breath out of me and I can't even speak to tell him I want to throw up, and suddenly Mrs Thing says, very clearly and distinctly, 'Well, thank you for calling but I've had enough of that.' And we are dismissed.

We loosen off. I feel all limp and foolish. 'I'd better be going,' I say, with minuscule dignity. 'I have to get back for Janey.'

Clyde has to lift me back over the fence and then I find I can't even stand so he carries me back into our house and puts me to bed.

The Start of the Eighth Week

I wake with a bloody awful hangover. Clyde tells me it's nearly ten. I reach out to verify.

'Where's my watch? The little one you gave me last year, with the enamel bangle.'

He says, 'Still at the repairs, I suppose. You were getting the clasp fixed.'

I think about this. It must be ready by now, it's been there weeks.

I get up, stumbling a bit, and go to the window to look out at the back garden. Everything is sodden. The barbecue has a murky pool of water in it and washed-down ashes stain the patio. The deadened garden torches still stand in the flower-beds, and all the leaves and petals are glittering with heavy raindrops.

'Yes or no?' Clyde is saying. His voice sounds distant like a memory. He comes back into the room and leans over me. 'D'you want breakfast, yes or no?' I put my hands to my head protectively as the thought bludgeons me. Clyde picks me up and puts me back on the bed.

He is so calm. It's very disconcerting.

'There ought to be . . .' I'm groping for the word *fanfares*, but I don't really know why. It's a perfectly normal thing for someone to know who they are in the morning, and also the thought of a fanfare hurts my head.

Clyde raises his eyebrows. 'Clowns?' he says. 'Tea, anyway. I'll bring you a cup of tea.'

I think about Leila saying *a gentleman*. It occurs to me that saying yes to Clyde wasn't simply scared capitulation because I was carrying Janey. Perhaps I had understood, once, the ephemeral thrill of dangerous games. I had chosen instead a gentle man. It's a pity I couldn't stick with that before it was too late.

I get up, delicately, and go into Janey's room. She's sitting up in bed reading. I sit beside her on the bed and lift up her long hair, still free and thick from the night. I hold it up loosely behind her head so that it shapes closely to her cheeks. She doesn't look up.

'D'you still want your hair cut?'

Janey turns a page methodically. 'Uh-huh.'

'Maybe we could get it done next week, at Sasha's, in town. If you like.'

She flicks her long-lashed eyes up briefly. 'Uh-huh,' says Janey.

But we both know that it was ages ago, before the beginning of the summer, that she last implored me about that cut. We both know Sasha's is the hairdresser's she longs to go to, although she hasn't mentioned it for a long time.

It's a small thing, but it's a start.

Still feeling somewhat precarious I make my way to the kitchen.

Clyde has tidied up and the dead wine boxes are crushed into the bin, their silvery bladders still glinting. He's standing looking intently at the kettle, as though it needs his moral support in order to boil, but his hand comes trailing out towards me as I pass him and I let it linger.

'I feel like I've been washed up on a beach after a long storm,' I say.

He nods. 'Now you've begun remembering, we can put a lot of that stuff behind us. We could start from here, from today.'

'Oh, Clyde.' I've climbed on to the stool and I drop my head on to my hands and let my arms spread across the worktop till my cheek touches its cool surface. I didn't intend to contrive this gesture, I simply can't help it when I hear his hopeful gauche prognosis. 'This is only the beginning. There'll be so much to sort through, before I can dump any of it.'

'We can do it together,' he says stubbornly. 'Now that you know what happened.'

I shake my head slowly. I can feel him stroking my hair, very gently.

'Sweetie . . . Kirsty?'

I lift my head. 'I'm sorry I was a bitch to you when I was Kirsten. But don't you see? I'd only do it all again.'

'Why?' he says. He sounds so miserable.

'Because we both know I can. Clyde, you deserve better than that.'

'I want you . . . to stay,' he says, after a hefty pause and with a pause in the middle too.

'Why? You don't know me. I'm not that Kirsten any more.'

Clyde says, 'I know. You're Kirsty.'

I feel so sorry for him. He's accepted he never knew me, me or Kirsten, and it doesn't make any difference. He still wants me. To stay.

But you can't base a relationship on pity. You can't use gratitude instead of love. Kirsten tried, and look what a bitch she turned into.

He pours my tea. He's used the mug Janey bought me with her birthday money. 'You're Kirsty Villiers,' he says stubbornly. 'We can talk about it all now – we can talk about whatever you want.'

'Can we talk about lions, Clyde? If a lion-tamer suddenly thought, What's the point? do you think that's when the beast would attack him?'

Clyde hesitates, but no longer than a heartbeat. 'Probably. Unless the lion was thinking, What's the point? too.'

I know it's stupid but there's something in the dry way Clyde says that which strikes me as funny. Not funny-hilarious, just droll.

'I don't know what I'll do,' I say. 'I'll have to think.'

He puts the mug of tea in my hands and moves away. I know he hasn't given up.

There's still a final coat of wood stain needed for this new rabbit hutch. The grass in the garden is dry already; the ground has soaked up last night's downpour and the waterdrops on the leaves have all evaporated. Janey is doing handstands while Clyde tests his brushes and tries to find a supple one by pressing them against his broad palm. She's got a delicate way of throwing her hands down and lifting her legs so that even though she can only hold the pose staggeringly for a moment or so she looks like a dancer. She has definitely got her father's breathtaking eyes.

It wasn't really rape, was it? I don't like to think of my little Janey being a rape-child. She's more of a love-child, really – a seduction that went wrong. *Kirsty should try to be more decisive.* She did, and nearly destroyed my world around me. And Paul, if he ever remembered his angry passion, never knew about the baby because I never told him. I never told anyone. I never even told myself.

I think about Leila saying, 'You sort of ignored the whole thing for months – you just wanted to go on having a good time.' I hated myself so much when she said that, but Leila was wrong. It wasn't a good time I wanted: it was a safe place where my desires would never be able to damage me again.

Maybe I should have thought that destroying one world is only a way of creating another.

I've been blaming myself so much, but it wasn't just me, it was all of us. Look at the muddle of the last few weeks, evasions and silences when I needed truths and certainties. Clyde just desperate to keep me, dripping hints like wringing out a blood-soaked cloth; Helen and Jeremy with their panic-stricken pact of secrecy, trying to cover the crack in their marriage that had split into an abyss. And long before that there was a tacit conspiracy. Debs and Miles have obliterated every awkward memory now, but nine years ago they let me drop like a stone in a lake. Even Mum and Dad allowed me to go without any real questions. Dad, of course, would have felt hurt and angry so Mum, to protect him, did as always – nothing. I'm beginning to realise the long trail that led me here, then left me a sleeping princess.

Clyde comes in and says, looking at me, 'What's funny?'

'Nothing. Not actually funny, just ironic. I was thinking how easy it is, once you find out what's happened, to find a way of blaming other people.'

'Are you going to forget again, then, or stick with the blaming?' That wry voice I used to think was grumpy, which sounds so vulnerable now.

'Is that the only choice I have?' I'm speaking lightly but he doesn't smile.

He says, 'I came in for the camera. Janey wants a picture of the hutch.' This is so obviously an attempt to involve me that I can't help saying, 'Wouldn't she rather have a picture of the rabbit?' and he hesitates in the doorway without answering. It's fairly clear what's on his mind: *Let me know whether you intend to take Janey away first, before getting another dependent creature to abandon.*

I fetch the Pentax. It's so unused that the strap still unfolds in creases.

'You could do a proper course,' Clyde says. 'Now you've packed in the pizza parlour, you could do evening classes.'

'You might as well use up the film,' I say. 'It's been in it since Christmas. Those snow shots, with Janey and Sam on the sledge – it's about time we got them processed.'

'See? Now you've started remembering, everything will go back to normal. You'll be fine.'

Beyond him in the garden I can see a small boy climbing over the back fence. It's Daniel. He approaches the hutch and squats beside Janey.

'I'll do them some drink and biscuits,' I say, and get a couple of cans from the fridge.

'We'll be OK, again,' Clyde persists, following me round the kitchen.

'Remembering is not enough,' I say, as gently as I can, rustling with the Hobnob packet. 'Knowing things is not enough. You have to do something too.'

'And what will you do?' says Clyde bleakly.

Daniel is stroking the hutch very gently as if it's a creature he's caught in the wild and brought here to tame.

'I don't know,' I say.

'Don't run away again,' he says.

'Would you have let me go, when you found out?'

'You can do whatever you choose,' he says, and then, less brittle, 'I was sure Helen would put a stop to it somehow. Every threat from the Child Support Agency to telephoning his new boss.'

Poor Jeremy. Poor Clyde, afraid of a fight. Afraid of his own strength. I sigh aloud at the thought of their panic and pain.

'How did you find out, anyway? After you found my letters, how did you find out who I was writing to?'

'I phoned the pizza place one night to speak to you, and Harvey said you were on a fag break. And you don't smoke.' This is not actually Columbo stuff. Harvey knows I don't smoke; Harvey says everyone is on a fag break if they aren't around. Nevertheless . . .

'So I phoned Helen to see if she could pop round for half an hour,' Clyde goes on, not looking at me, 'and she said, sorry, she was on her own, Jeremy had just gone out to see some client at the Design Studio.'

'So you put two and two together from that?'

Clyde does not reply. I get a long slow sensation of something indefinably like shame as I realise that he had collected more than a notional two and two. He must have trailed us doggedly into the woods, creeping quietly up to the old chapel walls, pressing his face silently to the leaded windows above the door. And I know exactly what he would have seen. There was only one time we had gambled with a night encounter, instead of using the anonymous afternoons for our secret meetings. So I know that what Clyde is not telling me is how he saw us naked, kneeling face to face, the evening light from that stained-glass half-moon above the lofty door decorating us like magical tattoos, giving us wings like angels. Except that we were close as Siamese twins, holding on and gasping like rock climbers reaching the last breathless crag.

'I told Janey I was nipping out to the pub for a four-pack,' says Clyde. 'I wasn't away long.'

Maybe he stayed long enough to see how Jeremy curled in my arms afterwards and I rocked him like a baby. Maybe he stopped wanting to kill him then. Maybe that's when he planned a better way to get me back.

I take out the tray to the children. Eleanor is in the back garden next door parking her mother in a deck-chair and she comes over to the fence when she sees me. 'I think this must be the end of the line,' she says, and for a surreal split-second I envisage that phantom washing-line filled with dainty lace and frivolous frocks from another century. In my mind's eye I see her mother slowly, triumphantly, hauling in her trawl, while Eleanor watches out for the end of the line.

'Last night,' Eleanor clarifies, and I say, 'Oh, yes. Your ma did get rather drenched.'

'Oh, it's not just the storm, though that was particularly unfortunate.' Her choice of adjective intrigues me – we only needed a blasted heath instead of a back garden and we could have staged the last act of *King Lear*. 'It's not merely the weather that worries me, it's the responsibility. I don't want to be responsible any more.'

'But . . .' I look back at Janey, kneeling beside Daniel and bossily helping him refit the pages they've managed to drop out of Clyde's spiral-bound wood-work manual. I want to say, 'Loving means responsibility, doesn't it?' but I don't think Eleanor needs a lecture right now with this decision to make. Perhaps she doesn't even love her mother – or, rather, doesn't love this strange woman who now inhabits her mother's body. Responsibility is a tough legacy.

'If I can help, at all . . .' I say feebly.

Eleanor says again, doggedly more than mournfully, 'I really think this is the end of the line. She's lost, you see. Miles away. Looking for things she hasn't got any more – she keeps going on about a mangle.'

But I know it's not mangle handles that Eleanor's mother is turning in her muddled mind. It is the mingled finger-writing of her long-gone years, fretted with corrections now and blotted with tears, that she is mourning. There's nothing I can really say to help. So I just say, 'Tell me when you find a place because I'd like to go and see her,' and Eleanor nods.

I hear the news van pass and decide to get some Sunday papers. 'Check our lottery numbers, will you?' says Clyde, as I pick up my purse, and I say routinely, 'OK.'

A grey Peugeot cruises past the gate. It slows. It stops. Jeremy is looking straight ahead, he doesn't turn towards the house but I know that he knows I am there. I know this, the way we always know, by the yearning osmosis of our proximity. His lean brown arm rests on the open window, his elbow against the hot grey metal. The gesture is achingly familiar. I could walk slowly down the path towards him. I know him so well. I know he will say, 'It's not too late for us, Kate,' and he will beg me like he did before. Only this time I will have decided.

I walk across the hallway to the front door and step into the garden. The road outside our house is empty.

When I get back with the papers Clyde comes in from the patio jiggling a handful of bright tomatoes, tiny as marbles in his big hands, proffering them like Jack's magic beans. He says, 'Shall I do us a salad for lunch, sweetie?'

'I'm Kirsty,' I say.

Clyde says, 'I know.'

'I'm not Kirsten and I'm not Kate.'

'I know.'

I want to tell him that what he said about running away has nothing to do with anything. I want to tell him that what I feel, now, is more important than whether I remember or whether I forget.

'I'm Kirsty Villiers,' I say.

I've filled a black bag with clothes I don't want any more and I'm leaving it out for Pol's jumble day. As I pass the phone I remember there's something I've been meaning to do. Dandy, sitting on the message pad as usual, moves disdainfully at my prompting shove. She's left the usual paw-prints on the scribbled notepad sheets. Eleanor's mobile, the number for the photography evening classes, the gym, the school. Here's the one, it was in the local paper, for lop-eared rabbits. The woman who answers the phone gives me her address. I tell her I know where that is, and arrange to go round to choose one this afternoon.